"Sweet ride," Craig said, running ~~~~~~~~~~~~~~ Mustang's fenders in a way that made my own fenders tremble a little. He had great hands, broad and long-fingered.

"She does the trick," I said, unlocking the door and slipping inside.

"I bet she does," he said in a voice that made wonder if we were still talking about the car. "I *will* call you."

It was always the ones that protested too much that you never heard from again. Best not to get my hopes up. "Sure," I said. "Whatever."

He leaned in and instead of turning my head at the last moment and giving him nothing but cheek, I lifted my chin and we locked lips.

Talk about zing!

He surged forward and my hands grabbed the pleated front of his shirt as if it was a lifeline. It might have been. It was one of those kisses that seemed to shut off all the oxygen to my brain. When his lips left mine, he bolted backward as if I'd given him an electric shock. He stared at me. "I will definitely be calling you," he said, his voice raspy.

I tried to look unconcerned, but my heart pounded so hard I was afraid it was going to leap right out of my chest. "Yeah," I gasped, trying to catch my breath. "Like I said, whatever."

Un-Veiled is also available as an eBook

Everybody's talking about the warm-hearted, wonderful novels of Eileen Rendahl!

Turn the page to read her rave reviews. . . .

In the tradition of Jennifer Weiner's *In Her Shoes* and Cara Lockwood's *I Do (But I Don't)*, Eileen Rendahl's captivating novels meld humor and heart!

Un-Bridaled

"Eileen Rhendahl's books are absolutely not to be missed!"

—*New York Times* bestselling author Victoria Alexander

"A heartwarming, humorous tale. . . . Eileen Rendahl writes with wit and warmth."

—*USA Today* bestselling author Cara Lockwood

"A wonderful and moving read . . . shimmers with the poignancy of love, loss, and inescapable family ties."

—Award-winning author Alesia Holliday

"Appealing. . . . Rendahl successfully blends romance and humor in this tale about starting over. . . . A poignant look at family relationships."

—*Booklist*

"Rendahl's best to date. . . . [She] displays a talent for creating warmly connected characters and a new determination to tackle emotionally difficult terrain without sacrificing her breezy style."

—*Sacramento News & Review* (CA)

Balancing in High Heels

"Hot action and hilarious antics . . . Rendahl crafts an enjoyable tale . . . that will appeal to fans of both romance and crime fiction."

—*Booklist*

"Humorous, but [with] plenty of depth. . . . A book about finding your purpose in life."

—*Romantic Times*

Do Me, Do My Roots

"Excellent. . . . Heartwarming and hilarious, and the characters jump off the page."

—*Romantic Times*

"A warm and touching novel."

—*Booklist*

"Moving. . . . An engaging relationship drama . . . [with] a wonderful cast."

—Thebestreviews.com

"Simply a winner. . . . Hilarious. . . . It makes me wish I had sisters."

—*Old Book Barn Gazette*

Also by Eileen Rendahl

Un-Bridaled

Balancing in High Heels

Do Me, Do My Roots

In One Year and Out the Other: A New Year's Story Collection
with Cara Lockwood, et al.

Un-Veiled

✴ ✴ ✴ ✴ ✴ ✴

Eileen Rendahl

*Teruko—
It was wonderful
to meet you!*
E Rendahl

doWn
tOwn
press

New York   London   Toronto   Sydney

Downtown Press
A Division of Simon & Schuster, Inc.
1230 Avenue of the Americas
New York, NY 10020

ISBN-13: 978-1-4165-3271-2
ISBN-10:   1-4165-3271-4

First Downtown Press trade paperback edition June 2007

10 9 8 7 6 5 4 3 2 1

DOWNTOWN PRESS and colophon are trademarks
of Simon & Schuster, Inc.

For information about special discounts for bulk purchases,
please contact Simon & Schuster Special Sales at
1-800-456-6798 or business@simonandschuster.com

Manufactured in the United States of America

Acknowledgments

As always, first thanks must go to my tenacious and classy agent, Pam Ahearn, and my thoughtful and perspicacious editor, Micki Nuding. You two always make me feel like I'm part of a team.

A huge thank-you to Eric Kiebler and Janice Solimeno for letting me hide in their condo while finishing the rough draft of this book.

An even huger thank-you to my darling Andy for making it possible for me to hide in Eric and Janice's condo, for never-ending patience in the face of my ubiquitous squirreliness, and for not panicking while I was watching endless episodes of wedding shows.

To Alesia, Beverly, and Cindy for the two most productive hours I've ever spent in a bar.

Un-Veiled

CHAPTER ONE

February 8, 2006

If it wasn't the wedding of the decade, it most certainly was the wedding of the year. Courtney Day and Brett Sedd vowed to love and cherish each other in front of a crowd so beautiful, it would have made Michelangelo weep. No one (except maybe the groom) was more beautiful, however, than the bride, who returned to her hometown of Santa Bonita, California, to have her hair done by her high school chums Cinnamon and Ginger Zimmerman at Do It Up for the lavish beachfront ceremony complete with fireworks.

Cinnamon's rune card for the day was Haegl, the Dark Goddess, the goddess of chaos and creativity.

"I don't understand," Cinnamon said, waving the card at me as she packed Sage's things up for a day at Grandma Rosemary's. We were thrilled to get the wedding business, but it did mean finding somebody to babysit Cinnamon's seven-year-old daughter, Sage. Keeping her at the salon didn't work. The last time we'd tried that, Sage had burned herself on a curling iron, spilled a soda all over the counter that almost hit the bride's veil, and generally pestered Cinnamon until I was afraid Cinn was going to duct-tape her daughter to a wall. Wouldn't that have given everyone something new to talk about? We could maybe even have made the *Santa Bonita Daily Mail* with that one.

"Courtney's a blonde. A white-blonde even. You can't be blonder than her without having no pigment in your hair at all," Cinnamon said, continuing to fret about her rune card. I wondered if I could duct-tape Cinn to a wall. But then, who would do Courtney's hair? I knew Cinn had something in mind already, probably something I wouldn't be able to pull off. And when an honest-to-goodness movie star is getting her hair done for her wedding at your salon, you want your A team playing. "She's even a real blonde, unless she started dying her hair in second grade, which I sincerely doubt. So this doesn't make sense. Why would I get the dark goddess?"

I resisted the urge to tell Cinn exactly what the odds were that she would eventually pick the goddess of chaos and creativity from the deck of twenty-five cards. I had taken statistics last semester and was pretty sure I could calculate that one in my head (four percent, if you'd like to know). I also wanted to tell her that because random chance dropped the goddess of chaos and creativity into our lives on that day didn't mean that anything chaotic or creative was going to happen. Or that the chances of the card she'd randomly picked having anything to do with what our day held were about as good as the chances of the alignment of the stars on the day we were born determining our personalities. Unfortunately, it wouldn't have worked. Cinn loves astrology almost as much as she loves runes.

I was pretty sure that the gravitational pull of Calista Flockhart probably had more impact on my birth than the stars Cinnamon consulted so regularly. My sister, however, doesn't allow facts to dissuade her from her favorite theories, and especially not from New Age-y belief systems, which she mixes and match-es like a kid with a new wardrobe full of Underoos.

We were born all of seven minutes apart, and looks-wise we are peas in a pod. Personality-wise? We could get into a "tastes great/less filling" debate at the drop of a hat, but then we'd just be one more set of twins in a beer commercial, and I really don't think the universe needs any more of that.

"I'm sure it will all be clear by the end of the day," I said, and gave the screen door a little kick at the bottom so it would un-stick. We all headed for the Mustang; I crossed my fingers that she'd start. That kind of chaos I did not need.

I twitched back the curtain of the shop and was nearly blinded by the flashes. "Geez, Courtney, I think every photographer in California might be out there."

Courtney giggled. It was good to know she still did that. It was less good to know that she also still tried to bum cigarettes, borrow jewelry, and cadge free snacks. "Isn't it great, Ginger?"

I tried to peer through the slit in the curtains without actually moving them and saw a sea of camera lenses trained unerringly on Do It Up. "I guess. If that's what you want." Having my ev-ery move recorded did not exactly sound like a good time to me, but then again, I wasn't trying to climb the ranks in Hollywood, and I have spent way too much time being the object of gossip here in Santa Bonita to make it sound like a good idea ever.

"It's not a matter of want or not want, Ginger," Courtney said from my sister's chair, her face a perky little ball on top of the purple cape Cinnamon had draped around her. "It's a matter of survival. This wedding will put Brett and me on the cover of every magazine in every grocery store for the next month, which means I'll be in front of every director and producer casting a movie. I'm getting tired of the sitcom schedule. Plus, don't you think half the girls we went to high school with are eating their hearts out?"

"No," Cinnamon said from behind Courtney as she slid Courtney's hair off her curling iron, using a comb so as not to damage the ringlet. "They all are. Every single one of them."

They could have gotten married anywhere. Hawaii. Greece. The Taj Mahal. Someplace where the morning mist would be guaranteed to burn off so no one's hair would frizz. Instead, they were getting married in Santa Bonita and everyone in town knew. Hell, everybody in the country knew, except possibly those who chose to live in caves.

Talk about getting the best revenge. After high school graduation, Courtney had left for Los Angeles as little more than the Santa Bonita version of trailer trash, and she was coming back the closest thing that America had to a princess without becoming a Kennedy, which as we all know can be detrimental to your health.

Her star had risen fast. First there'd been a toothpaste ad with her happy-go-lucky California-girl grin splashed on billboards all over the country. Then there'd been a guest appearance on *E.R.* as a bipolar college student whose blonde gamine looks captured the heart of Dr. Barnett. After that, there'd been an appearance on one of the *Law & Order*s as a rape victim whose pluck and courage helped the detectives catch her assailant. It seemed like those had barely aired when she got her big break: the part of Brandy, the feisty law-student-cum-cocktail-waitress on *Bar None,* the *Cheers*-meets–*The Paper Chase* sitcom that had been number one in the country three seasons in a row now.

Since then, there'd been a few movies, too. A clever indie to give her some street cred and a romantic comedy to test her box-office draw. But her biggest role to date was the fiancée of Brett Sedd, the pouty-lipped blond superstar whose name could make a thousand adolescent girls (and a few well past adolescence) swoon.

Having the wedding here was absolutely the perfect revenge on all the snotty rich girls who had gotten places on the pep squad instead of Courtney, despite the fact that she could jump higher and cheer louder, and on all the snotty rich boys who had wanted to spend time with her behind the stadium after the game, but hadn't wanted to take her to the Santa Bonita Country Club for the big winter dance.

Courtney could have had her hair done anywhere, or flown someone in. Instead, she was having her hair done right here at Do It Up, the shop Cinnamon and I own. I guess she felt partial to us. I had to admit, it was satisfying to play even a tiny role in serving up Courtney's sweet, cold dish of vengeance. It's not like Cinnamon and I went to the country club winter dance, either. After all, we're "those girls."

It's actually very unfair that we have slutty reputations. We are not slutty. If you start with Grandma, most of us are the exact opposite of slutty. It seems that Zimmerman women give their hearts once and only once. We just don't seem to give them to the right men.

Oh, and we seem to get knocked up as well. So far, I'm the exception to the rule.

Courtney settled back into the chair with a satisfied smile on her face. I tried to peer through the curtains without twitching them. Apparently, the photographers had seen that trick before and I once again received the supernova blast in my face. "I dunno, Courtney. I think I might get sick of having people watch every damn thing I do."

She shrugged. "There are ways to make sure they see what you want them to see and don't see so much of the other stuff. It's not so different from living here."

She had that right. Sometimes I felt like if I farted in the bathtub, they'd be discussing it over at Café Ole! before the bubble popped. Still, there were ways to keep a few secrets if you really tried. Cinnamon and I had certainly been privy to more than a few. "And you wanted them to see you ducking in here to get your hair done?"

"No. *You* wanted them to see me ducking in here to get my hair done. I'd be willing to bet you guys end up with more business than you can shake a curling iron at, after this." Courtney cocked her head, but Cinnamon straightened it back out immediately.

"It's true, Ginger," Cinnamon said. She'd seemed so absorbed in Courtney's hair that I hadn't realized she was still listening. Cinn often goes into almost a trancelike state when creating a particularly intricate updo, and Courtney's hair was nothing if not intricate. "This is great publicity for us."

I knew they were right. I wasn't sure it was going to translate into us making more money, but I hoped it would generate at least enough to replace all that grass that was getting trampled in front of the salon.

After Cinnamon finished Courtney's hair, she moved on to her entourage: her co-star from *Bar None* who played the downtrodden single-mother waitress, and another young up-and-coming actress who had played the quirky small-town girl slowly losing her mind while working at a fast-food drive-through in the indie movie Courtney had done. They were both pretty, but not nearly as pretty as Courtney, especially not after Cinnamon had created the deceptively simple, sweet, and romantic confection of hair on top of Courtney's head.

I'd always related to the single-mom character on *Bar None,* since I basically became a single mom along with Cinnamon. I was the birth coach and I was the first person to hold Sage.

I changed a heck of a lot of diapers and I took care of Sage for as many hours as Cinnamon did during the year and a half we were getting our cosmetology degrees. Let's not even start on the nights I stayed up watching old movies on AMC for the months (and months and months) Sage had colic.

So I really liked the spunky, strong, down-to-earth single mom in Courtney's sitcom. She was my kind of gal. Now, I know that the people on the TV screen are not necessarily real. I know that their dialogue has been written by other people and that they're being played by actors, but after allowing them into my living room week after week, I feel like I know them.

So, suffice it to say, when Miss Co-star sneezed, blew her nose in the tissue that Cinnamon handed her, and then—while looking me right in the eye—dropped the tissue on the floor, a major bubble burst.

Miss Indie Movie, whose nails I was doing at that moment, didn't even blink. "I hear Janelle Richards had some new work done," she said.

I love Janelle Richards! I love that movie where she plays the spunky reporter who has to solve the big mystery before she's killed by the evil corporation's lackeys, and the one where she plays the plucky law student who has to solve the big mystery before she's killed by the evil corporation's lackeys, and the one where she plays the gutsy legal secretary who has to solve the big mystery before she's killed by the evil corporation's lackeys. She's great. She's also so gorgeous that I knew better than to think everything about her was untouched and natural—but I didn't want to think she was completely a surgical creation.

"Oooh! What'd she have done? You know whatever she does, we're all going to end up getting done in the next six months. She is *such* a trendsetter," Courtney said, putting her hands under the nail dryer.

"I heard she had her cootch tightened," Indie said. "Apparently those twins she had stretched it all out down there. I've heard it was unsightly."

I froze and prayed that I had misheard, misunderstood, or mis-somethinged. It was bad enough to worry about my nose and my chin and my boobs and my butt. Did I actually have to worry that my, uh, you know, wasn't up to snuff either?

"Seriously? They can do that?" Miss Co-star Snot Rag asked. She twirled her chair around to look at Miss Indie Movie, causing Cinnamon to trot in a little circle to keep from pulling her hair.

Miss Indie nodded. "They use lasers."

Courtney and Miss Co-star nodded, serious expressions on both their faces. "Laser," they repeated. Then Co-star twirled back, with Cinnamon trotting behind her.

I started on Miss Indie Movie's toes. She pulled a candy bar out of her bag, took a big bite, chewed it, and before she swallowed, spit it out in a tissue, which she—big surprise here—dropped on the floor for someone else (me) to pick up. "New diet," she said. "I can eat anything I want as long as I don't swallow."

I really don't get people from L.A.

I heard the sound of footsteps outside the salon door and raced over to make sure it was still locked. The photographers were pushier than twenty-year-olds at a Bridal Barn blowout, and several of them had already tried to barge in. I squinted my eyes to protect them from the explosion of flashes that was sure to come when I peeked to see who was knocking. I was not disappointed. I wondered if I should wear sunglasses the next time. But the figure at the door came between me and the flashes, and there weren't many men in Santa Bonita who could block out a blinding light like that. I turned the lock and let the local law enforcement in.

"Troy!" Courtney squealed, jumping out of the chair and flinging herself at one of Santa Bonita's finest, who also happened to be Courtney's old high school flame, Troy Patu.

"Hey, Cor," he said, his voice a deep, soft rumble in his wide chest. "How's it goin'?"

"Seriously could not be better," Courtney said, flashing her patented toothpaste-commercial grin, the very one that had appeared in enough magazines to deforest small portions of Oregon.

"You want me to move those guys on the lawn farther back? They buggin' you?" Troy looked down at Courtney with his I-am-the-law scowl.

Courtney cracked up. I have to admit, it's kind of hard not to crack up when Troy acts like Mr. Tough Guy Law Man. Not that he wasn't always a hard-ass. Six foot five inch Samoans who work out tend to look like serious hard-asses, even in high school—but along with being Santa Bonita High's star wide receiver, he had also been Santa Bonita High's star stoner and general troublemaker. His argument when he joined the police force after blowing out his knee in his senior year at San Bernardino State was who knew better how to keep the little unreformed fuck-ups in line than a big reformed fuck-up? Since little fuck-ups were pretty much all the crime Santa Bonita had to offer, it was a pretty compelling argument.

"Bite your tongue, Troy! Just keep 'em at bay a little. We want to be tantalizing, but not completely inaccessible. Pretty much like I was in high school." Courtney winked. She stood back and gave him the big up-and-down look. "You look great."

That was true. Troy *did* look great. His shoulders had, unbelievably enough, broadened, and the last traces of boy had vanished from his face. Plus, he still worked out. A lot. It showed.

He countered with "You look amazing." Which was also

true. Courtney had always been pretty, but now there was a confidence in the way she held herself and walked that made her almost regal. Her teeth blinded with their whiteness and it was almost as if her skin had no pores.

Courtney did a little pirouette. "I eat right and do yoga every day," she said, her eyes wide and sincere. Then she winked. "And I know the number of a very discreet plastic surgeon in Beverly Hills."

I looked a little closer, trying to see if I could suss out where the surgeon's knife might have been helping Courtney. Whatever work she'd had done was good, because I couldn't see hide nor hair of it. Maybe she was joking. I mean, plastic surgery at twenty-four? What would she look like at forty? I thought about the last photo of Melanie Griffith I'd seen and shivered as if someone had walked across my grave.

Courtney sat back down. "So what've you been up to? Tell me everything!"

Troy sat down next to Courtney in my stylist's chair, which was presently empty, and it was everything I could do to keep my fingers out of that long, beautiful hair of his. These days, he keeps it back in a ponytail, but I'm not the only Santa Bonita girl with fond memories of it whipping in the wind as he drove through town in the old pickup truck he kept running with duct tape and baling wire.

"I'm an agent of truth and justice," Troy said, that slow bad-boy grin spreading across his handsome face.

"Girlfriend?" Courtney asked.

He shook his head slowly. "Sort of. Well, not exactly. It's complicated. I don't need to ask what you've been up to. I know pretty much everything, courtesy of those dopes out on the front lawn."

That surprised me. I hadn't heard about Troy seeing anybody, and Santa Bonita is the kind of town where you can't get your bikini line waxed without your mother knowing you have a date.

"Oh, you may think you know everything. I still have a few surprises up my sleeve," Courtney said.

"You always did." Troy smiled and leaned back in the chair.

"We had some good times, didn't we?" Courtney suddenly sat up straighter in her chair. "Do you remember . . ."

The rest of what she said was lost to me as she leaned over to whisper in Troy's ear. Based on the way the blush that started at his throat spread up his face to his hairline, it must have been a damn good memory indeed. "Yeah, Cor. That's not something a guy forgets," he mumbled.

Courtney laughed. "Do you still have those pictures?"

Troy's face went blank for a moment and then his eyebrows shot up. "I don't know, I haven't seen them in ages." He smiled at her. "I should look for those."

"You absolutely should," Courtney said. "Those puppies are probably worth some money these days. You could make a down payment on a house with those."

I looked up at that. Down payments on houses in Santa Bonita were not easy to come up with. I'd looked into it for Cinnamon and myself, and there was no way for us to amass a wad of cash that size. Of course, if you made a down payment, that meant you would have a mortgage, which implied putting down roots and staying. What was I saying? I was born with roots here. In fact, I was born rootbound.

Troy stiffened. "I think you're confusing me with someone else, Courtney. I'm not that kind of guy."

"Everybody is that kind of guy for the right amount of money, Troy." Courtney waved her hand in the air as if brushing away his comment. Her head tilted to the side as if she were listening to a voice from far off. "In fact, we should maybe talk about those photos, Troy."

"Yeah. Sure. Let's do that some time. Right now, I better go keep those chuckleheads in line." Troy stood, his shoulders rigid.

That was the other thing I liked about Troy. What a marshmallow. Courtney may not have realized it, but I knew she'd pricked his pride with that last comment. Whatever pictures she was talking about would never see the light of day.

Courtney said, "Hold on a sec, Troy. Give me your e-mail or your cell phone or something. You know, so I can get in touch some time, maybe."

Troy flushed again, which was completely adorable, I must say. His shoulders didn't relax though. "Sure, Cor. That'd be great." I gave him a pen and some paper, and he scribbled a few numbers out. I tucked them into Courtney's purse for her.

Then I let Troy out. The equivalent of a thousand suns glared into my face. Courtney didn't even flinch.

"You two stayed friends after you left?" Cinnamon asked Courtney.

Courtney shrugged. "Not really, but we didn't become enemies, either. My agent says never to burn any bridges."

She may not have burned it before, but I wondered if she'd just incinerated it now. Troy wasn't really joking when he said he was an agent of truth and justice. I think he really felt that way about his job.

See? Totally adorable.

By the time Courtney and her entourage left, I was seriously considering telling her exactly what I thought of her new Hollywood friends. Troy might still drive a battered pickup truck, but he would never expect someone else to pick up his half-chewed food or dig a booger out from underneath his fingernail for him.

It must have shown on my face, because Cinn kept giving me the hairy eyeball every time I started to open my mouth, and once when she walked by me she whispered in my ear, "Remember, we never, ever slap the bride."

It's one of our few rules at Do It Up, no matter how Bridezilla-ish they become. And let's face it, they *all* become Bridezilla at some point.

Our other rule is "Whatever happens at Do It Up stays at Do It Up." Remember that old Clairol ad? "Only her hairdresser knows for sure"? Well, there's a reason it resonated with women. As hairdressers, we're privy to personal information. People tell us stuff. Plus, we see it in your hair. Mindy DeMarco's hair was getting thin; my guess was her new real estate business was stressing her out. I'm not sure if Cathy Orton's husband was fooling around on her or not, but I knew she thought he was—why else would she get the new cut and color? It's almost always the first thing most women do. And Georgia Finkelbaum was tense about something; she'd been picking at her split ends and twisting her hair hard enough to pull it out. I'm also guessing that Joni Watts was depressed, since she hadn't washed her hair in several days when she dragged herself into the salon.

Having spent our lives as objects of gossip in a small town, Cinn and I made a pact when we opened Do It Up to never ever pass on what we learned while we snipped and plucked and dyed. So, no repeating that Janelle Richards had had plastic surgery on her private party bits. I'd bet money that all three of these women had laser vaginal rejuvenations scheduled within the month, though.

As the Hollywood harlots headed out into the paparazzi frenzy, Courtney threw her arms around me. "I can't tell you what this all means to me, Ginger. It really is the happiest day of my life. Thank you for being part of it."

I stood there, mouth agape, as she traipsed out the door.

"Shut you up, didn't she?" Cinnamon said, leaning against the counter, looking exhausted but triumphant. "She's always known how to do that."

I looked out the windows in time to see Courtney look back toward the shop. She saw me looking and winked at me. Damn it. I'd been manipulated.

I let the curtain drop and sighed, looking around the salon. It was trashed. Cinn and I had moved wedding parties with triple the people through Do It Up with half the mess, and that includes Jenna Thompson's wedding, where the bridesmaids showed up not only still drunk from the night before, but still drinking. Jell-O shots can make a terrible mess. If you allow Jell-O to sit long enough, it becomes a substance that you can cut glass with. Plus, it really should not be considered a nutritious breakfast for a bridal party.

Cinn looked around, too, the starch leaving her shoulders. "We could leave it for tomorrow."

Do It Up is closed on Mondays, like a lot of salons. It's my one day to focus on studying, writing papers, and that other life I try to lead, the one where I get an actual college degree. Although what I think I'm going to do with my bachelor's in biology in Santa Bonita is another problem altogether.

I shook my head. "I have class tomorrow."

"It's already three o'clock." Cinn bit her lower lip. I knew what she was thinking. Now that Sage was in school, Cinnamon didn't have nearly as much time with her as she used to during the week, making the weekends that much more precious.

"Go," I said. "I'll get it started and you can finish it tomorrow."

Cinnamon threw her arms around me. "Thank you! Promise you'll leave something really nasty for me."

"Don't tempt me." I wiggled loose. "Those girls are pigs."

"I think they get some kind of thrill out of making someone else clean up after them. It makes them feel important."

I looked at the tissues with the half-chewed food. "Then they must feel like they made it."

Cinnamon nodded, gathering up her purse and keys. "See you back at the apartment tonight."

"Where else would I be?"

I'd cleared the garbage off the counters and gotten the big chunks off the floor. All the combs and scissors were soaking in the Barbicide, and the nail equipment was in the sterilizer. I was trying to remember the ligaments of the elbow for my anatomy and physiology quiz at the end of the week when something smacked against the door. I turned and screamed. Something had plastered itself to the window. It looked a little like a woman.

Cautiously, I unlocked the door and opened it.

The she-thing stumbled into the salon. "You have to help me. The wedding is in an hour and a half. I can't go like this."

She could only have gone like that if she were marrying Frankenstein's monster. The woman's hair had been teased up into an enormous beehive. Her eyes were crusted with sky-blue eyeshadow and thick, dark eyeliner that made Baby Jane look like she'd been going for the natural look.

"How did this happen?" I asked, staring at her. "Who did this to you?"

"T-t-t-trudy. Over at ExcellaCuts."

"You had your wedding hair done at ExcellaCuts? What were you thinking?" *I* was thinking you get what you pay for. I was also thinking that I still had time to do the Sunday *New York Times* crossword puzzle on an actual Sunday if I left in the next fifteen minutes, although I never seemed to be able to finish it without Brian helping anyway, and I wouldn't be seeing him until tomorrow. I was also thinking that if you were foolish enough to have a woman who looked like Tammy Faye Bakker do your wedding hair, then it was not my responsibility to straighten out your life.

"I was thinking that I only had twenty dollars left in my wallet until my next payday, which isn't until the end of next week. Please, oh, please, don't make me go to my wedding looking like this. I'll find the money. I will. Or I'll work it off. I'll come sweep your shop floor every day for the next year." She looked around. "It looks like you could use a little help with that."

I narrowed my eyes. Ask a favor and insult my housekeeping in one breath? Not the way to make friends and influence Ginger. "You're not earning points here."

"I know. I'm sorry. Please make this go away." The woman gestured wildly at her head and then grabbed my hands in her cold, shaking ones.

The floor-sweeping thing was tempting. Cinnamon and I had talked about getting someone in to sweep and clean, but we weren't even close to there, financially. "Look, I see you have a problem, but we're closed already." I looked at my watch again. I could even potentially go running along the beach trail before it got dark if I left now. It was perfect outside. Seventy-four degrees and the sun had burnt off the mist.

"I know. I know. I know I'm asking too much, but please, I don't know what else to do. *Please* don't make me go to my wedding like this. It's not for me. It's for Ronnie. He deserves better. He deserves the absolute best, because that's what he is. The best." The Bride of Frankenstein grabbed the broom from my hands. "I'll start sweeping now. I'll be back every day. I'm a good worker."

I grabbed the broom back from her. "Look, I don't know . . ."

She grabbed the broom back again. She had a solid six inches on me, though that isn't exactly hard to do since I'm all of five foot four. "Please. I just wanted to look as beautiful on the outside as Ronnie makes me feel on the inside."

Her words took my breath away; I am nothing if not a sucker for a good line. I took the broom back from her. "No sweeping on your wedding day. I can't do this alone, though. I'm going to have to call my sister."

I called Cinnamon and told her she had to come back—we had an emergency.

CHAPTER TWO

From The Santa Bonita Daily Mail

Jolene Hampton and local businessman Ronnie Herbert wed on February 8 in the San Mateo County courthouse. The wedding was witnessed by the groom's friend and co-owner of Flush It Down, Kevin Whitman. The bride wore an A-line dress that she found on the sale rack at T.J. Maxx. The groom wore Levi's 501s, a snap-front cowboy shirt, and a bolo tie. The couple will reside in Santa Bonita.

Cinnamon took one look at Jolene and gasped. "Sweet Freya in all her glory. How did this happen?"

I pointed to the magazine over in the chair. "Check page twenty-nine." I took the sprayer attachment and began to rinse Jolene's hair. This was actually the third time I'd rinsed Jolene's hair. I'm not sure what Trudy used to glue it up into that hideous beehive, but I'm thinking maybe thinset.

"You asked for a basic bridal bouffant and she gave you a beehive? She is really going to have to get those hearing aids checked." Cinnamon stared back and forth between the magazine and Jolene. "And what's with the Cleopatra eye makeup?"

"I don't knooowww," Jolene wailed. "I said I wanted to look

pretty and sexy, and she did *this* to me. I should never have spent the money. I should have done it myself."

"Hush," I said. "Cinnamon's going to take over on your hair. I'm going to start getting this makeup off. Close your eyes and relax."

As Cinnamon took over, I could tell by the way that the tension left Jolene's face that Cinn's special touch had started to work instantly. I can't describe what it's like to have Cinnamon wash your hair. The closest thing to it I can think of is that moment when the wine hits your brain, and muscles you didn't know were kinked up suddenly relax. We often have to physically support clients as they walk from the hair-washing station to the cutting chairs because they're woozy.

"Where's Sage? Is she back with Grandma Rosemary?" I asked, as I took a seat on the other side of Jolene's head and started wiping away some of the bright blue eyeshadow.

Cinn shook her head. "She's with Mom at the shop. They're sorting the latest arrivals." Our mother owns Pass It On, a consignment secondhand shop by the corner of Willow and First. Sunday mornings in the spring are when she gets the vast majority of her donations. It's a spring cleaning thing. People clean their closets on Saturday and can't wait to get the stuff out of the house before the weekend is over, so Sunday afternoons mean a lot of sorting. I know I spent more than a few of my Sundays as a kid sorting items into piles by size and then by season.

Cinnamon started to hum something tuneless under her breath and Jolene relaxed a little further. Cinn smiled. "Mom's going to take her back to her house when they're done. So how'd you meet Ronnie, Jolene?"

"My toilet overflowed," she said, her voice dreamy and vague.

It wasn't the most romantic start to a story I'd ever heard, yet I was intrigued. "You met over raw sewage?"

"I'd just moved into my new place, and the toilet wouldn't work. I couldn't get the landlord on the phone so I picked a plumber from the yellow pages." Jolene's head tilted back a little more. "Hey, that feels real nice."

"That's good." Cinnamon smiled at me over Jolene. "So it was like fate or kismet or something that you chose Ronnie's ad?"

"Must have been. Ain't nothin' special about that ad, but I knew there was somethin' special about him the second he walked in the apartment." Jolene smiled. "He shook my hand. He called me miss."

"Respectful's good," Cinnamon agreed.

"Better 'n good. Nobody every treated me like that. Nobody ever assumed that I was the kind of woman who should be respected."

Cinnamon looked up at me again, and this time neither one of us smiled. We knew a little bit about how that felt. We were Zimmerman women, and everyone in Santa Bonita knew what that was supposed to mean. At least, we had certainly never been allowed to forget what it was supposed to mean.

"Good for Ronnie," Cinnamon said, rinsing Jolene's hair again. "You can sit up now."

"Good for me," Jolene said as Cinn wrapped the towel around her hair. "I don't know if I can tell you *how* good for me."

"Give it a try," I said.

"I'm no angel," Jolene said, her voice quiet. "I'm really not the kind of woman anyone should treat with respect. I done some bad things in my life."

"Who hasn't made a few mistakes?" Cinnamon said as she started combing out Jolene's hair. While she combed, I wheeled the makeup cart around and started trying to figure out what colors would work best on Jolene. She was a pale woman. She needed a little color, but too much and she'd look like a clown. Pretty much like she did when she walked in.

"No. Seriously. I been bad a lot. Real bad." She looked into the mirror, her eyes searching ours. "That's why I'm all alone here today, why I don't have any bridesmaids or flower girls or any of that stuff. My parole officer's been real clear about staying away from bad influences, and I'm not sure I have any good influences left. I pretty much managed to drive them all away. The pipe'll do it to you. All I got is Ronnie." Jolene's eyes began to well. "I told him he deserved better than me. He wouldn't hear it. He said I was exactly what he wanted, and he wanted to marry me and be with me the rest of my life."

I grabbed a tissue. All brides cry, but crying doesn't make anyone look good. Besides the puffy eyes, my big issue is what it does to your mascara. Hence the folded-up tissue, pressed gently under Jolene's lower lashes.

"I told him everything, too," Jolene went on. "He knows it all. All the things I done. The people I've stole from and the ones I hurt. He knows all about it and he still wants me. He deserves better 'n me, so that's what I'm gonna try and do; be better 'n me. He is like a knight in shining armor. I mighta gone back to the pipe if it weren't for him. It's mighty hard to stay away from it. Even if you really, really want to. Ronnie kept me strong. He saved me. He thinks I'm already worth it. I want to make sure he's right."

Whether or not Jolene was going to be better than herself would be up to her. She definitely looked better than she had by the time Cinnamon and I were done with her, though. In fact, she looked phenomenal. I put the last touches of blush on her cheeks and we whirled her around to see herself in the mirror.

"Holy crap!" Jolene leapt out of the chair. "I'm a freakin' goddess."

She was right. Cinnamon had smoothed Jolene's hair into the sleek, simple bridal bouffant that she'd wanted in the first place and added a little beaded comb at the top. I have to admit, I'd done a great job with her face. Jolene's eyes looked huge. She was thin, so she already had prominent cheekbones. Her skin—well, let's just say that if you have a parole officer, you may have been spending your time someplace that doesn't allow for a lot of fresh air. I smoothed everything out with some tinted moisturizer, gave her cheeks a touch of color, and plumped her lips up with some peach-toned gloss.

Jolene grabbed both of us in a hug and damn near knocked our heads together.

"You two are the best!" she howled. "The absolute freakin' best. It's like you took my inner self and put her all over my outer self. You made me look like Ronnie makes me feel inside. I will make this up to you. I will make you glad you did this. I will pay you back tenfold because you did it."

She released us and looked up at the clock. "Now I've gotta go. Ronnie'll be waitin' for me at the judge's office in half an hour and I don't wanna be late."

She ripped off the cape we'd put on her to protect her tank top and jeans and headed to the door.

"Wait," Cinnamon said, rifling through her purse. "Wait just a second."

Jolene turned.

Cinnamon pulled out a little bag. "You need jade. Jade is to heal the heart. Plus it's green, which corresponds to your heart chakra as well. I think your heart has taken a beating over the years, and this will help Ronnie heal it." She pulled a little green stone from her bag and put it in Jolene's hand.

"Cinnamon, it's a rock," Jolene said, with a look on her face that said she wasn't sure if a joke was being pulled on her or not.

"It may look like just a rock," Cinnamon said in the same voice she uses to explain to Sage how to use the microwave. "But it's really a crystal, and it's emitting special vibrations at a frequency that will make you feel better."

Jolene looked at the rock again, her doubt plain on her face; then she shrugged and tucked the rock into her jeans pocket. "I will not forget."

As the door slammed shut behind her, I looked over at Cinnamon. "Funny, I feel more satisfied about that than I did about Courtney."

"Amen, sister," Cinnamon said, starting to clear off the counters. "Amen."

It was close to four thirty. My Sunday was evaporating before my eyes. I must have sighed a little louder than I meant to as I started sorting the makeup brushes back into their holders.

"Go home," Cinnamon said, not looking up at me.

My heart leapt. "Seriously?"

"Yeah. Just do me a favor and pick Sage up from Mom's on your way."

"Thank you, Cinn. I really need the time." I was taking anatomy and physiology that semester and it was chewing up a lot of time. There is a huge number of itty bitty body parts in us, and memorizing them is a pain in the epistropheus vertebra.

"She can watch cartoons until I get back. I'll pick up some stuff for dinner, but you have to play Monopoly with us after."

Sage usually has me totally skunked within an hour, so that wasn't much of a problem. "Thank you, thank you, thank you," I said, dropping everything and grabbing my purse. "Can I take the Mustang?"

Mom lives a few blocks inland toward Our Lady of Perpetual Hope and Sorrow Cemetery. It's only about a mile, but I wanted to drive anyway. It would save time, plus Sage has a heck of a stubborn streak. More than once, she's decided she's tired on a walk and simply will not take another step. Then you're stuck with the choice of carrying her, sitting on the curb until someone you know stops and picks you up, or abandoning her. She's gotten too heavy for me to carry for more than a few blocks, I already feel enough like poor white trash most of the time without hitching rides, and if we abandoned everyone in our family with a stubborn streak, we'd all be living alone.

That, actually, was something worth considering.

"Go ahead. I'll walk," Cinnamon said as I headed out.

Technically, I suppose, the Mustang is Mom's car. It's been hers since the time she was blasting around Santa Bonita like a wild child of the seventies, but she gave it to Cinnamon and me when we were in high school so we could carry on the family tradition of blasting around town like wild children. I turned the key and listened to the engine growl with an appreciative smile. She'd been starting rough every now and then and it made me nervous. I didn't want to dig into my savings to fix her or to—heaven forbid—buy a new car. I had plans for that money.

I crossed Highway One and pulled into the neighborhood I grew up in. The streets were packed with single-family homes that had appreciated so much in the California real estate boom that the only people who could afford to live in them were the people who bought decades ago, and the people who had made a killing in the tech market and gotten out in time. I swerved to avoid a PT Cruiser that had been subjected to a particularly crooked parking job on the side of the road. It's possible that the driver had just been compensating for the Lincoln Navigator that was half up on someone's yard in front of it. The narrow roads really weren't made to be parked on, but since every house had about three cars to go with it, we all had to make do.

I maneuvered carefully through the obstacle course of cars that looked way too expensive to go with the tiny houses where their owners lived.

The parked car that stopped me in my tracks, however, was the battered white van parked in front of Mom's bungalow.

I didn't even slow down. I cruised past Mom's, pulled out my cell phone, and called Cinnamon at the shop. "Nice try, girl-friend, but no freakin' way."

"He's here for good this time." She knew what I was talking about. I knew she would. I knew it wasn't coincidence. I suppose I should have appreciated that at least she wasn't pretending it was, but mainly I was pissed at her attempt to manipulate me. Hadn't Courtney already done enough of that today? Come to think of it, Jolene had done a pretty crack job of it as well. It would have been nice to follow my own life course for once. I wondered what rune card Cinnamon would have to pull for that to happen.

"Really? I've never heard that one before. Wait. That's not true. I think I heard it every other week for a couple of decades. Why on earth would him saying he was back for good make me want to see him?" I slammed to a stop at the stop sign.

"He's really trying, Ginger. Maybe you should give him a chance."

I took a series of the deep, cleansing breaths I'd learned as Cinnamon's birth coach. They hadn't done much when she'd been in labor and they weren't working much better now. "I've given him a million chances, a million openings, a million every-thing, Cinn. I'm done. I've been done for ages."

"I think you should consider giving him another chance," she said.

I nearly threw the phone out the car window, but I'd opted not to get the extra insurance on it. *"Why?"*

There was a little pause at the other end of the line. Then she said, "Because he's our father, Ginger. That's why."

"Whoop-de-doo, so he was able to knock Mom up. I don't see why that should allow him into my life. Besides, why should I walk into his little trap when he's not even clever enough to hide his piece-of-shit van?"

There was a longer pause. Realization dawned on me like ice water being poured down my spine. "It's not his trap, is it, Cinn?"

"Not exactly." Her voice was really small, so small that it could almost crawl under the rock where our father belonged.

Let me explain a little about my parents. Our mother could be the poster child for warning young girls to never ever date a musician. And if you do, not to sleep with him. And if you *do* sleep with him, to use birth control, for the love of God.

Oh, and if you do date him, sleep with him, and fail to use birth control, maybe, just maybe, actually marry him so your daughters aren't a source of gossip for the whole town the second they enter the world.

It would almost be better if our father had been a complete failure as a musician. At least then he would have been around for dance recitals, school plays, award presentations, and parent-teacher conferences. Instead, he was always out on the road touring with his band, the Surf Daddies. Don't think Beach Boys. Think Dick Dale. Think the Mermen. Think Jeff Spicoli in *Fast Times at Ridgemont High.* Think about having Jeff Spicoli, on his perpetual search for tasty waves, as your father.

It's not so funny when it's your dad falling out of the van in the cloud of marijuana smoke, now is it?

The other decent option would have been to have Dad be wildly successful. No such luck. The Surf Daddies were successful enough to have gigs nearly every week during the year, but not so successful that they could say no to them or not be on the road six months out of the year. The part of his mind Dad hadn't turned into tapioca pudding with dope and booze thought he was Living The Dream.

"*You* did it, didn't you, Cinn? He didn't know I was coming over. He probably couldn't have cared less if I did or didn't." I tamped down the little wave of sadness that went with that thought. It would have been nice to inspire some kind of emotion, even if it was devious and scheming. Cinn and I had never been much more than inconvenient curiosities for Dad though. The fact that we were in our twenties didn't change that one bit.

"That's not true, Ginger. He would have cared," she said. "If he'd known."

"I'll drop the car off in front of the shop, but then I'm going home. You can get Sage yourself. By the way, I can't believe you let him near her. If the school calls because she's teaching the first grade class how to roll a joint, I'm not picking her up." I snapped my phone shut, cutting the connection.

CHAPTER THREE

"Why?" Sage asked, her hands open in front of her as if she were begging for alms rather than an explanation. "Why do you do this every time, Auntie G?"

"Because Park Place rocks," I said. It also tends to bankrupt me. I will wheel and deal and sell my Monopoly soul to get it. Then I do the same for Boardwalk and slather them with hotels. It has been my strategy since I was Sage's age, and has proven to be a reliable method to extricate me from any and every Monopoly game as quickly as possible. Sometimes people just don't understand your true goals.

"Park Place bankrupts you. You're out of the game." Sage said this with a level of disgust usually reserved for green beans and early bedtimes. "Again."

"Someday I'll learn, I'm sure," I said, pulling out a textbook and settling in to study while Cinnamon and Sage strove to prove who was the biggest capitalist pig in the apartment.

"What's that picture?" Sage said, looking at my open book.

"Layers of skin," I said. "Strata germinativum, spinosum, granulosum, lucidum, and corneum."

Or as my study buddies have taught me to memorize it: Good Sluts Get Laid Constantly. It's like a mnemonic.

"I have all those layers on me?" she asked, looking at her arm and then twisting it around in the light as if she were going to be able to see through it.

"You bet," I said. "You also have your mother sitting on Marvin Gardens."

Sage whirled, curls flying out around her head. I'd like to say how completely darling she is, but it would be conceited. She looks exactly like Cinnamon, which means she looks exactly like me, so extolling her adorability is a little like extolling my own. And my mother's as well.

It's as if my mother reproduced without taking any genetic material from my dad at all. It's one of the many things for which I'm grateful to her. Other things on the gratitude list? First pick of the best clothes at her shop, her salsa recipe, and the Mustang.

Having extracted the requisite thirty-five dollars in Monopoly money—which was the only kind of money we had in abundance—from Cinnamon, Sage turned back to me. "What will you do once you know about all the layers of the skin? Will it help you make people's skin prettier?"

An excellent question, as many of Sage's were.

"No. It'll help me pass the test I have to take at the end of the week, which will help me pass the class so I can graduate." What I would do then with my extensive knowledge of skin layers, well, that was another question altogether. Maybe there was a chance I could strip through all of them and figure out what I was underneath.

"Hey! I'm surprised you're here!" Natalie Vu, one of my co-suffering biology majors, plopped down next to me.

"Where else would I be on a Monday morning?" I know it came out cranky. Who wouldn't be cranky when the best mnemonic that anyone had given them for memorizing the cranial nerves was Ooh, Ooh, Ooh, To Touch And Feel Virgin Girls' Vaginas, Ah, Heaven!

"I don't know. Basking in the sunshine of your new celebrity status?" Natalie said, twirling my notebook around to face her. 'Virgin Girls' Vaginas'? Where the hell did that come from?"

I closed my eyes and thought hard. "Vestibulocochlear, glossopharyngeal, vagus."

"Cranial nerves." Natalie flipped the notebook back around. I love Natalie. She's forty-eight years old and divorced, but looks about my age. She chalks it up to Vietnamese genetics. She claims her mother still gets carded buying booze. Natalie's kids are both in college and she decided, after years as an emergency-room tech and a surgical tech, that she might as well be in school, too. She's planning on getting a nursing degree. "There are better mnemonics."

"Like what?" There was no way I could study with Sage even in the apartment with that as a mnemonic. Of course, the "Good Sluts Get Laid Constantly" one wasn't exactly Sesame Street–friendly, even if you could convince Elmo to sing it. Now there was a picture. An annoying little orange creature singing the cranial nerves. Maybe I'd be able to memorize them after all.

Natalie chewed on the end of her braid. "I don't know. I'll make one up."

"Let me know how that goes," I said.

"Hello, ladies. Ginger, I can't believe you lowered yourself to be part of Foster City State after hobnobbing with the likes of Courtney Day and Brett Sedd over the weekend." Brian MacEgan plopped down at the table.

Natalie snapped her fingers. "I've got it. "Out Of Office To Take A Fine Vacation. Going to Vesuvius And Hiking.'"

I thought for a second. "You added a 't.'"

"Only one, though," Natalie said, affronted.

"That's better than 'Virgin Girls' Vaginas' how?" I asked.

Brian put his head in his hands. "How is it that I always walk into the middle of these conversations?

"Cranial nerves," I said, ruffling his blond hair. He always seemed like a puppy, probably because of his perpetual glad-to-see-you grin.

"I guess that's a relief." He grinned at me. "It's kind of a disappointment, too, though."

We may not be the likeliest of study groups, but we are definitely the best I've had so far in my six years at Foster City State. Everybody was always prepared. Everybody had always done the reading. No one breathed through their mouth, or at least not noticeably. Natalie often brought cookies. Brian often brought booze. I loved them.

"How do you know who I hobnobbed with, anyway?" I hadn't exactly been advertising the Courtney Day thing. The press was intense enough as it was.

"You pretty much have to have been in a coma not to know about what you did this weekend. Didn't you see any of the photos in the paper?" He flipped open his own notebook.

I shook my head. "I was trying to learn the layers of the skin and the cranial nerves, thank you very much. Oh, and trying to lose at Monopoly as fast as possible."

"Try buying Park Place and Boardwalk," he said. "Then throw a bunch of hotels on 'em. That usually works for me. I think they're called board games because they are bo-ring."

I love Brian. "Me too. Sage adores them, though. So does Cinnamon." I cannot count the games of Sorry, Trouble, Clue, and Chutes and Ladders I have let the two of them wheedle me into playing. I routinely thank my lucky stars that neither of them likes Risk; Risk makes me want to drive sharp objects into my eyeballs.

"Hey, did you get your applications?" Brian asked.

I nodded. "Fat lot of good they'll do me, but yes, I've got all the paperwork." Brian and I were applying for physician assistant programs. I once again wondered what was possessing me to consider wasting the money on application fees. Even supposing I got in, how would I pay for it?

"You can't go if you don't apply," Brian said.

"And you can't go and run a beauty shop and help raise a kid at the same time either," I answered, feeling uncomfortable that he guessed what I was thinking so easily. Again.

"So don't." Brian shrugged, looking down at his notebook.

"Don't what? Run the beauty shop, raise the kid, or go to school?" I asked.

"I don't know. You figure it out."

"Excuse me," Natalie broke in. "Cranial nerves, anyone?"

We both groaned, but started chanting "Out of Office . . ." anyway.

I didn't go back to the salon until eleven on Tuesday after my microbiology class. We didn't officially open until noon. I'd have a few minutes to sift through the mail and figure out which bills we could get away with not paying this month. I dumped my stuff on the desk and hit the answering machine button to hear what messages we had.

"You have forty-three messages," the mechanical man's voice said.

Forty-three messages? I didn't know Mr. Machine could even count to forty-three. He'd never had to count higher than fifteen before, and that was when Connor Daley was leaving prank messages on our machine asking if our refrigerator was running and if we had Prince Albert in a can. We'd cleared that little problem up at his mother's next cut and rinse. We let her know that we'd be all booked up when she called for an appointment if we kept getting phone calls. She'd have no choice but to go to the only other salon in town.

Nobody wants to have to go to Trudy at ExcellaCuts for their highlights—at least, no one under the age of eighty who isn't legally blind—Connor hasn't called here since. In fact, he crosses to the other side of the street when he sees me coming.

I sat down with my pen just in time to hear a breathy voice say, "Hi, my name is Ellie. I saw the photos of Courtney Day's wedding on E! and I have to have that updo at my wedding. I mean, I just *have* to."

I scribbled down Ellie's number and the date she requested as the next message started. "This is Valerie Wang? I'm calling because I want to have the same hairstyle that Courtney Day had? I think that was your salon that I saw on E!? My wedding is July twelfth? Please tell me you're not booked already?"

The next forty-one messages were nearly identical. If we booked all these brides, we'd have one or two weddings a weekend for the next four months solid!

I guess Courtney had been right. We did want all those photographers on the street, after all.

CHAPTER FOUR

Ashley Cristina Elliott, daughter of Hope Deaton Elliott and Dr. Lawrence O. Elliott of Santa Bonita, C.A., was married on April 23 to Justin Llewelyn Esposito, son of Missy Semple Esposito of Carmel and Daniel Barcroft Esposito III, also of Santa Bonita, at the Coastside Community Church in Santa Bonita.

It wasn't the first time I'd seen a bride turn green, and it probably wouldn't be the last. The poor things had usually been dieting for months, living on lettuce leaves dipped in lemon juice and running miles and miles through the hills around Santa Bonita in an effort to fit into a size tinier than they'd been since junior high on their big day. Then the festivities around their big days arrived and one margarita turned them sloppy drunk and woefully hungover the next day.

That said. Ashley's shade of green was almost cute. It figured. Everything about Ashley was cute. Cute little face. Cute little hands and feet. Cute little ears. If I thought I could get away with it, I'd slap her.

"Are you all right?" Cinnamon was pinning Ashley's specially streaked blonde hair into an elaborate fantasy of twisting strands and ringlets.

Ashley held one finger up, asking to be given a second. "I

don't know. I haven't been feeling so great since the bachelorette party. I think maybe I got a bad piece of fish at the sushi place."

"Or a really good Red Bull and vodka at the bar afterward," suggested Stephanie, her sister and maid of honor.

I was pinning up Stephanie's brunette hair into a simple yet elegant chignon. Simple yet elegant chignons are my job at Do It Up. I can do those, a basic French twist, and a serviceable bridal bouffant. You want something fancier? Take a seat at Cinnamon's station. You want the books to balance? Make sure I'm the one keeping them. Cinnamon thinks double entry bookkeeping sounds dirty and treats it as such.

"Or three Red Bull and vodkas," suggested Jessica, Ashley's bridesmaid, while having a pedicure done by Natalie, who was now our new nail technician. When business had boomed enough that we had enough money to hire someone, Natalie had volunteered. Between an aunt and three cousins who were all nail technicians, she'd had plenty of training, and she wanted the extra money to pay for books.

"I think that's how many I had," Jessica continued.

Natalie grunted, but I wasn't sure if it was to second how many Red Bull and vodkas Jessica might have had or because of a particularly stubborn spot on Jessica's heel.

"That was three days ago!" Ashley protested. "We had the girls' night early so I wouldn't be hungover and puffy on my special day. It is not the Red Bull and vodkas!"

Stephanie winced. "I'm sorry," I said. I didn't think I'd poked her or pulled a hair, but sometimes you did things without realizing it. It was quite possible that my fingers had tightened involuntarily after hearing the phrase 'my special day' fall from Ashley's fashionably plump lips—had she looked that Angelina Jolie–ish in high school?—for about the bazillionth time that day. It was only ten thirty, too.

I looked into the mirror to check that I hadn't made Stephanie's bangs lopsided. Her gaze met mine and she gave the tiniest of eye rolls. I bit back a grin.

I liked Steph. Only her legend had remained by the time I'd gotten to Santa Bonita High. Track star, valedictorian, scholarship to Swarthmore. To think there was a time that I thought I might take the world by storm, when I thought I was smart enough and pretty enough to do all those great things too. I looked at Steph's smooth face and wondered why I felt so old at age twenty-four.

"Speaking of three days ago," Jessica said, "where'd you disappear to that night, Ashley? I thought we were going dancing and all of a sudden you were gone. Then two hours later you were back like nothing happened."

Ashley turned pink. "Yeah. Sorry about that. I . . . uh . . . saw someone I knew and went outside to talk."

"For two hours?" Stephanie asked. "Who was it?"

Ashley turned pinker. "Oh, nobody. Just someone from high school I hadn't seen for a while."

Jessica frowned. "The only person I saw from high school was Troy Patu. I feel like I see him every time we turn around. He never smiles anymore, either. He's totally lost his sense of humor since he became a police officer. Ouch!" She drew her foot back and glared down at Natalie. "That hurt."

"Your feet too rough, Miss Jessica," Natalie said. "How you gonna get man with feet so rough?"

Natalie grew up in Modesto and her English is as good as mine. What had Jessica done to tick Natalie off? She doesn't usually break into her pidgin English unless a client has really annoyed her. I think she sometimes believes that being of Vietnamese descent allows her to insult clients with impunity.

Sometimes she's right.

I gave my head a little shake and hoped Natalie got the hint. This wasn't a bridal party I wanted to piss off. It looked like she got it. Her lips tightened a bit, but she grabbed Jessica's foot and stuck it back in the tub. "Sorry, Miss Jessica. I be careful."

I rolled my eyes but turned away. I pinned the last loose tendril into Stephanie's updo. "What do you think?" I asked, giving her the hand mirror and twirling her around so she could see her hair from different angles.

"It's beautiful, Ginger," she said and smiled up at me. "It's perfect. It's exactly what I wanted for Ashley's Special Day."

It was a good thing I hadn't taken a sip of my Diet Coke; it would have been a shame to spray it through my nose all over Stephanie's perfect hair.

Meanwhile, Ashley had gone back to green again. "Oh, man," she groaned.

Cinnamon stepped back, alarmed. "Are you going to be okay?"

Ashley shook her head. "I don't think so." Then she bolted.

Cinnamon raced after her, squealing, "Let me hold your hair!"

Today, Cinn had gotten Beorc, a card of birth and new beginnings, and she was all happy because she'd decided that boded well for Ashley. As far as I was concerned, Ashley had already had more than her fair share of good beginnings in life.

She had still been at Santa Bonita High when Cinnamon and I had entered as freshmen, thinking that the world was at our feet and only the fact that our mother chose to give us stripper names would hold us back. Well, that and the fact that everyone always seemed to stop talking when we walked into a room.

Ashley had been a sensation in her own right, although she'd taken a different tack than Stephanie. Ashley had sailed off in the direction of being a Popular Girl. She'd been homecoming queen, was on the pep squad—all the stuff that makes you high school royalty.

As much as I wouldn't have minded following the trajectory of the Stephanie Elliotts of Santa Bonita, I'm pretty sure Cinnamon would have preferred to follow Ashley—and I don't mean to the bathroom to hold her hair as she was presently doing.

Cinnamon, however, blew all those dreams big-time when she got knocked up the summer after junior year. They don't make really terrific prom dresses in maternity styles, and seventeen-year-old boys don't generally ask pregnant girls to be their dates, especially girls who won't give up the name of their baby-daddy. Yep. Pregnancy pretty much killed Cinnamon's prom queen dreams. As much as I love my niece, Sage, her advent into the world derailed a lot of people's plans, mine included.

It would have helped a lot if Cinn would have told us who the father was, but trying to get something out of my sister when she doesn't want to tell is like trying to get blood from the proverbial stone. Sage is seven now, and while I know what color toenail polish my sister is wearing at any given moment (Mango-A-Go-Go as of last night, for instance) and what she had for breakfast. (Frosted Mini-Wheats and half a banana), even I—her identical twin—cannot tell you who put the bun in her oven that summer. As I recall, she was in a heavy-duty surfing phase and wasn't even dating anybody special at the time.

I looked over at Stephanie, whose frown creased her makeup as she gazed toward the bathroom, where her sister was clearly not feeling well. "Nerves?" I suggested.

"Ashley?" she said, incredulity clear in her voice. "There are no cooler cucumbers than Ashley."

"Maybe it was the sushi," Jessica suggested from over at the nail dryer. "One bad piece is all it takes."

Stephanie took her place at Natalie's nail station, casting a worried glance back toward the restroom. "I don't think she ate much of anything last night. I'm not really sure if she's eaten in weeks."

"We see it all the time," I said. "The brides eat so little for so long, and when they start to party, things get away from them."

A paler Ashley emerged from the back room, with Cinn still holding her hair. "Sorry about that," Ashley said. "That was so weird. I feel better now, though."

Cinnamon got Ashley situated back in her chair. "I'm glad you feel better, but I'd feel better if you'd hold on to this," she said, pulling a crystal from a leather pouch that hung from one of her drawers. "Malachite has soothing powers for the stomach and it's linked to your third chakra, which is right there in your tummy."

Ashley let Cinnamon place the stone in her hand and stared at it. Then she looked up at Cinn. "Uh, thanks, Cinnamon. Thanks a lot." Then she leaned forward and peered into the mirror. "I think we're going to have to start over, Cinnamon. It's not right."

"The front is fine, Ashley. I'll repin these places in the back and everything will be great." Cinnamon started taking out the bobby pins holding the last twisting tendril.

"No. We have to start over. It's not right. I want the Courtney." Ashley's voice was rising.

"I know you want the Courtney," Cinnamon said in a soothing tone. "You're going to have the Courtney. I invented the Courtney, remember?"

The irony of Ashley, who would not have invited Courtney to her house for one of her famous summer pool parties, now having a little hissy fit over whether or not she was going to get a real Courtney for her wedding day was not lost on me.

Sadly, it probably was lost on Cinnamon, who, rather than

further upsetting Ashley, was taking out the whole thing and starting over. I glanced at the clock. The girl better not barf again, or there was no way we were going to have all three girls ready in time for their photos.

Steph took Jessica's place with Natalie at the nail station as Jessica swung into my chair for her French twist, and I started to brush out her hair.

"Hello, one and all, I come bearing sustenance." A vision of the tall, dark, and handsome variety strode into the salon and every estrogen molecule I had stood up and saluted. One look at the shaggy dark hair and melting brown eyes had me all shook up. Okay, maybe it was the nicely proportioned body beneath the slightly worn Flogging Molly T-shirt and the faded jeans. Whatever it was, everything girly in me knew it the second he walked in the door.

Apparently, I was not the only one with that reaction, because Cinnamon froze, curling iron still stuck in Ashley's hair. Damn. Were we going to have to toss a coin? I don't think we'd had to do that since we were fifteen.

Ashley squealed. "Craig! What are you doing here? Justin's not here, is he? He's not supposed to see me until the wedding."

"Nah. Just me and some bagels," Tall, Dark, and Handsome said. "Seriously, Justin was afraid you would all be starving and he asked me to bring this stuff by. I believe there's a cinnamon-sugar bagel with a schmear of light cream cheese expressly for you, Ashley. Before you say anything else regarding carbs and fat content, he also said to tell you that one bagel isn't going to keep your dress from zipping and that he's worried about you. So eat."

He tossed a paper-wrapped package into Ashley's lap. She looked at it as if it were a snake.

"And for you, Miss Stephanie, I have a sesame bagel with

veggie cream cheese and sliced tomato." Another paper-wrapped package came out of the brown bag. He dropped this one in Stephanie's lap.

"Thank you, Craig," Stephanie said quietly. "It's nice of you to remember what I like."

"You're quite welcome, but I am only the errand boy." He smiled at her. "Justin placed the order."

"What about me? Did he remember me?" Jessica chimed in.

Craig turned and stalked across the salon. "How could he forget a woman of such fiery beauty? Especially one who favors jalapeño-cheddar bagels."

Jessica squealed and clapped her hands.

Something smelled funny. I hoped it wasn't the bagels, because my stomach was growling. It didn't look like Ashley could bear to touch hers, so I was hoping I could score that one. I'm not that fussy. If it's bread, I'll probably like it.

He turned his attention to Cinnamon, Natalie, and me. "We didn't know what you'd want so I brought a selection. Some sesame, some plain, and another jalapeño-cheddar in case someone is as crazy as Jessica here."

I smiled. "Thanks. I'm sure we'll find something we can choke down."

I peeked in the bag. The bad smell definitely wasn't coming from there. I turned to Cinnamon to ask what she wanted and Ashley began to scream.

Cinnamon was still staring at Craig with her mouth open, and the curling iron was still tucked in Ashley's Courtney. The smell was burning hair.

I knocked the curling iron out of Cinnamon's hand and quickly inspected the back of Ashley's neck. It was a little red, but nothing that a quick touch-up with foundation wouldn't hide. "Are you okay?" I asked, not sure whether I was more concerned about Ashley, who was repeating "ouch, ouch, ouch," or Cinnamon, who was still staring at this Craig guy like she'd seen a ghost.

Was there a reason that everyone had to lose focus when we had the closest thing to a society bridal party that Santa Bonita had to offer? We could lose all our new Courtney business with bad word-of-mouth from someone like Ashley Elliott.

"I'm fine," Ashley said, sounding irritated. She looked down at her bagel again. "I don't want this. Did you say there's a jalapeño-cheddar bagel in there? Is there any peanut butter?"

I looked back into the bag and pulled out a little packet. "Right here."

Ashley trotted over with Cinnamon trailing behind her, still sticking bobby pins into the latest set of curls.

Craig handed Ashley a plastic knife and then turned his attention on us. "You two must be the famous Spice Girl twin hairdressers."

As he turned to look at her, Cinnamon flinched away. Okay, the Spice Girl crack was uncalled for, but it wasn't like we hadn't heard it before. Trust me, when you're named Ginger or Cinnamon, and your mother's name is Cassia and your grandmother is Rosemary and your niece or daughter is Sage, Spice Girl jokes are ubiquitous. Still, physically recoiling like that seemed like a bit of an overreaction. I looked back at him. I couldn't see a single solitary problem there. Maybe Craig had a murky aura or something. What did I know?

"I'm Craig, cousin of the groom, best man, and gopher extraordinaire," he said, sticking out his hand. Cinnamon took another step back, her eyes narrowing. His aura must be really nasty.

I stepped up and took his hand. Mmmm. Warm, dry, and slightly rough. It enveloped mine completely. I'd have liked to find out if he truly *was* the best man or not. "Hi," I said. "I'm Ginger."

"And I," he said, "think I might be in love."

Looking up into those yummy brown eyes, I decided that would be fine with me.

"Don't mind him. He's been living with monkeys for a year in Sierra Leone, and he's forgotten how to hang out with humans," Steph said between bites of her bagel.

"Hey, I'm not picking things out of her hair. Although food offerings are a pretty common mating ritual among all the lower primates, I suppose," Craig said, still not letting go of my hand. "I forgot how incredibly beautiful the women of Santa Bonita are."

"You're a giant goofball, and you have been since I met you in third grade and you stuck straws in your mouth and pretended to be a walrus," Steph said.

Craig dropped my hand. "Hey! That's pretty high humor for a nine-year-old. Have a heart, Steph."

"So if you've been around here since third grade, how come I've never met you?" I asked. As in, where have you been all my life, you handsome hunka hunka burning love?

"The curse of the Esposito men," Craig said, dropping his eyes and crossing his hands in front of himself fig-leaf style. "My father and my uncle were sent off to Thatcher at fourteen, and they did the same to their sons. Justin and I both went to boarding school in Ojai. We only got back here for summer vacations and holidays."

He said it as if it had been a punishment. Thatcher. My heart bleeds. It's only one of the most prestigious prep schools in the United States. No wonder I'd never seen this guy. Not only were he and his cousin just enough older than us to be off our radar in school, Cinn and I simply didn't run in the same league. They were all junior cotillion and country club. Of course, that's not a surprise when you're the mayor's son and nephew.

Cinn and I were all part-time jobs at Dairy Queen and public swimming pools. That's no surprise when you're a Zimmerman girl. Actually, Craig and his cousin Justin were a step above even the lofty heights of Ashley and Stephanie. Good for Ashley. She was marrying up. That wasn't so easy to do in Santa Bonita, where the caste system sometimes seems as strict as the one in Calcutta.

"And where are you now?" I asked, looking up from beneath my lashes since I know that's a good look for me.

He smiled broadly. "Right here. I'm back for Justin's wedding and to write up my notes from Africa. In September, I'm back to Stanford."

"Sounds nice," I said. It sounded like heaven. It sounded like getting out of Santa Bonita, something it didn't seem I'd ever do.

"I am indeed a lucky man," Craig said. "In every area but one."

"Oh, here it comes," Steph said, rolling her eyes and taking a bite out of her bagel. "Brace yourselves, girls."

"I am unlucky in love," Craig said, ignoring Jessica and Stephanie's boos. "I have no date for the wedding."

"He has been whining about this for two weeks. Ever since he came back, all we've heard about is how poor Craig doesn't have anyone to dance with at his cousin's wedding." Jessica whirled around in the chair. "But does he do anything about it? Oh, no. He's passed on all the perfectly decent dates I've suggested."

"I didn't want decent," he said, still not letting go of my hand. "I wanted special. I wanted magical."

"I've dangled two out there and he hasn't bitten for either of them," Stephanie said.

"Well, I'm about to bite now," Craig said. "Miss Ginger Zimmerman, would you do me the honor of being my date tonight?"

I stared at him. "Are you nuts?" I asked.

"The jury's out on that," he said, smiling. "The question still stands."

I looked over at Cinnamon, who was putting bobby pins and clips back into their compartments at her station and seemed not to be paying attention at all. Whatever I'd seen on her face when Craig had come in was gone, but I knew I hadn't imagined it. "I don't know," I demurred. "It's awfully short notice."

"Oh, do it!" Steph said. "It'll be fun. I'll have someone to talk to. Only our most annoying cousins are coming to the wedding."

"And you'd be right there if something happened to our hair," Jessica said.

Oh, great.

"Please," Craig said, the smile gone and those luscious chocolate brown eyes gazing into mine. "Seriously. Please."

"Okay," I said.

"That was delicious," Ashley said.

We all turned. She was over by the bag of bagels, peanut butter smeared all over her hands and chin. "A jalapeño-cheddar bagel with peanut butter was exactly what I needed to calm my stomach. Maybe we should pick up some extras on our way to the church."

We watched the bridal party take off for their pictures and Cinnamon looked at her watch. "You have enough time to get to Mom's shop and get a dress if you hurry. I'll be waiting back here for you."

"I won't," Natalie said, gathering up her purse. "I'm going to memorize the muscles of the lower leg. I'll make up a kick-ass mnemonic for you though."

"Thanks," I told her, gathering up my purse and keys.

"Just one word of advice," Natalie said, that mother tone coming into her voice. "No kissing on the first date. When he swoops in for that big wet one, turn your head so it lands on your cheek."

Having heard about a few of Natalie's dating escapades, I turned and stared at her.

"What?" she said. "I never kiss a guy on the first date."

I continued to stare at her.

"Fine," she said. "A lucky few get a blow job on our first date, but never a kiss."

When I hustled out of the shop, I saw Tessie Hamilton by the shop's mailbox. Tessie runs the watch repair and trophy shop next door to Do It Up. She firmly believes in alien abduction, that Bill Clinton profited from drug smuggling at the Mena airport while he was governor of Arkansas, that we never landed on the moon, and that regardless of age, temperament, or coloring, blonder is always better. She is seventy years old if she's a day and looks like a wizened little monkey wearing a wig, with a cigarette permanently·dangling from her lips. Never ever mention Marilyn Monroe in her presence. It can go only one of two ways. You can get an hour-long discourse on the life and times of Norma Jean or you can get an hour-long discourse on the Kennedys, the mafia, and how Marilyn was murdered.

I am so grateful that she goes to ExcellaCuts. I cannot imagine a worse walking advertisement for hair care than Tessie Hamilton.

"Hey, Tess," I said. "What are you up to?"

Tess jumped as if I'd poked her with a pin. "Nothing. Why would I be up to anything?"

Okaayyyy. "It's just a saying, Tess. Everything okay?"

She nodded, her lips tightening into a skinny line. "Why wouldn't they be okay?"

This was bad even for Tess, so I waved and kept moving. I ran the few blocks to Mom's. It was early in the day and the fog hadn't burned off yet. I wrapped my hoodie a little closer around myself.

"I need something to wear to Ashley Elliott's wedding," I said as I burst into Pass It On.

"You're going where?" Mom asked.

"To Ashley Elliott's wedding," I repeated. "And I need something to wear. Now." I tried to duck around her to get to the cocktail dress I could see on the rack behind her. It looked like something Audrey Hepburn would have worn in *Sabrina,* which would be perfect on so very many levels. First, the dress would fit like a dream. Second, it would be perfectly appropriate for a spring wedding. Third, I'd be just like Audrey in the movie: the poor girl who gets to go to the ball like Cinderella. Now I just had to get Mom to give me the damn dress.

Secondhand may not sound like the way to go for a society wedding, but trust me, Mom's shop is more vintage than hand-me-down. It's where all the wealthy ladies of Santa Bonita and the surrounding little towns that dot the California coast go to dump their wardrobes each year.

If you think hairdressers know everyone's secrets, you are underestimating the information available to the owner of your local secondhand store. She knows if you've lost weight because you're too nervous and you've stopped eating. She knows if you've gained weight because your husband is more interested in his golf score than scoring with you, and you've been hitting the Ben & Jerry's pretty hard at night. She knows if you've got a will of iron and are still wearing the same dress size you did in high school. She knows if you've turned forty and have decided to give up miniskirts. She knows if your husband left you for a younger woman and you've gotten rid of all your sensible knee-length skirts and are wearing things that would get you kicked out of the local high school for violating dress code.

Or you would know if you weren't my mom, who lived in a haze of happiness when my dad was in town and in a daze of depression when he was gone. I honestly wondered how she stayed in business sometimes. It was like she had a fairy godmother or something.

Some of the stuff in the shop has barely been worn. In fact, the dress next to mine still had the price tags on it. The only real problem with picking a dress from Mom's shop would be if I showed up in a dress that had been dumped by another wedding guest. "Whose dress was this?" I said, reaching toward it.

"I have no idea." Mom deftly switched position to block me. "Since when are you and Ashley such great friends that you got invited to her wedding?"

"We're not. She didn't invite me." I fell back, hoping to lull her into a false sense of security. Then I'd lunge and snag the dress. It was sheer gold fabric over a solid underdress. It was sleeveless and looked like it would fit snugly down to the waist and then flare in one of those fabulous fifties-looking skirts. "Seriously, who dumped it?"

"I don't know and I don't care." Mom crossed her arms over her chest and shook her head. "You're crashing Ashley's wedding? I don't think so."

Honestly, it made me want to laugh, but that would have hurt Mom's feelings and she's always been a bit . . . fragile. Cinnamon and I were never afraid of being spanked or grounded. We lived in fear that we would make Mom cry. Still, the stern propriety bit coming from her was pretty laughable.

"I'm not crashing, Mom. One of the groomsmen just moved back here and didn't have anyone to take as his date. He asked me today and I thought it would be fun." I edged the teensiest bit to my left. If I could make it a few more inches without Mom noticing, I was pretty sure I could reach around her to get the dress. "Stephanie said I'd be doing them all a favor."

"He asked you today? That doesn't seem very respectful. Why didn't he ask you earlier?" Mom edged with me, damn it.

"He couldn't ask me before today. He only met me today. Plus, he's been out of the country for the past year." I decided to go for the full frontal attack. "Please, Mom, please, can I try on the dress? I already told him I'd go and I really don't have anything I could wear." I let the tiniest wobble shake my voice.

I saw her shoulders sag and knew I'd won. She didn't like to make Cinnamon or me cry any more than we liked to make her cry. I grabbed the dress and trotted off to the dressing room. "Thank you thank you thank you. He is sooooo cute, Mom. And he's going to Stanford in the fall!"

Mom sighed. "So what's this dreamboat's name?"

"Esposito," I said, shimmying out of my jeans, dumping my hoodie, and pulling my top off over my head. "Craig Esposito."

The curtains of the dressing room flew open. "You're going to the Elliott wedding with an Esposito?"

"Mom!" I squealed, trying to cover myself with my arms. "A little privacy?"

She stepped into the dressing room with me and pulled the curtain behind us. "This is not a good idea, Ginger. It's not a good idea at all."

That was an understatement. The dressing rooms at Pass It On were not particularly spacious. "Mom, get out and let me try on the dress. I already know what you're going to say."

"You do?" She crossed her arms over her chest and looked down at me. Mom's got at least three inches on me.

"Messing around with a boy like that is only going to bring me heartbreak. Everyone has their place in the world and mine is not with those people, and they will never let me forget that. Rich boys who ask out girls like me are only looking for one thing."

"You know all that and you still said yes?"

"Yes. Now can I try on the dress or not?" I squared off with Mom. A little height inequality didn't intimidate me. Not when I had a chance to get my hands on what looked suspiciously like vintage Dior.

"There are things you don't know about the Espositos." Mom pressed her lips together and flounced out of the dressing room. Fine—she could squeeze her lips together until they fused, as long she let me try on that dress. "He'll break your heart. The Espositos are not nice people," she said from outside the curtains.

"I don't believe in broken hearts, and Craig is different. I can tell." I unzipped the dress and carefully stepped into it.

"I know what you're thinking, Ginger, and it's not going to work out that way. This isn't a movie."

"I know it's not a movie. If it was a movie, I'd have a soundtrack." I zipped up and then turned to the mirror.

"It's not going to get you what you want."

The dress fit like a dream. I looked amazing.

I stepped out of the dressing room. "Are you sure about that?" I asked.

CHAPTER FIVE

I ran the couple of blocks back to Do It Up with the dress slung over my shoulder, practically skipping. The way I was feeling, I was surprised that woodland creatures weren't scampering out of the flowering hedges and frolicking around my feet as I went. Linda Johnson waved as I went by. She was hanging out the window of her second-story bathroom, having a cigarette. I couldn't believe Norman hadn't figured out she was smoking again yet. I didn't think the smoking-out-the-bathroom-window-with-the-fan-going thing would work for that long. On the other hand, maybe he didn't want to know. "You look happy," she called.

"You look guilty," I called back.

She laughed and closed the window.

I rushed into the shop. Jolene had come for her usual clean-up duty. True to her word, after a four-day camping trip in Lassen Volcanic National Park, Jolene had started showing up every day for an hour or two. She swept, mopped, wiped down counters, and occasionally answered the phones, but she'd more than worked off her updo and makeup.

"Hey," I said. "What are you doing here? I thought you were a free woman."

She blushed. "I had Natalie give me a pedicure. I didn't want my feet scratchin' Ronnie's legs at night, so I'm working that off now."

"You won't believe the dress I found at Mom's," I squealed at Cinn. "It's fabulous and it fits us perfectly." I lifted up the plastic garment bag so Cinnamon could see it.

She smiled. "It's not exactly my style. I don't think you'll have to worry about me stealing it out of your closet."

It was true. There were no sequins, fringes, or tassels, no bell sleeves or flowing velvet. Still, it would have looked great on her. "You never know when you might want a change of pace."

"It's beautiful," Jolene said, leaning for a moment on her broom. "I bet you look like a million bucks."

I grinned. "I do."

"Does it have to go on over your head or can you step in?" Cinnamon asked.

"Step in."

She made a sweeping gesture in front of her stylist's chair. "Then sit on down, sweetie, and let me do you up."

"Up is definitely the way to go. Up and sleek."

"Audrey Hepburn in *Sabrina*?" Cinnamon asked.

We do have that weird twin psychic thing. I can't rely on it for anything practical, like mental messages to pick up bread and milk at the grocery or to pay the electric bill, but it almost always works for hair. "Exactly," I said.

Cinnamon started the long, arduous process of straightening my curls. I couldn't help smiling when I realized the straightener had already been plugged in and heated up before I walked in. "So that Craig guy is cute," Cinnamon said as she slid the paddles down the length of my hair.

"Is it okay?" Our eyes met in the mirror, which was always trippy. Most people think Cinnamon and I are identical. Mostly, they're right. We're both the teensiest bit lopsided and our lops side off in mirror-image ways. My left eye is a tiny bit lower than my right. Cinnamon's right eye is a tiny bit lower than her left. When I look at her straight on, it's like looking at me in a mirror. When I look at her in a mirror next to me, I get a teensy bit confused about which one of us is which. It makes me a little sympathetic to all those people who can't tell us apart. "You didn't want him, did you?"

"Him? No way!" Cinnamon separated off another hank of hair.

"Don't say it like that! You make him sound diseased or something."

"He's not diseased," she said quietly. "He's fine."

"Cinnamon, are you really sure? You didn't want him?"

"I didn't want him." She slid the paddles down my hair.

I hesitated. If she said she didn't want him, maybe she truly didn't want him. "It's just that you looked kind of funny when he first walked in."

"I don't know what you mean. What kind of funny?" Cinn kept straightening.

I tried to think of a way to describe it. "Funny like you'd seen a ghost."

Cinnamon stopped and shook the straightener at me the way a schoolteacher would shake a finger at a naughty student. "You know how I feel about that kind of talk, Ginger."

I scowled at her. "Fine. You looked like you'd seen the spirit of someone who had passed."

"Better," she said with a smile.

"So?" I asked.

"So what?" Cinnamon asked back, already busy with my hair. See what I mean about the psychic thing not always working for me?

"So what was the business with almost burning Ashley's hair off the back of her head?"

"Oh, that." Cinnamon's brow furrowed and she pursed her lips. "I thought he was someone else."

"Who? Who have we ever met who was that cute and that smart and that funny?"

"No one. Like I said, I made a mistake. He wasn't anybody I knew." Cinnamon's jaw started to jut, a sure danger sign, and I knew I wasn't going to get anything more out of her. Besides, it didn't really matter. All that mattered was that I wasn't poaching anyone my sister might have felt she had dibs on, because dibs would negate the whole coin-toss thing. Dibs were sacred.

"So he didn't have a murky aura or anything, right?" I don't really believe most of Cinn's New Age crap, but it never hurts to hedge your bets.

"No. Not at all. He had a lovely aura, a kind of throbbing turquoise."

"Throbbing, Cinnamon? His aura throbbed?"

"Absolutely. He's a man of great passion. And turquoise is the stone of communication. It's supposed to make the speaker more eloquent and more honest."

Crystal shmystal, I thought. "We're not talking euphemisms here, are we? When you say his aura throbbed you're not talking about . . . you know . . ."

Cinnamon swatted me. "Don't be gross. I'm speaking meta-physically."

"Well, as long as he only throbs metaphysically, I guess that's okay."

"Bet he throbs plenty the other way, too. He looked like a throbber to me." Cinnamon started to giggle.

I started to giggle, too. "One can only hope . . . Wait a minute, he's not gay, is he?" I have no gaydar. None.

"Nope, definitely not gay. Definitely a throbber."

Cinnamon finished my hair and I headed back to our place to finish getting ready. I didn't have a whole heck of a lot of time left. In forty-five minutes I was due to meet Craig at the church, but my hair was up and my makeup was on. I just needed the right underwear and shoes, and to put on the dress.

I was golden.

I stepped into the dress and I really did feel golden. Santa Bonita is not the kind of town where people dress up much. The annual Artichoke Festival is not the kind of affair that demands formal wear, and that's our big event. Well, that and when the little Latino girls all dress up on Mary's birthday in September and troop down the street in their little white dresses. On top of that, my life was not the kind of life that involved formal wear.

I tried not to let it bother me, but sometimes it seemed like I spent all my time getting everyone else ready for their life except me.

But today I was standing there, all dressed up to go to the best wedding in town with the cutest—and let's face it, probably richest—guy I'd met in a long, long time.

Maybe Cinnamon's card for the day was exactly right: Beorc, the card of births and new beginnings.

I heard the door to the apartment open and shut, and Sage came bouncing into my bedroom, all bedazzled jeans, swinging braids, and tiny little pink high-top Converse sneakers with hearts on them.

"You look like a princess, Auntie G!" she exclaimed, heading toward me with fingers outstretched to touch the fabric of my dress. She's a very tactile child.

I took a step back. "Let me see those hands first," I demanded. We were still working on the personal hygiene thing, and the last thing I wanted was peanut butter, dirt, or snot smeared on me right before it was time to go. I'm a professional and I can say with great authority that having boogers on your dress completely ruins the Audrey Hepburn look. Audrey was not a booger kind of gal.

Sage stopped and held them up for inspection. They didn't have any big chunks on them.

"Okay, then," I said, and she rushed over to run the sheer overdress through her hands. I turned to look in the mirror again.

"So I hear you've gone and caught yourself an Esposito boy," a raspy voice said behind me.

I didn't have to turn around. The voice, the comment, and the unannounced entry into my home all added up to one person: Grandma. I knew she was watching Sage while we did the Elliott wedding. Dad was, inexplicably, still hanging around Santa Bonita, and that made Mom a much less reliable babysitter these days. Although admittedly not as unreliable as she usually was, based on the number of times each week Sage and Cinnamon had dinner over there. Personally, I was glad of the quiet in the apartment so I could study without paying for every minute with a minute of Monopoly.

Anyway, back to Mom and her relative reliability. It's been that way since I can remember. Once Dad would show up in town, it was as if the rest of us became transparent. Mom simply didn't see us anymore. Or at least not very clearly.

"I wouldn't say caught, Grandma." I was a little surprised that she knew about Craig. That news traveled fast in Santa Bonita was not news to me. I knew Georgette Reynolds's husband was having an affair long before she did, for instance, although how a supposedly intelligent man could think it was possible to use a public pay phone without arousing suspicion is a complete mystery to me. Clearly, he couldn't call from home or his office, and he didn't want the call to show up on his cell phone. Either he was a spy or he was having an affair. It wasn't my fault he'd used the pay phone right in front of our shop. I'd also known that Bradley Cranston had been arrested at school for sneaking in wine coolers before his mother did. I'd had to answer her cell phone for her, since her nails were wet.

But who had spilled about Craig? I didn't think Mom would have said anything, or at least not this quickly. Grandma Rosemary was no more happy about Dad's reappearance than I was, and the two of them had been pretty chilly with each other lately. I prayed that by the time I was in my forties I would be done rebelling against Mom. Although, since rebelling against Mom often took the form of taking college classes and refusing to have an illegitimate child with a name from a grocery category, perhaps I should adjust my hopes and prayers to something less destructive. Still, I don't think she would have dialed up Grandma the second I left her store with the dress.

Then I remembered Tessie by the mailbox, looking like a guilty little monkey who had just stolen somebody's banana. Despite the fact that she looked twenty years older than Grandma R, Tessie was about the same age. Maybe she'd been acting so weird because she'd been eavesdropping. Lord help me if my life ever became small enough that listening to someone getting their hair done would be considered entertainment. It was already small enough to make me feel smothered. "Maybe temporarily ensnared rather than actually caught," I said.

She laughed her throaty laugh. She quit smoking back in the

seventies, but the cigarette voice was here to stay. "Good for you, girl. Good for you. Step carefully though. Those Esposito men have quite a reputation around here."

"As much of a reputation as the Zimmerman women?" I countered with a smile.

My grandma is notorious, in a sexy, soulful, Ingrid Bergman kind of way. When she was seventeen, she won the local beauty pageant. There may never have been a more fiery and delicious Artichoke Queen in all the history of Santa Bonita. She was beautiful and feisty and so tender that all the men wanted to dip her in butter and eat her up. At least, that's the way she tells it.

That's why the judge from Santa Barbara fell in love with her. He proposed hours after she was crowned, and because he was dashing and handsome and worldly, she'd said yes. They were in Reno by the next day and were married and off to New York on their honeymoon the day after that.

It was in New York that Grandma had discovered that her dashing, handsome, and ever-so-worldly beauty pageant judge already happened to be married to someone else.

It really was a shame. It was even more of a shame that she also happened to know where he kept his little gun.

"More of a reputation than us," Grandma said, letting her voice drop to its lowest register, which is pretty darn low.

"Who could have more of a reputation than us?" I said. I tried not to mind the reputation thing anymore. In junior high and high school, it had been torturous.

I am completely unlike my mother—who'd been the teenage-girl equivalent of Halley's Comet—and, of course, Cinnamon. I had pretty well kept my nose clean. Someone had to.

"Trust me, darling." Grandma seated herself on my couch in a move that Anne Bancroft in *The Graduate* couldn't have pulled off with more panache. "There are reputations and then there are reputations. Let's just say that I was acquainted with the Esposito brothers in their younger years. Before Daniel married that simpering Semple girl. It's her blood that makes the young pup so weak."

"Grandma, you're talking about the groom."

Sage's face creased with confusion. "Someone's marrying a puppy? Does that mean I could marry a unicorn? 'Cause Annabelle Rodriguez says that I can't and I'd really like to marry a unicorn. I think they're pretty."

"Annabelle's right. You can't marry a unicorn. First of all, they're pretend. Second, you're pretty much required to stick to your own species. Grandma Rosemary doesn't mean that the groom is really a puppy."

"Oh." Sage's face fell and she went back to playing with the overskirt of my dress. "That's too bad. I like unicorns."

"You look lovely, by the way." Grandma got up off the couch and came to stand behind me. "An absolute vision."

"Thanks," I said, a warm glow in my tummy. Grandma Rosemary didn't hand out compliments like candy. If she said I was a vision, I was a freakin' revelation with an angel choir behind me.

Cinnamon hurried in with a bag of groceries in her arms.

"Mama!" Sage cried, and rushed over to Cinnamon and threw her arms around her legs.

"Hey, sweetness," Cinnamon said, hobbling over to the table with Sage stuck to her legs. "How was your day?"

"Good. I filled all the salt and pepper shakers and then Grandma and I played cards."

"She owes me nearly fourteen thousand dollars now," Rosemary said. "I'm planning on retiring soon."

"Can't get blood from a stone," Cinn said as she pulled macaroni-and-cheese boxes and some apples out of her bag.

"It's like anything else, darling," Grandma said in that throaty voice that still sounded sexy. "You just have to know how to wring it." Then, before she turned and sashayed out the door, she swatted me on the ass and said, "Knock 'em dead, kid."

No wonder that jury acquitted her. Who could lock up a magnificent creature like that?

The actual wedding went smoothly. Ashley looked gorgeous. Justin, Craig, and their friend, Phillip, all looked devastating in their tuxes. What is it about a man in a tux? It's almost as good as a man in a tool belt, and I love a man in a tool belt. I wonder if they could make a tool belt cummerbund for a tuxedo?

Craig looked like he'd been born in his tuxedo, and I bet it wasn't a rental. The material looked too fine, and there were no shiny spots where too many dry cleaners had had to try to get out spilled wine or beer, or other fluids that didn't bear thinking about. It clung to his broad shoulders and draped to his narrow hips, and the sight of him in it was enough to make my knees wobbly.

No one fainted. No one forgot their lines. The flowers all arrived on time.

It was slightly embarrassing to see the confused look on Ashley's mother's face as I went through the receiving line, and I got it again from Justin's mother a few handshakes later. I felt like I could see thought bubbles over their heads: Who is that? What is she doing here? Oh, dear lord, did someone invite one of those Zimmerman women? Where is security?

Like I said, Cinnamon and I are pretty much carbon copies of Mom, and her apple didn't fall far from Grandma Rosemary's tree. We're recognizable, especially in a town the size of Santa Bonita.

Outside the church, I had one of those awful moments where you don't know what to do next. Should I head to the restaurant without Craig? Should I wait for him? Meanwhile, the crowd on the lawn seemed divided into two groups: one that recognized me and wasn't sure why I was there, and one that didn't recognize me and couldn't figure out why I was there. Neither group was exactly welcoming me in, so I stood by myself under a jacaranda tree and waited for a sign.

"Wow! You look even more gorgeous than you did this morning," Craig said as he hurried toward me across the lawn.

I felt my face flush. It's not like I never get any attention from men. It's just that it always feels so damn good, especially when it comes from one who looks like Craig. "Thanks. You don't look too shabby yourself. You should consider wearing one of those every day."

"Yep." He nodded. "That's one of the things I love about living in northern California. Tuxedos and painful shoes every day. They're perfect down at the taqueria."

"I suppose there could be some pitfalls to my plan," I acceded.

"Listen, Ashley says we've got at least another thirty minutes of photos before we can go to the restaurant, and every shot needs to be perfect, so if we want to eat before midnight we'd better stop clowning around." He stuck his hands in his pockets and rocked back on his heels. "The girl is a dictator, and not a benevolent one."

"We call it bridal disease at the shop. A perfectly reasonable young woman gets engaged, and by the time the wedding actually starts, she becomes the Nazi Bride from Hell." I cannot count the number of times we've seen it happen. It didn't even surprise me anymore.

Craig's brows furrowed a little, which only made him more

handsome. "I don't know Ashley that well. I'll have to take your word that she was ever perfectly reasonable. Today wouldn't exactly be a good example of that."

Fine. "Perfectly reasonable" was not a description I would have applied to her ever. Still, it didn't seem nice to dis the bride on her Special Day. "Do you want me to wait here?" I looked around outside the church for a place to sit.

Craig shook his head. "That's why I came out. Why don't you head over to the restaurant? I'll meet you there."

An hour later, it occurred to me that I could have gotten dressed up and hit the bar at the Moss Beach Distillery by myself without being invited by Craig Esposito.

"You want another Diet Coke?" Manuel Hwang asked me. Manuel and I go way back, like maybe second grade. His mom, Rosarita, used to cook at Grandma R's restaurant, and his father, Mingtung, owned the flower farm where Grandma got all her arrangements. He was way more my people than the rest of the folks at the restaurant. I was beginning to feel like I would be a lot happier behind the bar, too, even if I didn't know how to mix a decent martini.

I shook my head. "No thanks. I think three is plenty."

"You're looking good, *mi hija*." He glanced around. "It's not your fault these people are such snobs."

I tried to smile back, but it was difficult. The way the Cinderella story is supposed to work is that when Cinderella shows up at the ball, everyone wants to dance with her because she's so beautiful. They're not supposed to all form little clumps and whisper while casting furtive glances her way over their shoulders. Someone should at least talk to her, someone besides one elderly lady with elegant, if thinning, snow-white hair who patted me on the arm and told me I looked lovely until someone else dragged her away while whispering in her ear. To her credit, the older lady shook the other person off and gave her a disapproving look, but she also didn't come back to chitchat.

At least someone could try to steal Cinderella's shoes. Which didn't seem likely since mine came from Payless.

I'd seen the wedding party swan in about five minutes ago, but I hadn't been able to catch Craig's eye. I'd caught a peek of Ashley's beautifully coiffed blonde locks as she was hustled by in the center of a throng made up of her bridesmaids and her mother.

Then suddenly Craig put a hand on my shoulder. "Hey, there you are!"

"Yep," I said, trying not to sound pathetic. "Right here. Waiting."

His brow furrowed a little. "Why are you all by yourself?"

Because the rest of the guests are snobs? "Oh, I was catchin' up with Manuel here," I said, tipping a head toward the bartender.

Craig looked up, brow still furrowed, and stuck out his hand. "Hi, Manuel. I'm Craig Esposito."

Manuel set down the glass he was polishing and dried his hands on a towel before taking Craig's. "Nice to meet you, sir."

Craig didn't bat even one long-lashed eye at the deferential title. I suppose if you're born to it, you're used to it. "There's apparently some form of beauty emergency in the back room, and there was some hope that you could come back and consult," he said to me.

Ah, yes, and perhaps I could pass around a tray of hors d'oeuvres when I was done. "Sure," I said. "Then I think I should probably get going."

Craig's eyes opened in surprise. "Going? The party hasn't even started yet. I haven't gotten to know you yet." He leaned in and I felt heat surge through me. "And I'd really like to get to know you."

I leaned toward him, too, so our foreheads just barely touched. "I'd like to get to know you, too, but maybe this isn't the place. Maybe we should wait and go someplace more private where there isn't such a crowd."

"Hold that thought," Craig said, touching his finger ever so gently to my lips, making me shiver right down to my toes. "I want to hear more, but first I'd like you to meet the groom. Justin, hey, Justin, over here."

"So," a voice behind me said, "I'm finally getting to meet this incredible woman that you stumbled on today? The most beautiful woman in Santa Bonita? Which you'd better not say in front of Ashley again on her Special Day, or she's likely to smack you upside the head. She might be tiny, but she's been working out and she packs a wallop."

I turned to say hello. The man who looked almost like a twin to Craig took one look at me, turned white as a sheet, and started to crumple to the ground.

"Dude!" Craig grabbed Justin's arm and guided him onto a bar stool. "Have you eaten anything today?"

Justin's Adam's apple bobbed up and down a couple of times before he choked out an answer. "Not much, to be honest. Wow. That was embarrassing." He turned toward me. "I'm so sorry. It's nice to meet you."

It was a nice recovery, considering that he'd taken one look at me and almost passed out. "Nice to meet you, too. Would you like me to get you a glass of water? You look a little pale."

"No. No, thank you. You're . . ." He looked over at Craig, more than a hint of desperation on that dark, handsome face, then back to me, full in the eyes. "Tell me again, please. I'm so sorry."

"That's okay," I said. "It's your wedding day. Of course you're a little overwhelmed. I'm Ginger Zimmerman. My twin sister, Cinnamon, did Ashley's hair. I did Stephanie's and Jessica's."

"Ashley?" Justin looked confused for a moment. "Oh, yes. Ashley. Your sister? Your twin sister? An identical twin?"

"Yep. Identical. We can tell ourselves apart; everybody else has trouble." I turned to Craig. "Speaking of trouble, didn't you say there was some kind of trouble with the bridal party?"

Craig jumped. "Oh, yeah. Ashley's having a hissy about something with her hair and they were hoping you'd come fix it." He paused. "Are you sure you don't mind?"

I suppose he got points for realizing that it was an odd request to make of a wedding guest. I shook my head. "It's fine. I'm happy to help." I'd be happy to be out of that bar, with the groom looking at me like the Ghost of Christmas Past and everybody else looking at me like something they'd found on the bottom of their shoe. The dress was great, damn it! I knew it was. Wasn't it?

"They're in the back lounge. Do you know where it is?" Craig cast a worried glance at Justin. I wouldn't have wanted to leave him alone right then, either; it wasn't a good best man thing to do. More points.

"Got it covered," I said, and hopped down off my bar stool. I sidled through the crowd, which was getting thicker and hungrier based on the mutterings I was hearing. I hoped Ashley's hair emergency was minor. If she didn't come out soon there was going to be a riot.

Once I made it to the hallway I could walk more freely. There was a sudden chill and the hair on my arms stood up. I froze for a second.

The Moss Beach Distillery is haunted. I know that makes me sound like a total flake, but everybody who spends any time at the Distillery meets the Blue Lady. Cinnamon has had a number of lovely chats with her in the downstairs bathroom. I have never seen her, despite busing tables in the dining room the summer I was fifteen. The story is that the Blue Lady was the wife of one of the Distillery's bartenders back when it was a speakeasy and a major smuggling stop during prohibition. She'd had a car accident on her way to meet her lover, the piano player, and wouldn't cross over to the afterlife now because she didn't want to spend eternity with her pissed-off husband.

There were worse places to spend eternity than the Moss Beach Distillery, though. They make a mean hot chocolate and the view from the deck is amazing. The Blue Lady wasn't malicious. I'd heard she was a little mischievous. The other busboys and girls complained about being pinched or tickled as they walked with their trays. The worst thing I'd ever experienced was an unfortunate sneeze while carrying a bowl of French onion soup. Cinnamon suggested that the Blue Lady could have tickled my nose, but I was pretty sure it was just the almond blossoms someone had stuck in a vase in the hall.

I caught a sweet scent on the air. Slightly decayed roses? Or was that Axe body spray? A large dark shape emerged from the alcove where the phone booths were with a smoothness usually reserved for particularly nasty demons on *Buffy*. My heart leapt into my throat.

"Troy!" I said, my hand over my heart. "You scared me."

He blushed a little. "Sorry. I didn't mean to leap out at you like that. I've been waiting there for a while and I didn't think about it."

"Waiting for what? Somebody whose heart you could stop?"

"No. I was waiting for you. Or anybody else I knew and could talk to. There aren't so many here that I pal around with."

He blushed harder. He shoved a folded-up piece of notebook paper into my hand. "I was hoping you could take this note to Ashley."

"You're sending a note to Ashley?" I didn't mean to sound incredulous. It's just that Troy sending a note to Ashley all folded up and sweaty from his palms seemed about as likely as Barack Obama waiting around to send a note to Britney Spears. "Does it have two boxes marked Yes and No, and does it ask if she likes you?"

Troy blushed harder and I felt terrible. "Please, Ginger. Just give it to her. Try not to let anyone see you do it." Then he glided away with that curious light-on-his-feet thing that certain big men have.

I went on to the back lounge, repeating with each step the little mantra that Mrs. Owens tried to teach me in second grade: "Think before you speak. Think before you speak." One of my faults is a tendency to let what is on the lung be on the tongue. Being straightforward may be a virtue, but being blunt is not, especially if you're in the profession I currently reluctantly am in. Nobody wants to hear it if you don't like their highlights or don't think their new moisturizer is making a damn bit of difference in the lines around their eyes.

I slipped through the door to the lounge, not bothering to knock.

"Don't touch me," Ashley shrieked. "I need a professional."

As near as I could tell, Ashley's hair emergency was a single ringlet that had come loose. Granted, it was near the front and it did look a little silly hanging down like a Hasidic side curl with a dangling bobby pin. Still, it was one ringlet. It wasn't like she'd set her hair on fire or anything. It would have been funny, except that she was hyperventilating and looked near tears.

I'd spent a fair amount of time on that makeup, and no ringlet was going to make my little ice princess look like a raccoon. Not on my watch.

I threaded my way through the bevy of women who were circling just out of reach of her French- tipped claws. "Ashley," I said, taking her hands in mine and slipping the note into one of hers as I did it. "Calm down."

She looked down at the note and then up at me, confusion clear on her face.

"Troy," I mouthed at her, I hoped subtly. It was the least I could do after hurting Troy's feelings in the hallway.

She inhaled a quick, sharp breath. "Ginger, you're here! Can you fix it? Can you put it back?"

This was not rocket science. But logic and common sense were not what was called for here. I stepped back and took a long look at the side of Ashley's head. Then I extended my hands so that they hovered inches from her scalp and closed my eyes. I hummed a little.

Cinnamon did this crap all the time. She'd make this little humming noise, then open her eyes, clap her hands, and say she knew exactly what whoever was in front of her needed. Invariably, the woman left our shop convinced that she had indeed received the haircut of her life. In all honesty, she often had.

Some people have visions of the future or know when someone's going to die. My sister knows your perfect haircut. She claims it just pops into her brain. The only reason she needed to go to beauty school was to figure out how to make her visions a reality. That, and to get a license. She already knew which cut would go with which face shape, and what hair texture could withstand what kind of styling regime.

I opened my eyes, clapped my hands, twirled the ringlet up, and pinned it with a bobby pin. "There," I said.

Ashley's hands flew to her mouth. "Oh, Ginger, thank you! It's perfect again. It's just right for my Special Day."

The rest of the women surged forward and I saw that some of Stephanie's hair had come loose as well. "Hey, Steph," I said. "Let me fix that for you."

"Thanks, Ginger. You don't have to," Steph said.

"Sit down." I gestured to a chair a few feet away from where everyone was swarming Ashley. "I don't mind. Mingling hasn't exactly been working real well for me."

Steph turned to say something, but before she could, Craig came in, slipping between the ladies to come stand next to me.

"You're not supposed to be here, Craig," Steph said.

"I wanted to see how Ginger is doing," he said. "I've had to leave her alone too much as it is."

That made a little warm glow in the pit of my stomach. The cute, smart, rich guy didn't want to leave me alone. "So how am I doing?" I said.

"You're like a bonobo," he said, sounding amazed.

"Craig!" Stephanie smacked him with her tiny beaded purse. "Never call a woman a bonobo. That's insulting!"

"What's a bonobo?" I asked, pinning Steph's hair smooth again.

"A monkey," Stephanie said. "A very slutty monkey."

"I wasn't talking about that part of being a bonobo!" Craig protested.

"Slutty?" I asked Stephanie.

"Very slutty," Stephanie said, her face a mask of horror. "I told you he wasn't used to being around humans again."

"Exactly what part of bonobo-hood was I exemplifying?"

"First of all, bonobos are genetically the animal most similar to us," Craig said, his voice picking up.

I was not entirely without monkey knowledge myself, though. "I thought that was chimpanzees."

"Them, too, but bonobos are every bit as close, and while chimpanzees are matrilocal—daughters stay close to their mothers—bonobos aren't. Young bonobo females are forced to go off and find new tribes to live with."

"In that case you're definitely mistaken about me and bonobos. There's nobody more matrilocal in Santa Bonita than the Zimmermans," I said. Cinnamon and I had moved all of one mile from Mom; we were still in the same zip code. Mom, in turn, was no more than six blocks from Grandma Rosemary's condo. Granted, Grandma had moved there after Mom had moved from her house, but that house was just around the corner. We were stuck to each other like white on rice, with our noses so deeply in each other's business I often felt like my throat was going to swell shut with claustrophobia.

Craig continued talking about slutty monkeys. "Ah, but look at you here, helping groom the other females, finding ways to soothe them, fitting into their group as if you were born to it. That's one hundred percent bonobo behavior. Bonobos are good at making girlfriends."

Maybe I should have started grooming people in the bar. I would totally have done it, too, if I'd known that would be all it would take to get them to talk to me.

"And making out with their girlfriends, too," Steph said. "Take the bonobo comment back, Craig, before I kick your butt. In fact, get out of here entirely. Ginger will meet you in the bar in a few minutes."

Craig shook his head, but did as Steph asked and left.

"All done," I said, patting her back.

"You have to forgive Craig," Steph said. "He means well. He's just a bit of a doofus."

"There's nothing to forgive," I said. "Everything's fine."

Which was precisely when everything went to hell. Stephanie and Ashley's mother chose that moment to approach us.

"And you are?" Hope Elliott turned her parboiled blue eyes toward me. Sweat prickled instantly in my armpits. Imagine facing Blythe Danner if Blythe had eaten only lemons for the past two decades. Imagine facing the lemon-eating Blythe when she was wearing a mother-of-the-bride dress that probably cost more than three months' rent on my apartment. She frightened me.

I took a deep breath and held out my hand. "I'm Ginger Zimmerman. It's nice to meet you, Mrs. Elliott."

She didn't take it. Instead, she looked around, her gaze finally settling on Stephanie. "The hairdresser is here dressed as a wedding guest? Would someone care to explain?"

CHAPTER SIX

I dropped my hand, wishing I could sink into the floor.

"Mother!" Stephanie said, getting up and stepping between us. "Ginger is here as Craig's date."

"You can't be serious," Hope said. If she could have pursed her lips further, she would have. "What was he thinking?"

"Mother!" Stephanie repeated more sharply.

I didn't stay to hear more. I ducked out of the room and fled down the hall. I stopped at the bar to catch my breath. Craig was there.

So was a blonde. Okay, it's California. There are lots of blondes. This particular blonde happened to be hanging on my date as if she were an invertebrate and needed support, which made her somewhat more noticeable in my personal universe.

Craig looked up as I walked over. "Ginger, I'd like you to meet Kendra Lewis."

I didn't need to meet Kendra Lewis. I was well acquainted with her. Kendra's the kind of girl who gives rich girls their bad reputations. Kendra's the kind of girl on whom you should never ever turn your back—unless you like to have sharp things sticking out of it.

"We've met," I said, trying to muster a smile.

Kendra blinked her baby-doll blue eyes at me. "We have?"

Oooh. Nice one. Pretend I'm so unimportant that she doesn't even remember me. Pretend like she doesn't remember lighting my hair on fire in chemistry class. Pretend like she doesn't remember spilling iodine on my lab bench when I was up asking Mr. Hoffman a question. Then again, do sociopathic little boys remember every fly whose wings they've pulled off? Maybe she really *didn't* remember me.

"I sat in front of you in Mr. Hoffman's chemistry class."

Kendra snapped her fingers and blinked like she'd had a major brainstorm. Right. I'd lay odds she not only knew who I was, but knew whose date she was hanging on before I ever walked up. "I remember now. You have a twin sister. She's the one who had a baby our senior year." She pursed her big red lips into an O and then covered them with her hand as if she'd made a social gaffe. "Or was that you?"

I nearly smirked. She'd known who I was all along. "Nope. My sister is the one who got knocked up in high school."

"So how about you?" Kendra asked with a slithery smile. "Do you have any children yet?"

"Nope. Still single."

Kendra pretended to examine her fingernails, but I knew she was looking up at me from under those lashes. "As I recall, that's not exactly a deterrent to having children in your family."

Simply lovely. I had to admire the deftness with which she skewered me with my family's history.

I knew a little bit about Kendra's kin, too. "How's your sister, by the way? I haven't seen her in any of the local shops recently."

Do It Up was one of a score of local shops that finally banned Kim Lewis from entering. She was well known for taking the proverbial five-finger discount. It had started with little things when she was a kid—a lollipop from the Sugar Shack, a lipstick from Dolly's Drugs—but the last time she'd been in Do It Up, she'd stolen a bottle of expensive conditioner and two nail polishes off our rack. Now we were always booked solid when she called for an appointment.

Kendra's eyes narrowed. "She's, uh, taken to shopping in the city."

"Smart move," I said, not smiling this time.

Kendra glanced over Craig's shoulder and said, "I hope you two will excuse me. I just saw Jessica and I really must catch her."

I stood aside and let Kendra sweep past.

"What just happened there?" he asked. "I'm pretty sure something went down, but I can't figure it out."

"It's pretty simple. She insulted my family, so I reminded her that her family has a skeleton or two in its closet, which reminded her that those of us way down on the social ladder may know more about her than she's comfortable with."

"Wow. It was like watching two Old World cercopithecine monkeys battle for position, except a lot more verbal." He shook his head. "Steph's right. I spent too long in Africa. The more I watch people, the more like monkeys they seem."

"Well, this monkey is going to make like a banana and split. I'm sorry. I've got to go." The understatement of the year.

"Why? Not because of that thing with Kendra? She's not worth stressing over." He stood, positioning himself between me and most of the wedding guests.

"It's a little bit because of Kendra. I can't explain. I don't belong here. This was all a mistake." I looked up at him and regret stabbed my heart. I *so* didn't want to go. He was so handsome.

Craig's eyes narrowed. He took my arms in his hands. In a rush, I imagined what it would feel like to have him pull me against him. It was really good, in my imagination. I shivered.

"Tell me what happened," he said.

I thought about lying. I thought about refusing to answer, but I looked up into those melting brown chocolate eyes, and those big warm hands on my skin felt so very good. "Hope Elliott put me in my place in front of everybody."

"That bitch." Craig dropped his hands and his eyes narrowed. "I told Justin he was marrying into very questionable stock."

"Don't, Craig. That's exactly what Hope would say about me. Let's face it; she's right. We're poor white trash and the Elliotts are local royalty."

"No. You're bonobos and the Elliotts are a band of particularly nasty chimpanzees. You know, a mother chimpanzee of a certain rank will kill the daughters of a lower-ranking chimpanzee to assure that her daughters will have less competition." Craig nodded as if he'd made a particularly persuasive point in a debate.

I sighed. "I'm not competition for Ashley Elliott. I am Ashley Elliott's hairdresser. Actually, I'm not even her hairdresser. I'm her hairdresser's assistant. Even if the Elliotts were chimpanzees, they'd have no reason to notice I even exist. I don't have enough bananas to worry them."

"You don't see yourself the way others do. Trust me, you have tons of bananas. I know exactly what Hope Elliott is thinking: with you here, there's no way her daughter will be the center of attention." He slid his hand around my waist and I felt that amazing *zing!* race through my veins. "Stay. Please. I won't let any of those Elliott chimps near you. Stay and be my beautiful bonobo girl."

Now, how often does a girl get an offer like that?

It turned out that Craig's offer of keeping everyone away from me was an easy promise to keep. After Hope Elliott's performance in the back lounge, which I'm sure had been repeated and redramatized over and over, nobody wanted to come near me. It was handy when I wanted to get to the bar or the buffet, but not exactly a fun time. Except that Craig Esposito stuck to me like particularly handsome glue. That was nice. Maybe even a little better than nice.

Still, there are moments when a girl needs to be alone, like when she's heading for the bathroom after too many glasses of white wine. I was going down the hallway toward the restrooms when a young man in a well-cut suit careened out of the men's room. I knew I was in trouble when he tried to focus his eyes on me and failed. Sometimes you just have a feeling, you know?

"Hey, I know you!" He made an attempt to snap his fingers and was momentarily distracted by his failure to get a noise from them.

He was right; he did know me. Not that I would have expected him to remember. Lamont Gilman's father ran *the* insurance agency in Santa Bonita. Everybody got their insurance from Gilman and Associates. Even we did.

Lamont had disappeared from my radar around seventh grade. He had probably wound up at some place like Thatcher, like Craig. "Hey, Lamont," I said, trying to slide past him to the ladies' room.

Lamont shifted and effectively blocked my way. Based on the alcohol content on his breath, I may have miscalculated. Maybe he ended up at Mt. Bachelor, the boarding school for bad boys, instead of Thatcher. "You're one of those Zimmerman twins."

If I'd lit a match, we probably would have gone up like Fourth of July fireworks. Lamont pressed closer and I considered the fact that self-immolation might be preferable to being trapped by a sweaty, drunk, overgrown rich boy when I really needed to pee. "Guilty as charged."

I tried to wriggle past, but Lamont grabbed my arm and squinted closer. "I could never tell you two apart. Are you the snotty one or the one who got knocked up?"

There really wasn't a good answer to that one. "I'm the one who needs to get to the ladies' room, Lamont. If you'll excuse me . . ."

Lamont wasn't going to fall for any kind of polite ruse. "Whatcha doin' here anyway? You're too cute. Ashley wouldn't want you here. And you sure as hell aren't one of her friends. Not that she actually has friends. It's more like a posse." He pressed closer against me.

I tried to shove him away, but Lamont wasn't going anywhere. "Get off me, Lamont."

He pressed even closer. "Seriously, why the hell are you here?" His hands started creeping up to my waist.

I tried to shove them away, but he was like an octopus. "Let me go, Lamont. I mean it." God damn it. My voice quavered like Billie Burke's in *The Wizard of Oz*. I hate that. The more serious I get about something, the more likely I am to sound like a cartoon character.

He giggled. Is there anything creepier than grown men giggling? "Whatcha gonna do if I don't?"

A big hand clamped down on Lamont's shoulder. "She's gonna tell your mother that you still haven't learned any manners." Craig spun him around as if he were a toy top and shoved him down the hall.

Then he turned back to me. "You were gone awhile. I wanted to make sure you were okay."

"Thanks. I wasn't." The quiver was still in my voice.

He grimaced. "I'll stand guard if you want to go to the bathroom."

When I came out, we stepped outside to get some air and cleared the deck. Even the couples curled up under blankets on the deck chairs headed in. Craig slung his arm across my shoulder. He'd tossed the jacket and the tie pretty early into the reception, and with a glass of scotch in his hand, he looked like an ad for high-end living. Still, I knew I couldn't take much more.

"Craig, I've really got to go. This is too hard."

His lips tightened. "Are you sure?"

"Yeah. You can't be having fun either." Wasn't shunning the absolute worst thing the Puritans did to people? You had to stay and live with them, but they'd pretend you weren't there. It had to be worse than being put in stocks, although probably not as bad as being tried as a witch.

"You underestimate the pleasure I take in being the thorn in my family's side." His grin was a white slash against his tanned face. "Can I call you?"

Did I want to be someone's thorn? Then I looked up into that face that looked like Michelangelo had sculpted it and I smiled. Aw, hell, what's a slutty monkey to do? "You know where to find me."

As Craig walked me down the street to the Mustang, I pulled my wrap tighter around my shoulders. I waved to Troy, who sat in his cruiser watching a group of kids with skateboards head toward Il Pignoli Pizza. He nodded but didn't wave back.

Maybe he was waiting to catch the guests in a giant drunk-driving dragnet. Not that any of them would end up paying their tickets or losing their licenses; the mayor could make those things go away. In this town, he could pretty much make anything go away. Between being the mayor, running a profitable law office, and his substantial real estate holdings, I think Mayor Esposito could have walked down Willow Street naked and had us all talk about his grand new clothes.

"Sweet ride," Craig said, running his hand down the Mustang's fenders. He had great hands, broad and long fingered.

"She does the trick," I said, unlocking the door and slipping inside.

"I bet she does," he said in a voice that made me wonder if we were still talking about the car. "I will call you."

The likelihood of a guy calling always seemed to be inversely proportionate to the number of times he said he was going to call. Best not to get my hopes up. I closed the door and rolled down the window. "Sure. Whatever."

He leaned in, and for a second I thought about Natalie's advice. Then I figured this might be my only chance, so instead of turning my head at the last moment and giving him my cheek, I lifted my chin and we locked lips.

Talk about *zing!*

He surged forward and I grabbed his shirtfront. It was one of those kisses that seemed to cut off all the oxygen to my brain. When his lips left mine, he bolted backward as if he'd gotten an electric shock.

He stared at me. "I will definitely be calling you," he said, his voice raspy.

I tried to look unconcerned, but my heart pounded so hard I was afraid it was going to leap right out of my chest. "Yeah," I gasped, trying to catch my breath. "Like I said, whatever."

I drove home wondering if maybe I was wrong. Maybe he would call.

Sage was asleep in bed when I came in. Cinn was watching *Sandcastles,* a movie she saved for truly dark nights of the soul.

I sat next to her on the couch and slipped out of my high-heeled sandals. "What's wrong?"

"Nothing." She patted her lap and I put my feet on her legs, then leaned back and moaned as she started massaging them.

"Then why are you watching *Sandcastles?*" I asked.

She shrugged. "I just needed a young Jan-Michael Vincent fix."

Right. And Naomi Campbell just needed a little anger manage-

ment course. If she didn't feel like telling me, though, I wasn't going to bang my head against a brick wall any more this evening.

"How was the wedding?" she asked.

"Miserable. Though it pains me to say this, Mom was right. I shouldn't have gone. I didn't belong there and several people were extremely invested in making sure I knew that." I closed my eyes to better appreciate the way she was removing all the soreness from the soles of my feet.

Cinn made one of those little noises in the back of her throat that she usually reserves for shampooing a particularly jumpy client or getting Sage to let the pediatrician give her a shot.

The warm melty feeling in my feet was spreading rapidly up my body, and I didn't care if she was manipulating me or not. Maybe being manipulated wasn't all that bad.

"Troy Patu gave me a note to sneak to Ashley." I was still kicking myself for not reading it. It wasn't any of my business, but I was still curious.

Cinn didn't even ask what was in it. "That's interesting. Did Ashley look pretty?" she asked.

I settled back against the arm of the couch. "Ashley looked very pretty. Her hair was perfect, of course, and her dress was amazing. A strapless Vera Wang."

"One of the mermaid gowns?"

I nodded. "The modified mermaid with the spiral flange detail on the bodice and skirt."

"She must have been gorgeous," Cinnamon agreed. "I wonder why she doesn't want anyone to know that she's pregnant."

I stumbled down the hallway toward the front door. It was two fifteen; whoever was pounding on my door had better be having an extreme emergency, and it better have nothing to do with their hair. "Who's there?" I asked through the door.

"It's me, Ginger!" a male voice said.

I couldn't think of any male who had earned the right to show up on my doorstep at two fifteen with only an "it's me." But the voice did sound familiar.

I peered out the living room bay window to see who was on the porch. Ewww. It was Lamont. I opened the window and spoke through the screen. "Go away, Lamont."

Lamont spun around so fast he nearly tripped himself. Great. That would be just my luck. Drunken Lamont would fall, break something, and then sue Cinnamon and me. His father would cancel our insurance policy retroactively and we'd lose everything.

"Wh-wh-where are you?" Lamont asked, looking around as if he were Noah and God had just told him to build an ark.

"It doesn't matter where I am. It matters where you are, and you shouldn't be *here*. Now go home." I grabbed the afghan off the back of the couch and threw it over my shoulders against the cold air.

"Is that you, Ginger?" Lamont said, facing the wrong direction.

"Yes. It's me. Now go away."

He whirled, now facing the window. He held up a bottle. "I brought a bottle of wine."

"I don't care if you brought a whole case of Dom Perignon. Get off my porch and go home, before I call the cops." Un-freaking-believable! He was here for a booty call in the middle of the night with nothing but a bottle of wine? I knew our rep was bad, but I didn't think it was *that* bad.

Lamont's shoulders slumped. "Oh, okay." He turned and headed down the stairs. At the third step he stopped and turned back. "Is Cinnamon home?"

"Lamont!"

"Okay. I'm going."

I watched him slink down the stairs. I shut the window, turned to head back to bed, and saw Cinnamon and Sage standing in the hallway. Sage had on her Blossom Powerpuff Girls jammies, and both her eyes and Cinnamon's were nearly Powerpuff Girl–sized.

"Is the man gone?" Sage asked.

I nodded and she skipped over to me and snuggled inside the afghan. Cinnamon, in Edwardian jammies made of hemp, followed more slowly. I offered her a corner of the afghan and she slipped under it.

"Why was the man here?" Sage asked. "What did he want?"

I looked at Cinnamon. How was I supposed to explain to a seven-year-old that because her great-grandmother had been a particularly delicious Artichoke Queen and her grandmother had a thing for musicians, we were forever branded as the town floozies, and men would periodically show up on our doorsteps at inappropriate hours howling like wolves? The fact that we never let them in had no impact on this whatsoever. I realized *I* didn't understand it, either. Maybe I should call Lamont and have him explain it to all of us.

"He wanted to come in and spend time with Auntie Ginger," Cinnamon said softly.

Sage scowled. "Didn't his mama or auntie ever explain the nine-to-nine rule to him?" One of the banes of her existence was that she wasn't allowed to call anyone—even her grandma—before nine A.M., unless it was an emergency. It seriously galled her that looking particularly adorable in a new outfit was *not* an emergency, even if her grandma would definitely want to see it. After nine P.M. was also off-limits, but since her bedtime was still eight thirty, that was pretty much a moot point.

"No," I said, shaking my head and putting on my best sad

face. "Apparently his mama and aunties neglected to teach him any manners at all."

Sage shook her head in disgust. "Well, we're not inviting him to my birthday party. Annabelle says that boys with no manners are worse than dogs, and she doesn't like dogs one bit. She says they drool and lick themselves in private places. Would someone make me some hot chocolate?"

My eyes flew open at seven thirty. I'd planned on sleeping in, but that clearly wasn't going to happen. My mind kept flitting from one topic to the next. Kendra draped over Craig. Whether or not Ashley had the beginnings of a baby bump. How many bones were in the hand.

I closed my eyes and tried to imagine myself by a crystal-blue pool in a woodland glen, but it was no use. I dragged myself out of bed and went to the kitchen.

I started the coffeemaker, and went to get the paper. I opened the front door, and nearly fell over the two cases of Dom Perignon.

Attached was a note from Lamont: "Now can I come in?"

CHAPTER SEVEN

I was dying to tell Natalie Cinnamon's suspicions about Ashley. I hadn't seen anything that made me think Ashley was pregnant, but that meant nothing. Cinnamon had been nearly five months along with Sage before I figured it out. We managed to keep it hidden from Mom for another two months. It hadn't been terribly hard. The Surf Daddies had lost their bass player and were auditioning replacements so Dad had been around all the time, which meant that Mom's head was in the clouds. Or perhaps up somewhere else, depending on your view. Anyway, I'll never forget Mom's reaction when the doctor told her Cinnamon was due in eight weeks. I can still hear her howling, "How am I supposed to decorate a nursery properly in the time you've given me?"

We all have our own priorities, I guess. My mother's tend to run toward what paint colors rather than prenatal vitamins. It was okay anyway, I'd researched it on the Internet and had had Cinnamon taking folic acid as soon as I found out.

At any rate, I felt Cinn was a pregnancy concealment expert, and if she thought Ashley was pregnant and not telling anyone, Ashley probably *was* pregnant and not telling anyone. Which meant that *I* was dying to tell someone.

When I found Natalie at school the next day, Brian was there,

too, but it didn't matter since Natalie leapt up and started bab-
bling the second I got to the table. "So how was it? How did it
go? How far did it go? What did you end up wearing?"

"I'm not even done with my coffee yet. Give me a second," I
said, pulling a chair up to their table.

"What is she talking about?" Brian asked me, the confused
puppy look on his face.

"Her date," Natalie crowed. "Her big date."

"She had a big date?" Brian directed the puppy gaze back at
Natalie.

"You should have seen it!" Natalie waved her arm through
the air as if to create the panorama. "Picture this. We're all in the
salon, primping this particularly hateful group of snobby rich
girls—"

"They weren't all snobby or hateful," I said. "Stephanie is
perfectly nice, and I have no idea what Jessica did to piss you off.
What was with the Vietnamese nail girl act?"

"Stephanie was nice in a condescending kind of way, as if
we should all be grateful for her down-to-earthness. And I *am*
a Vietnamese nail girl, even if the closest I've ever been to Viet-
nam is getting take-out from Sunrise Restaurant," Natalie countered. "Besides, that's not the point. We're all in there, working
on their feet and their hands and their skin and their hair, and
in walks this bootylicious vision of dark hair and dangerous eyes
and broad shoulders—and he's got food with him!"

"What kind of food?" Brian asked.

"Bagels," I said.

"Any particular flavor?" he prompted.

I took a sip of coffee. "A bunch. I think I had sesame."

"Sesame's good. A little basic though, don't you think?" he
asked. "I like some imagination in my bagels. Sun-dried tomato.
Jalapeño-cheddar. Something."

"Are you pregnant?" I asked, thinking about Ashley's upset tummy and what settled it for her.

"Not that I'm aware of," Brian said. "Although I have been a bit tired lately and I did cry at one of those Hallmark commercials the other night."

"Seriously?" I asked, a grin splitting my face. He was such a softie. I bet he got sniffly at holiday movies, too.

"No, I *do* have testosterone coursing through my bloodstream; I only cry at beer commercials."

"To get back to the point," Natalie said. "He took one look at Ginger here, practically fell to his knees, and asked her to go to the wedding with him."

Brian looked to me for confirmation, his brows arched. I nodded.

"Kind of corny, don't you think?" he said.

I shrugged. "It works for him."

Brian looked dubious. "If you say so. Sounds to me like a guy who'd stick straws in his mouth and pretend to be a walrus."

"How did you know?" I said, opening my eyes wide. That was so Brian. He tapped into things without having them explained to him. He reminded me a little of Cinnamon that way. Maybe that was why I was so comfortable with him. I don't have a lot of guy friends. For me, guys seem to fall into two categories: the ones I want to date who don't want to date me, and the ones who want to date me who I don't want to date. Brian was the exception. Come to think of it, Craig was, too. Each in their own way.

"You're not telling me how it went." Natalie bounced up and down in her seat, pounding on her microbiology textbook. "I want details. Now."

I took a long sip of my coffee, savoring the way they both sat on the edge of their seats for a moment. It was so rare for me to be the center of positive attention; I wanted to bask for a teensy bit. "It was god-awful."

Natalie sank back in her chair. "Ohhh. I wanted you to be like Cinderella at the ball."

"And I wanted to be like Audrey Hepburn in *Sabrina*. We all have to live with our disappointments." I didn't even bother bringing up Lamont's booty call.

"What happened?"

"I shouldn't have gone. I didn't belong there." I pulled Brian's notebook over to me so I could see what they were working on, then opened up my pack to get my notebook out.

"You've been talking to your mother." Natalie grabbed Brian's notebook back.

"Yes, but more than that, I've been talking to Ashley's mother and Craig's mother and all the mothers of all the other people at the wedding who acted like I had the bubonic plague."

Brian took his notebook back. "Then they're all booger-eating morons."

I smiled at the *Bad News Bears* reference.

"And did anything else exciting happen?" Brian asked.

"Like what? Do you want to know if I let him get to first base?"

From the look of horror on Brian's face, apparently not. "Did you send anything off in the mail?" he asked.

I smiled. "Yes, I did. Did you?"

A smile spread across his face, too. "I sent in my application to San José State University on Friday."

Natalie looked back and forth between the two of us. "Really? Both of you? Me, too! Everyone up! Group hug!"

Which was when my coffee ended up all over my T-shirt.

Brian looked at my chest. "Sorry about that."

I looked, too. "Does that look a pair of scissors to you?" Was it an omen? Was I destined to cut hair forever?

"You know, it sort of does," he said, tilting his head to the left.

"No way," Natalie said. "It looks totally like a man with a big nose and glasses."

"You see Groucho Marx in my coffee stain?"

"No. Not that kind of big nose and glasses. More like Henry Kissinger. More of a I'm-so-intellectual-I-can't-be-bothered-with-my-eyebrows look."

Brian shook his head. "I still see the scissors. Maybe it's one of those foreground/background things. You know, which one do you see, the vase or the two faces talking."

"You couldn't be more wrong if you said it looked like two puppies chewing on a shoe. It's a guy with glasses." Natalie leaned forward to take a closer look.

I was starting to feel uncomfortable with my friends both staring so openly at my chest and began to imagine what the rest of the day would be like. Natalie was not above taking a poll in Microbiology to prove her big nosed guy with glasses theory.

"That's okay. I've got a tank top in my gym bag in the car. It's a little stinky, but that's better than having everyone use my chest as a Rorshach test." I gathered up my notebooks. "I'll see you in class."

I was halfway to the door when I heard Natalie call my name. I turned around.

"So did he?" she called.

"Did who what?"

"Did the hunky guy get to first base?"

Only Natalie would yell something like that across a crowded room. I gave her the thumbs up, and headed for the door again.

When I turned and pushed it with my back to open it (my hands being too full), I saw that Brian's head was down on the table and Natalie was patting his back.

I smiled, wondering what crazy mnemonic she'd made up that had flustered him this time.

There was only one message when I got home from school on Monday: Grandma Rosemary asking if I could come and see what was wrong with her computer. There were none from a certain tall, dark, handsome, wealthy young man who had kissed me good-night through my car window and made me quiver all the way down to my toes.

I wasn't surprised. Really, it was to be expected. I wasn't even disappointed. At least, that's what I told myself as I flipped open my microbiology book.

Microbiology is not the easiest course I've ever taken. Right now I think that might be biotechnology, which is also hella boring. At least microbiology is entertaining in its own way. I hardly noticed the time passing until Sage and Cinnamon banged into the apartment and I realized it was nearly eight o'clock.

"Hey! Where have you two been?" I demanded.

Cinnamon turned red. Sage skipped over and announced, "We had dinner with Grandma and Grandpa."

I shot a look at Cinnamon, who turned an even darker red. "You're sneaking out to see Mom and Dad?" This was so wrong. It was wrong enough that she was spending time with Dad and having Sage spend time with Dad. It was worse that she would two-time me with Dad. It just made the whole thing sordid somehow.

"We didn't sneak. We just went." Cinnamon stayed in the doorway. "Sneaking implies some sort of subterfuge."

I leaned back in my chair and gave her the stare I give Sage when I know she's lying about having brushed her teeth or putting on clean underpants. "How'd you get there?"

"We drove there." Cinnamon stood a little straighter. "In the Mustang."

"Uh-huh," I said. "So you walked Sage home from school and, without even coming up here, hopped into the Mustang and drove over to Mom's."

"You make it sound so sneaky!" she protested.

"If the shoe fits, girlie girl . . ."

She held out the big grocery bag she was holding. "Mom sent you some leftovers."

I considered snubbing the leftovers, but I could smell that it was something with red sauce, which probably meant lasagna. I took the bag and started pulling out the Tupperware containers. The lasagna was still warm. Cinnamon got a fork from the drawer and handed it to me.

"Grandpa said he was sorry," Sage said.

"For what?" I said through a mouthful of lasagna. I grabbed the salt. Mom never puts enough salt in anything. There was salad in another container and a foil-wrapped bag of garlic bread. The salad wasn't even soggy yet. Mom must have set some aside and then put the dressing on right before Sage and Cinnamon left for home. That was weird. In fact, the whole thing was weird. Mom remembered to send me leftovers when Dad was in town?

Sage's little lips pursed. "I'm not sure why he was sorry, but he said it a lot."

I looked over at Cinnamon. "I can't begin to guess what he was apologizing for. The list of possibilities is too damn long."

"It's a step." Cinnamon got another fork and sat down across from me.

I knocked her fork away. "Hey. You already had yours."

"I just want to pick. Don't be selfish."

"Fine." I sighed and pushed the container toward the center of the table so she wouldn't drip marinara sauce on my study notes. I took another bite. Mom had done something different. It didn't taste like her usual lasagna. It was good, though. "So what do you mean about it being a step? A step in the right direction?"

"No. I mean one of the twelve steps." Cinnamon went for a particularly cheesy portion of the lasagna, like I knew she would. That's okay; I like Mom's sauce. She spends hours on it. Had she put more basil in it?

"Like A.A. twelve steps?" I switched to the salad.

"The very same. He's trying to make amends." Cinnamon put her fork down. "Come on, Sage. It's time to get ready for bed."

"Already? We just got home!" Sage complained.

Cinnamon looked at her watch. "It's still bedtime. By the way," she said, turning back toward me, "Dad's the one who packed up the leftovers for you."

Cinnamon and Sage headed off, their bedtime argument the background noise of my life.

So Dad was home for good and was in A.A. That was new. Packing up leftovers for me was extra new. I shrugged. It wouldn't last. It never did. Daddies who come home and make everything right are for fairy tales and Hollywood movies.

I'd reimmersed myself in the mysteries of microbiology when the phone rang. I have to admit, when a male voice said, "May I speak to Ginger?" I was thrilled.

"This is she." I hadn't meant to sound quite that coy. I'd wanted to be coy lite. I definitely hadn't hit it. My voice had come out full-fat coy.

"Hey, Ginger. This is Lamont Gilman. Remember me? Did you get the cases of Dom? Can I come over now?"

According to my anatomy textbook, it wasn't anatomically possible, but it felt like my heart sank right down to my toes.

"What are you doing here?" I asked Natalie as I let myself into Do It Up on Tuesday morning.

"I believe I work here." She was sitting behind the computer at the front desk.

"But generally only when there is work for you to do." I dumped my books on one of the chairs in the waiting area. "We don't have any nail appointments on the books today, and you're in my spot."

"I thought I'd take advantage of any walk-ins that might drop by, and see if you wanted to study for that microbiology test together." She pulled a sheaf of index cards out of her backpack and waved them tantalizingly in the air. "I made flash cards."

She had me at "flash cards." I love flash cards.

Cinnamon came in from the back room with an armload of towels that she plopped down on the desk between us. We started to fold.

"So what's new, Natalie?" Cinnamon asked. "How's school?"

"It's great!" Natalie enthused. "This semester's been tough, but I'm keeping my fingers crossed that I'll get accepted to the nursing school at San José State. Then all I have to do is pass the classes I'm taking this semester and I'm in!"

"Will you move?" Cinnamon asked, a towel pressed to her breast. "Will we have to get a new nail girl?"

"I'm afraid so," Natalie said. "You'll have to get more than that, anyway, if Ginger decides to go to P.A. school."

I folded up the last towel and before Cinnamon could say a word, I took the whole stack and shoved them into her arms. "Better go put those away! You know how Ken gets when he finds towels laying around a salon. We'll get a citation for sure."

As soon as Cinn was out of the room, I whirled on Natalie. "Ix-nay on the aduate-gray ool-schay in front of Cinnamon," I hissed.

"Are you speaking pig Latin to me?" Natalie shook her head as if to clear her ears.

"I'll be speaking smack-down if you don't shut up," I said as quietly, yet as menacingly, as I could. "Cinnamon doesn't know I'm thinking about going away to school."

"You haven't told Cinnamon you applied to the physician assistant program?"

I bit my lip. "I haven't even told her I was thinking about it."

Natalie sat back in her chair and blinked a few times. "You've been planning this for two years. You've been saving for it for longer than that. You've been working toward leaving here and going to graduate school since I met you. You've got great grades and kick-ass references. You're definitely going to get in. Don't you think she's going to notice when you aren't here anymore?"

"There won't be anything to notice if I don't get accepted or can't afford to go," I said.

"Didn't you apply for financial aid?" Natalie asked.

I thought for a second. I didn't remember financial aid forms. "Was I supposed to do that?"

"Uh, yeah." Natalie rolled her eyes. "What is your advisor doing?"

I sighed. "Mainly telling me that it would be a waste of time and money to get that degree and then just get pregnant." My advisor was a couple years behind my mother in high school and knew the Zimmerman women too well for comfort. Every time I walked into her office she asked me when I was due. I'd considered taking it personally for a while and then decided it had more to do with my family history than my waistline although I did stop wearing those babydoll cut blouses.

Natalie shook her head. "Call the financial aid office at San José State and get them to send you the paperwork. That'd be a start."

"What would be a start?" Cinnamon asked as she came back in.

"Natalie's flash cards. They would be a start to studying for the microbiology test," I said quickly.

"Ooh, flash cards." Cinnamon smiled. "You love flash cards."

She knew me so well. I couldn't understand why she didn't know I was lying.

Natalie and I had worked our way from the muscles in the face to the nervous system, and Jolene had sterilized all the nail equipment and was looking through one of the style books we keep around for indecisive clients, when the door to the salon swung open.

"Hey, miracle girl!" Cinnamon said, running across the salon to throw her arms around the frail blonde who'd come in on the arm of a handsome young man. "It is so good to see you. How are you feeling?"

The blonde looked from Cinnamon to me, and from Natlaie to Jolene, then questioningly at the young man. Cinnamon backed away, a confused look on her own face. We'd been cutting Laura's hair for at least three years. She didn't look like she knew who we were at all. Seven months ago, the van Laura was riding in on the way back from Chico had been hit by a tractor trailer whose driver had fallen asleep behind the wheel. Three of the other girls in the van hadn't made it and Laura had been in a coma for several weeks. We'd heard there had been some brain damage, but we didn't know how much. Clearly, there'd been enough that she didn't recognize us.

I barely recognized her myself. Her face had been badly injured in the accident, and while I'd heard through the grapevine that she'd had to have extensive plastic surgery, I wasn't prepared for the horrible bruising and swelling on her face. If she hadn't walked in with her fiancé, Monroe, I wouldn't have thought it was her at all.

"This is Cinnamon and this is Ginger," Monroe said in a soft voice, resting his hand reassuringly on the small of her back. "Ringing any bells?"

Her lips quirked up in a bit of a smile, or maybe she was trying not to cry. With her pinched little face, it was hard to tell.

Cinnamon rushed forward and hugged her again. "Don't you worry about it, Laura! You'll remember us soon enough. The important thing is that we remember how you like your hair done. Right, Monroe?" Cinnamon turned to Laura's fiancé.

Laura and Monroe had gotten engaged about six months before the accident. Word was that he had barely left her bedside.

"You need to feed this girl some French fries, Monroe," I said, stepping forward to give Laura a quick squeeze. She felt even thinner than she looked, like a little bird in my arms.

Monroe shook his head. "Good luck with that. She barely eats anything these days."

Laura smiled—or maybe it was a wince, since her hand went to her stomach as if it hurt. "I don't do anything all day except sit around. I don't do anything to get hungry."

"Or sleepy." Monroe's brow furrowed. Clearly, Laura wasn't entirely out of the woods yet and he knew it.

Cinnamon slid in between Monroe and Laura and put an arm around Laura's shoulder to shepherd her into the shampoo room. "You're not sleeping?"

Laura shook her head. "Not much."

"Have you tried lavender?" Cinnamon said as they left the room.

"She's not sleeping at all," Monroe said to me under his breath. "And when she does sleep, she wakes up screaming."

"She's been through a lot, Monroe. You need to give her time."

Monroe sat down on one of the waiting-area chairs and put his head in his hands. "I know. I've tried. I even suggested we postpone the wedding. She started crying so hard, I was afraid she'd stop breathing."

Yikes. Wedding planning was stressful enough for a perfectly healthy person. Doing it while recovering from multiple surgeries for everything from pinning your leg to rebuilding your face would put anyone over the edge. "How's that going?"

Monroe grimaced. "It's a nightmare. She doesn't remember anything but the most vague details of what we'd already planned, and she's changing her mind about everything."

"Like what?"

"You name it and she's decided she doesn't like it. Colors, flowers, time of day, everything." Monroe ran his hand through his slightly messy brown hair. When he'd walked in, I thought he'd gotten one of those trendy spiky haircuts that so many guys are wearing right now. Unfortunately, I don't think it was a style choice. I think it was a man at the end of his rope. "I get it. I really do. An experience like that changes a person. I mean, she almost died, right?"

I nodded. Laura was wildly lucky to be alive.

"I just don't get how a near-death experience changes what a person's favorite flower is or what colors they like or what they like in their coffee." Monroe stopped speaking as Cinnamon and Laura came back into the room.

I went back to my bookkeeping, letting Cinnamon's chatter and Laura's almost monosyllabic responses fade into the background until Laura was blown dry and ready to go.

"Thanks, Cinnamon," Laura said, then stumbled against the desk.

I rushed out to help steady her, but Monroe was already there. "Are you all right?"

"Just a little tired. I get clumsy." She rubbed her elbow where she'd smacked it.

"Let's get you home," Monroe said, taking her arm and leading her to the door.

"Not right away though, right?" Laura looked up at him.

"Yes, right away. You don't have to do that today."

Tears started pooling in Laura's eyes, and I already knew Monroe had lost the argument, whatever it was about. Hell, that look was pathetic enough that *I* would have taken Laura wherever it was she wanted to go. "I do, Monroe. Please."

Monroe's shoulders slumped. "Fine, but this has to stop soon. We don't have to go to the cemetery every day."

"If we don't, who will?" Laura asked.

Monroe shook his head. "Jamie had family. If they wanted to put flowers on her grave every damn day, they would."

Jamie hadn't survived the van accident. She'd lived up the coast a ways, and even though I hadn't known her, the whole thing made me teary every time I thought about it. I looked at Laura, wondering how strange it must be to have survived when her friend had not.

"They live too far away," Laura said. "It's up to us."

Monroe shook his head, opened the door for Laura, and waved good-bye to us.

I watched them go out to their car and then turned back to Cinnamon. "You didn't give her any crystals."

Cinnamon shook her head. "It's going to take a lot more than a bunch of rocks to cure whatever's wrong there."

Natalie and I quizzed each other on parts of the brain and nerve root ganglia while Cinn did a cut and color on Maria Delgado.

"Jorge's nephew is joining the business," Maria informed Cinnamon. Maria's husband, Jorge, owned one of the many flower farms along the coast. His specialty was agapanthus. I always thought they looked like they belonged on *Star Trek,* with their huge purple heads on their long slender stalks, but apparently much of California wants their front yards to look like a *Star Trek* paradise.

"That's nice," Cinnamon said, combing Maria's hair back and snipping off the tiny bits of dry ends. Maria has gorgeous hair, so there wasn't much to snip.

"He's very smart. He's going to be a big asset in the business," Maria said, staring into the mirror. "A very big asset."

"Mmm-hmm," Cinn murmured, clearly more interested in getting Maria's layers right than wondering what was going on beneath the layer of polite conversation. My spidey sense was tingling, though.

"He's very handsome." Maria crossed her legs.

"Uncross your legs, Maria, or your hair will be crooked," Cinn said.

"He's single," Maria answered, obediently putting her feet flat on the footrest.

"Who's single?" Cinnamon stopped cutting.

"My husband's handsome nephew who is coming to help with the flower farm," Maria said. "He's single. And lonely."

"I'm sure he won't stay that way long," Cinnamon said. "A young, successful man will have girls crawling all over him in a matter of days."

"Maybe you'd like to help with that?" Maria asked.

"No, thank you." Cinnamon got out the blow-dryer and started styling Maria's hair.

"Why not?" Maria asked, her brow furrowed.

Cinn pushed Maria's head down to start blowing it dry from underneath. "I'm just not interested."

"How can you know that without meeting him?" Maria asked in a voice muffled by layers of hair.

"Because I'm not interested in meeting anyone. I'm fine."

"You are not fine. You have no man!" Maria started to sit back up.

Cinnamon shoved her head back down. "That's not true. There's my dad. He's back in town for good, you know."

Natalie looked at me, one eyebrow raised. I shrugged. So he'd actually stuck it out for more than a week. Big freaking deal. It wouldn't last. There was no reason to talk about it.

"Pah!" Maria said. "I'm talking about a man for *you*, Cinnamon. Raul's people are fine, upstanding citizens. He's a hard worker and he's smart. He has a degree in business agriculture from U.C. Davis."

"I don't need any other man." Cinnamon jutted out her jaw, and I went back to the flash cards. Once that jaw juts out, you may as well give up.

Maria, however, didn't know that. She turned the chair around and put her hand on Cinnamon's arm. "One mistake at sixteen doesn't mean you have to spend the rest of your life alone, Cinnamon."

"Mistake?" Cinnamon said. "Are you implying that my daughter was a mistake?"

Maria's cheeks flushed. She put up her hands as if to ward off an attack. "I'm sorry, Cinnamon. I didn't mean anything by it."

Cinnamon nodded stiffly, grabbed her sweatshirt from the coatrack by the door, and left.

I grabbed the blow-dryer and silently finished blowing out Maria's hair.

She kept trying to apologize, even as she was writing me a check—onto which she tacked an enormous tip. "I'm so sorry. I didn't mean to offend her. I just thought that she and Raul would make such a cute couple. I thought—"

"It's okay, Maria," I said. "Don't worry about it. She'll get over it."

"I feel terrible. Sage is such a great little girl."

"Of course she is."

She stopped and looked me over. "I don't suppose you want to meet Raul, Ginger?"

"Good-bye, Maria," I said, taking her check.

"I've gotta go. I've got a date." Natalie picked up her bag and hoisted it onto her shoulder.

"Who's the lucky guy tonight?" I asked, sinking down in my chair behind the computer. We were done studying, but I still had some bookkeeping chores to do. Jolene was sweeping up.

"Tom Marshall." A smile curved Natalie's lips.

"Tom? From In the Lube?" I liked Tom. He ran the oil-change business off of Eucalyptus and Pine. He was closer to Mom's age than ours, but I guess Natalie was, too. He and his wife had split up about two years earlier, and he was sort of cute. "How'd that happen?"

"I was dropping off my Camry to get its oil changed. He asked if I knew about their top-off policy. I told him I didn't, and asked him if he wanted to know about mine."

"Natalie!"

"Buh-bye!" she said and blew me an air kiss as she went out the door.

I glanced at the clock. I had about half an hour before I had to leave for school. Jolene had finished sweeping and was in the back room. I picked up the phone and dialed.

"Hello, my name is Ginger Zimmerman and I'm applying to your physician assistant program."

"Congratulations." The woman on the other end sounded bored.

"I need to find out about applying for financial aid." Duh— why else would I be calling the financial aid office?

"Full-time—that means eight or more units—students with high financial need who meet all application deadlines can be considered for Federal Perkins Loans."

For a second, I thought I'd been switched to a recording. That's how much life sparked in her voice. "A loan? How long would I have before I need to start repaying it?"

"Repayment begins nine months after the borrower ceases to be enrolled at least half-time."

And apparently warm blood would flow through the veins of financial aid office clerks about the time hell froze over. "Is that all you have available?"

There was a pause. "Subsidized and unsubsidized Federal Stafford Loans are also available. Repayment begins six months after the borrower ceases to be enrolled at least half-time."

Okay. Loans were it. I've had worse news. "How do I apply?"

"To be considered for the Federal Perkins Loan and work-study program, the federal processor must receive the Free Application for Federal Student Aid—FAFSA—or Renewal FAFSA. In addition, the financial aid office must receive the completed Supplemental Financial Aid Form for Graduate and Professional

Students. The financial aid office must also receive a complete copy of the student's (and spouse's, if applicable) signed federal income tax return including all schedules and W-2 forms or the student non-filing statement form. Non-filing statement forms may only be submitted if the student and/or spouse are not legally required to file a federal tax return. Graduate students must also submit any additional documents requested by the financial aid office. Law, dental, medical, occupational therapy, biokinesiology, and physical therapy, physician assistant, and pharmacy students should check with their departments for additional application requirements."

Physician assistant. That was me! "Okay. Anything else?"

"The Federal Work-Study Program enables eligible students to earn part of their financial aid award either on campus or with an approved off-campus employer. Only full-time students with high financial need who meet all application deadlines are considered for this program."

The woman droned off a series of due dates for all the different applications and I scrambled to write them all down. Maybe Natalie was right. Maybe I could pull this off.

My half hour, however, was up, and it was time to head to school. Cinnamon still wasn't back, but she didn't have anything scheduled. Any walk-ins would simply be out of luck. I hustled Jolene out the door, grabbed my backpack, and locked the door behind me.

I slid inside the Mustang, turned the key, and got nothing but a sputter. From hard experience, I knew to sit back and count to ten. It was easy to flood her engine and once you did that, you were truly screwed. I finished my count to ten and tried again. Still, nothing but a sputter.

At least it wasn't the battery; that much I knew. I got out, opened the hood, and gazed at the mystery that is my car engine.

"It's probably the alternator," a male voice said behind me.

It was inevitable. Santa Bonita is a small town. If he really was back for good, we were bound to cross paths sooner or later. It was a minor miracle that we hadn't bumped into each other before this.

I turned. "Hi, Dad."

"Hey, Ginger. Long time, no see." Considering that he was supposedly changing his whole life, he didn't look a whole lot different than the last time I'd seen him. Maybe the hairline had crept infinitesimally back on his forehead and there was a touch more gray on the side. He still had that athletic build, like a surfer who hadn't quite gone to seed. He still wore those faded 501s and a plain white T-shirt. He still looked like he didn't know quite how to deal with me.

"I've been busy," I said.

"So I've heard." He looked down into the car's inner workings. "Do you have a screwdriver?"

On closer inspection, he looked a little healthier than he had when I'd stood in the middle of the street six years ago and screamed that I never wanted to see or talk to him again. He'd lost that slightly puffy look around his eyes; his face was tan and taut.

"In the trunk," I said, walking around the car to fish out the toolbox. "Phillips-head or flat?"

"Flat." He leaned farther in, peering at the engine. "She used to do this every once in a while to your mother, too."

I handed him the screwdriver and watched while he laid it across one metal thing that had a whirly item on it and then another metal thingie. He gestured with his chin that I should get back in the car. I did and turned the key in the ignition.

The Mustang's engine coughed and turned over. Dad closed the trunk and then came over to the driver's-side window and handed me the screwdriver. "There you go."

"Thanks," I said. The word nearly stuck in my throat, but I choked it out. I'd say it to a stranger, so I should probably say it to him.

"Any time," Dad said and backed away from the car.

I put it in reverse and pulled out of the space. I swear the only reason I checked my rearview mirror as I drove out of the parking lot was because I am a safe and prudent driver. I didn't do it to see if he was still standing there, watching me.

I'm sure it was just a coincidence that he was.

By the time I got through microbiology and biotechnology, the incident with Maria Delgado was completely out of my head. Cinn, however, was still stewing when I got home from school. Sage was having a playdate at Annabelle's, so Cinnamon didn't have to curb her words.

"Imagine the nerve, implying that Sage was a mistake, an error of some kind. The nerve, Ginger! The sheer unmitigated nerve!"

"Maria didn't mean it that way, Cinnamon."

"In what way did she mean it, then?" Cinn tends to get very grammatically correct when she's riled.

"She probably meant that maybe you meant to wait until you were out of high school or even until you were married or something. She just meant that you didn't exactly plan to have Sage when you had her."

"I would have planned her if I'd known," Cinn said.

Oh, great. I was undoubtedly about to be treated to one of Cinnamon's long, complicated discourses on what we're all fated to be, and how it was better to follow that inevitable course than fight against it. Maybe she was right. Rather than fight the inevitability of her explaining this all to me, I decided to play along. "Known what?"

"Known what it's like to have something to love. Something to love that loves you back. I'd have had her when I was fourteen if I'd known that." Cinn sank down on the couch into the lotus position and clutched a throw pillow to her chest.

I sat down next to her, but didn't attempt the yoga pose. I was too stunned. "That's why you had Sage? So you'd have someone to love?"

"You're making it sound like a Jefferson Airplane song, Ginger. Besides, why do you think any of us are here?"

I had no reply. I looked around the apartment we shared, like we'd always shared everything, including Sage. Had I chosen any of it? I certainly hadn't chosen my sister's pregnancy at sixteen.

Since then, choice hadn't played a huge part in my life. Necessity had ruled. What was I going to choose?

I thought about my phone conversation with the financial aid drone that afternoon. It sounded like I might be able to piece together what I needed to go to graduate school and carve out a whole new existence for myself—away from here, away from my sister and mother and grandmother, in a place where no one would make assumptions about me based on my last name, away from other people's hair and other people's scaly feet.

I looked at my sister's sweet, open face and felt shocked at how different she really looks from me, considering how identical we are. At least I knew what she was keeping secret. She had no idea what dark things I was hiding in my heart.

CHAPTER EIGHT

T'Fan (Tiffany Shaw) and Stanok (Stanley Hyslop) honored their Pon Farr on April 30 at the Santa Bonita Outrigger Grill in a *Star Trek*–inspired ceremony. The bride wore a red minidress and black boots inspired by Lt. Uhura. The groom opted for the more up-to-date uniform. All hope the bride and groom live long and prosper.

"You. Can. Not. Slap. The. Bride." I held my sister's hands trapped between my own and spoke slowly and clearly. I did not want to be misunderstood.

It has always been our rule. Hell, Cinnamon *made* the rule. I'm usually the one who wants to break it. Cinnamon wants to give them all crystals and herb packets and introduce them to their spirit guides, not bitch-slap them across the room.

"She needed it, Ginger." Cinnamon stared into my eyes with just as much vehemence as I was trying to convey to her.

I contained the urge to slap my sister the way she'd cracked Tiffany Shaw across the cheek moments ago. I had an odd feeling she was doing her best to contain the same impulse.

This has been the story of our lives. Same impulse, way different reasons. Same face, different expressions. Same hair, different style. Same body, totally different actions. I realize the sameness comes with the identical twin territory, but it cheeses me off for a variety of reasons, not the least of which is if you poke more than a single millimeter under our skins you couldn't find two people less identical than Cinnamon and me.

Cinnamon had not been herself this week and I had no idea why. I hadn't been my usual happy-go-lucky self either. I know I said I wasn't expecting Craig to call, and I wasn't. At least, not in my rational, conscious brain. Apparently the slutty monkey lurking inside me had had different expectations.

"She's right, you know," Tiffany said from behind me. "I needed to be slapped, just like Spock needed to be slapped by Nurse Chapel in 'A Private Little War.' Scotty didn't understand and tried to stop her. He thought he was helping, but he wasn't."

I turned to look at Tiffany, who was three quarters of the way to becoming T'Fan, her Vulcan persona. We'd dyed her hair a deep blue-black earlier in the week. I'd waxed and tweezed her eyebrows into slanted slash marks, and Cinnamon was nearly done cutting her hair into the ever-so-unflattering bob preferred by fashionable Vulcan and Romulan women the universe over. Oh, and there was a big flaming handprint on her cheek.

"Why do I always have to be Scotty?" I swear, in every analogy that day and in the days leading up to the wedding, I'd ended up being Scotty. I *hate* being Scotty. He's just one rung above the geologists who always get toasted the second they land on a new planet. If I'm Scotty, I'm one bit-player away from getting hit by a phaser set on "extreme explosive disruption."

Tiffany sat back down in Cinnamon's chair and shrugged. "We are who we are, Ginger. In the *Star Trek* world and the real one. I'm feeling much better now, by the way. We can continue."

Jolene shook her head from where she was cutting new waxing strips, a job she'd pretty much taken over completely. She thought Tiffany must have been hitting the crack pipe to decide that a *Star Trek* wedding was a good idea, but this was one of the few non–Courtney inspired weddings we'd had lately and we needed to keep them coming in. Eventually the Courtney phase would die. Although who knew? Maybe the Courtney would end up being to wedding hair what Pachelbel is to wedding music, and Cinnamon and I would be pinning up ringlets on fresh young things when our own curls were thin and gray.

Just the thought sucked all the air out of my lungs and made me feel like I couldn't breathe.

The good thing about theme weddings is that the bride knows exactly what she wants.

"Is that too layered?" Tiffany said. "Because it shouldn't be too layered. It should be more blunt across the bottom."

The bad thing about theme weddings is that the bride knows exactly what she wants.

"It's going to be great," Cinnamon said.

Tiffany leaned forward in the chair and scrutinized herself in the mirror. "Okay," she said. "Go ahead. Are you sure these are Vulcan ears and not Romulan?" Tiffany held two plastic ears up to either side of her head with a suspicious look on her face.

It was hard for her not to look a little suspicious at this point, what with her eyebrows waxed and tweezed into big accent marks over her eyes.

"I am absolutely sure they are Vulcan ears," I said with great authority. "Romulan ears slant backward much more."

Tiffany settled back in the chair. "Okay," she said, but I could tell she was only partly mollified.

That could be because I was totally talking out of my ass. I have no idea what the difference between a Vulcan ear and a Romulan ear is. Sometimes sounding authoritative is much more important than actually being an authority.

Cinnamon took a deep breath and made her next cut. If Tiffany jumped one more time she was going to need those fake ears, because Cinn was going to chop one of hers off.

She didn't jump, but she did tremble. She looked like she was going to burst. Then suddenly she flung her arms out. "I can't help it! I'm just so darn excited!"

Cinnamon stepped back and shook her comb at Tiffany. "Am I going to have to slap you again, T'Fan? Get your emotions under control."

"I can't stop! I'm so darn in love with him and today he's going to be mine. I feel like dancing!" She flung her arms out wide as if to embrace the whole world. Then she burst into tears.

"No!" I screamed. "No crying!"

With the amount of eyeliner and mascara we had caked on Tiffany, anything more than dewy eyes was going to end up turning her into an Alice Cooper look-alike. I grabbed a tissue, folded it up, and held it very gently under first one eye and then the next.

"You're right. This is serious business. Stanley has to do battle for me and everything. I can't ruin it now with this . . . this . . . emotion." She said the last word as if it left a nasty taste in her mouth.

"There's going to be fighting at your wedding?" I had no idea you could actually plan out the fighting at a wedding. My experience from behind the scenes was that it generally took a more free-form, organic structure stemming from long-held resentments and rivalries. How refreshing to have it all scripted!

Tiffany/T'Fan nodded vigorously. "He has to do ritual combat. He and Oliver—that's his best man—have been working out the choreography for weeks now."

I raised one eyebrow in my best Spock imitation—which is not all that impressive, but it's all I had in this particular instance.

Talking seemed to calm Tiffany down.

"So is Oliver hot?" I asked. "Are you sure you want Stanley to win the kalifee?"

"Stanley and I are soul mates," Tiffany said. "Total soul mates."

Cinnamon motioned to me to keep talking.

"Really? Soul mates? How do you know?"

Tiffany held up her index finger. "First of all, when I met Stanley, he had a framed print of the original *Enterprise* over his bed. I also had a framed print of the original *Enterprise* over my bed. I mean, can you believe the coincidence?"

"No," Cinnamon said, turning the chair just a little bit. I don't think Tiffany even noticed. "I can't believe it."

I glanced back at her, but she seemed intent on cutting Tiffany's hair. I could have sworn I heard a touch of sarcasm in that voice though. Not that I knew what sarcasm would sound like in Cinnamon's voice. I pretty much had the corner on all the sarcasm genes that we were supposed to split. Cinn has all the sincerity ones. I must have misheard.

"Anything else?" I asked, trying to sound casual.

"We both had Starfleet dishes. Now, that wouldn't have been any great coincidence, except that we each had service for four."

Cinnamon stopped snipping to look at Tiffany in the mirror and check the cut to make sure it was symmetrical, symmetry being high on any Vulcan's list of must-haves. "And?"

"Don't you see? Once we combined our dishware, we had service for eight. Eight. Turn eight on its side and it's infinity. Plus, it's the perfect number for a dinner party."

"Meaningful and yet practical," I observed.

Tiffany practically leapt out of her chair. Damn. I'd gotten her too excited. Cinnamon frowned at me. Like it was my fault that we had an overemotional Vulcan on our hands. "That's it exactly. Meaningful, yet practical. It all makes sense. Especially since we're soul mates. Which is why we're having our Pon Farr today and I'm going to be his wife and I'm just so darn happy and excited that I think I'm going to cry."

"Noooo!" Cinnamon and I yelled in unison, both rushing to hold tissues under Tiffany's eyes.

"Sorry. So sorry," she whispered. "I can't seem to stop myself."

Cinnamon made cooing noises to Tiffany and shooed me away.

At least Cinnamon wasn't slapping her anymore.

"Do you think she'll make it through the whole thing without crying?" I asked Cinnamon after we sent T'Fan and the rest of her Vulcans on their way.

"It's going to be fine. In fact, it's going to be great. I got Gyfu today as my rune card, and there simply isn't a better wedding card than that one. Plus, I gave her some lapis, although that's really supposed to be for anxiety. Still, I figure if it calms you down, it calms you down."

I nodded, although I thought a nice Xanax might have been more in order. Come to think of it, I'm not sure I would have said no to a Xanax myself at that point. "That was exhausting."

"You just don't like weddings," Cinnamon said, picking up the broom and starting to sweep up Tiffany's hair.

I started tossing the combs into the jar of Barbicide. "That is not true. I love weddings. Weddings bring in the big bucks. I'm thrilled to have a wedding every weekend."

"I'm not saying you don't like having the wedding business. I'm saying you don't like the actual weddings. You don't believe in them."

"Weddings are not fairies, Cinn. I don't have to clap my hands and repeat 'I do believe, I do believe' over and over."

"I know they're not fairies, Ginger. I also know they're not movies, and you're selling me short if you think I don't know why you really don't believe in them."

I shot my best hard look at Cinnamon and she countered with her best I'm-not-backing-down stare. "I give up. Why don't I believe in weddings?"

"Because you don't believe in marriage." Cinnamon pinched up her mouth and went back to sweeping.

"You're right, I don't believe in marriage. Which is completely shocking, considering how well the whole marriage thing has gone for the women in our family."

"Don't blame that. We've never even tried marriage." She had a point there. "You don't like weddings because you don't believe in what they symbolize. You don't believe in lasting commitment between one man and one woman."

"Maybe because our grandmother shot our grandfather on their honeymoon, and because our own father is about as committed and reliable as a grasshopper in the summer?"

He'd been around so much lately, it was starting to really grate on my nerves. It had to be some kind of record for him, but I still wasn't buying it.

"We are not typical," Cinn maintained.

"Thank goodness for that." We *so* had had this argument before. It seemed absurd to me that she still believed in fairy-tale weddings with happily-ever-afters, but logic, reason, and experience were no match for Cinnamon's enduring belief in fate and love.

"At least Tiffany is willing to come out and say what she wants and to go for it." Cinnamon swept a pile of bobby pins into her drawer.

My face burned. "What the hell is that supposed to mean?"

Before things could escalate further, someone knocked at the door.

"Can't people read?" I grumbled as I marched to the door. "I flipped the sign to Closed."

I flung the door open and stopped in my tracks.

It was Craig, looking scrumptious in a System of a Down T-shirt that had been washed so many times it was gray instead of black, and faded jeans whose cuffs looked frayed in just the right way. He held up a bag that looked suspiciously like the one he'd brought the day of Ashley's wedding. "I brought another food offering. It worked so well last time, I figured I'd do it again."

I knew it shouldn't, but the slutty monkey in me stood up and cheered.

"I'd kind of given up hope of hearing from you," I said, nibbling at my sun-dried-tomato-and-basil bagel. I was betting Brian would totally crack up when I told him. Just thinking about making him laugh made me grin.

Craig grimaced. "Sorry about that. I should have warned you. This week was filled with the whipping of the prodigal."

I licked some cream cheese that had squeezed out from between the two bagel halves, and realized that Craig had stuttered to a halt. "I assume you're the prodigal, but you don't exactly seem like prodigal material to me."

Craig's Adam's apple bobbed up and down a couple times. "Yeah, well, you're not an Esposito. I'm not following The Path. Every time I come home, there is a concerted effort to try to get me on it."

"The Path? What are you guys, some kind of cult?" I did the cream-cheese-licking thing again to see if I'd get the same reaction. Poor guy; he almost choked. It made a warm feeling in the pit of my stomach to know I could get that response so easily.

He set his bagel down. "I'm supposed to be a lawyer, like my father, uncle, and grandfather. We're all supposed to be lawyers. Then we're all supposed to spend some time in a firm in a big city. After that, we come back to Santa Bonita, join the family firm, and get married. I'm twenty-eight. At this point, I should have my L.L.D., have passed the bar, and be getting married some time in the near future to a girl of appropriate social and economic standing."

I blinked. "You should be Justin?"

Craig nodded. "Justin is definitely on The Path. He is not backpacking around Africa recording monkey behavior or pursuing meaningless degrees." He paused. "I'm also not entirely sure he's happy."

Pffft. "What's not to be happy about in Justin's life? A cushy job in the family firm and a pretty wife?" I held my hand to my forehead. "Oh, sweet Lord, have mercy upon me. I must drive my Mercedes to the country club for drinks again. The horror! The horror!"

"It's still a prison, even if the bars look pretty from the outside. It's probably why he . . ." Craig's words trailed off and he lowered his eyes.

"Why he what?" There's nothing like someone only half saying something to pique my interest. Maybe it's from knowing what goes on beneath the surface for so many people in town. I've gotten to the point where I feel I have a right to know. I felt like my ears had perked up even though there are no muscles in a human ear. They're made entirely of cartilage, skin, and connective tissue. Still, I felt like one of those scruffy little dogs that are always so inexplicably popular on TV shows.

Craig waved my question away. "It doesn't matter. I can tell that he's unhappy. Whatever he's doing, from where I stand, it looks like suffocation."

"I know all about that." I gave a little snort.

Craig looked back up. "You, too? How so?"

I gestured at my body. "I am twenty-four and have not yet procreated. It may not exactly be rebellion, but it's definitely bucking a trend. I certainly know about the suffocation thing, too. I'm not exactly crazy about spending the rest of my life in Santa Bonita and eventually having an illegitimate child that I name after an herb or a spice."

"What is with the Spice Girl names, anyway?"

I rolled my eyes. "It's a long, stupid story."

"I got time and I'm not all that bright, according to my father." Craig leaned back in his chair and put his hands behind his head.

"My grandmother's name is Rosemary. My grandfather—"

"The one your grandmother shot?" Craig asked.

I nodded. Was there anyone in town who didn't know that story? Of course not. It was a local legend. Seriously, sometimes tour buses stop at my grandmother's restaurant. "His name was Basil."

"Like the herb?"

"More like the English actor in those Sherlock Holmes movies, but the herb connection was apparently simply too enticing for Grandma Rosemary to ignore. When she found out that she was pregnant, she named my mother Cassia."

"Is that an herb?"

"It's more of a spice. It's related to cinnamon. Anyway, that would have been fine except my mother decided to make bearing illegitimate children with spice names a family tradition. Cinnamon followed in the family footsteps by getting pregnant in high school and naming her daughter Sage."

"So by getting pregnant in high school she was actually being the good, obedient daughter?" I could see the wheels turning in his head.

"Go figure," I said. "We've confused more than a few high school counselors in our day."

He laughed. "Listen, I'm actually capable of buying food that doesn't have a hole in the center. Do you want to grab a bite to eat and see a movie or something?"

I set my bagel down. "You really have been hanging out with monkeys too long. You've forgotten the rules."

The poor guy looked kind of frightened. "I have?"

"It's Saturday afternoon and you're asking me out for Saturday night? Tonight?"

"Yeah. I'm not doing anything, so I thought—"

"Ah, but you also thought *I* wasn't doing anything. You assumed that I would be at home awaiting your call?" I crossed my arms in front of my chest.

He held his hands up in front of himself as if to ward off an attack. "No! Clearly, you're not. You're here. I just hoped—"

"Hoped I'd be at home awaiting your call?" I started to tap my foot.

He frowned. "You're twisting this around."

"No, I'm just putting it in human-speak. No matter how often you try to convince me otherwise, I am not a bonobo. I read up about them on the Internet, you know."

Craig shrank down in his chair. "Steph thought saying someone was a bonobo was a pretty egregious dating error, and she should know. It's just . . ."

"Just what?" I wasn't ready to let him off the hook so easily yet. He was cute when he was flustered.

"When we, uh, said good night after the wedding." His voice was soft and a little bit raspy all of a sudden. I could appreciate why. The memory of that kiss left me a little flustered, too.

"I remember," I said.

"It's not always that way for me." He threw his head back and groaned, tilting his chair onto its back legs. "I sound like an idiot. Maybe it was just a kiss for you."

I decided I liked Craig too much to play games about the important stuff. "No. It wasn't just a kiss," I said.

He snapped his chair back to the floor and gave me a grin. "Good. Then you'll go out with me tonight." He leaned forward, elbows braced on his knees, his lips almost close enough to kiss.

I grinned back. The tingle was growing into a full-blown fire, but I didn't want him to know that just yet. I leaned in, too; sparks practically flying off our lips. "You're lucky that I'm such a forgiving woman. What exactly did you have in mind?"

"Clearly, I'm going to have to come up with something better than dinner and a movie at this point. It may take some thinking." He leaned back in his chair. "And thinking may require some blood actually reaching my brain."

I leaned back, too, a little sad to let all that electricity dissipate, but a little relieved, as well. Too much longer and I might have pushed him to the floor and had my wicked way with him. I looked at my watch. "You don't have much time."

He grinned wider. "I'll pick you up at six. Dress casually."

I looked down at the California coast spread out beneath me, the blue-gray water to one side and the rolling green of the mountains to the other. I turned around to face Craig in the basket of the hot air balloon that was sailing us along the coast as the sun set. "This is definitely grace under pressure, Esposito," I said.

He slung his arm around my shoulders and took a sip of champagne. "Thank you. It makes writing term papers hell, but it pays off in other ways."

"How'd you get it set up so fast?" I nestled in a little closer. It was a bit chilly up here for my tank top and cotton circle skirt. Plus, the champagne was making me the tiniest bit dizzy.

"Never underestimate the power of name-dropping. The Esposito name has a way of opening doors." He shifted a little.

I looked up at him. His gaze stayed on the horizon. "With great power comes great responsibility."

A smile quirked at the edge of his lips. "Precisely what I'm trying to dodge—according to my father."

"The power or the responsibility?"

"Both." He looked down at me. "You're very beautiful."

A warm glow blossomed inside me. "You're changing the topic."

"I am." Then he leaned down and kissed me.

Zing! At 1,500 feet with a champagne buzz, it's a miracle I didn't fall right out of the basket.

I hadn't planned on asking Craig in. It's not like I have a chart detailing how many dates before I allow access to a specific body part. First of all, I'm a Zimmerman woman; I make my own rules. Second, it's important to be flexible. So, while normally I would probably not have dragged a guy into my apartment after the second date, I also normally didn't feel physically dizzy just from a guy's kiss. I figured it wasn't really only our second date if you counted the two lunches he'd bought me, and the dizziness thing was a fascinating physiological reaction that should be studied further.

Besides, Cinnamon and Sage weren't home. That was both good and bad. On the plus side, the presence of a seven-year-old can damp most guys' libidos pretty quickly, since she's a living and breathing warning about the dangers of premarital sex.

Unfortunately, Cinnamon and Sage's absence had enabled Lamont to express his artistic side. He had used Sage's sidewalk chalk to write CALL ME with his phone number on the sidewalk, festooned with hearts and flowers. I was going to have to ask Troy about stalking laws in California.

"Wow, you really made an impression on Lamont," Craig said, inspecting the artwork.

"Any hints on unmaking it? I'd really like him to go away." I thought about trying to scuff the whole thing out with my shoe, but it needed a good hosing off. Lamont had done a very thorough job of coloring everything in. Sage was going to be super-impressed. She liked a tidy coloring job.

"Definitely don't kiss him," he said. "He'll never leave you alone once he finds out what it's like to kiss you."

Then he kissed me. Every time our lips met, it felt like my brain shorted out.

After Craig and I came up for air from our doorstep kiss, I banged the top of the screen door to unstick it, opened it, and then unlocked the front door.

"Was that some kind of warning shot?" he asked, following me in and looking around.

"No. The door sticks unless you make it pop by banging it," I murmured as he pulled me close to him again. An electric tingle ran through me as our bodies touched, and all I could think was *more*.

We stumbled together to the couch and the wicker creaked beneath him.

"Whoa. Am I going to break this?" He started kissing my neck, his hand sliding up my torso. I thought I was going to burst into flames.

"Nah. Cinnamon, Sage, and I sit on it together all the time."
I caught his lower lip between my teeth and nibbled on it.

"AhfinwaymorevanFinnmonthage," he murmured.

"What?" I said, letting go of his lip.

"I said I think I weigh more than Cinnamon and Sage combined." He smiled. "It's not exactly designed to support a bunch of guys watching the game."

"That hasn't exactly been an issue for us."

He kissed me again. His fingers traced along the edge of my tank top's neckline, pausing just for an instant in my cleavage. "I find that hard to believe. You probably have guys lined up around the block, begging for a chance to come in."

I froze. "What do you mean by that?"

"Hmmm," he said, looking up from where he was starting to follow the line that his finger had made with his lips. "Just that you're very beautiful and I bet a lot of guys are interested in you. You certainly made a conquest out of Lamont."

"Lamont is not my fault," I said, feeling a little cold.

He snorted. "Lamont is his own fault, and his own worst enemy, too."

I settled back down. "Fine. As long as you understand that. Just because we're necking on the couch on our second date doesn't mean that I'm easy."

Craig sat up a little and looked me in the eyes. I felt both sad and good at the same time. My boobs kind of missed him. "Why would I think you're easy?"

"Because of who I am and who my family is."

"I'll make a deal with you." He dipped his head back down to where my breasts swelled out of my tank top and ran his tongue right along the edge. "If you won't judge me based on my family, I won't judge you based on yours. Don't assume I'm a dickhead and I won't assume you're easy, deal?"

"Deal," I gasped, because what he was doing along the edge of my top felt so good.

"I understand your concern, though. Statistically speaking, girls from households with no father sexually develop earlier than girls from households with stable father figures."

"You're kidding." His hand was sliding under the edge of my top, warm against my skin. I wasn't sure how much longer I could string together cogent sentences.

"I know, it makes no sense. A household with only one parent, and that parent being female, will generally have fewer resources and less stability. Any self-respecting monkey would take longer to start being reproductively viable, rather than shorter."

I toyed with the top button of his shirt and it popped through its hole almost of its own accord. I went for the second one. "Perhaps that's part of the problem. Maybe the girls who grow up without daddies aren't self-respecting monkeys. Maybe they're monkeys with no self-respect at all."

He pulled me closer to him. "I respect you." He kissed me, long and slow. "And I'll still respect you in the morning."

He pulled me into his lap and I went all liquid and warm. "Promise?"

"Promise," he murmured into my neck.

CHAPTER NINE

I woke up with Craig's arm around me, my head tucked into that perfect indentation on his chest, our legs twined together like pretzels. I must have shifted, because he pulled me closer and planted a kiss on top of my head.

"Is there some monkey instinct that makes us want to wake up this way?" I asked. It felt so good and so right; clearly it had to come from some ancient part of my brain.

"Possibly the same instinct that makes bonobos have sex a gazillion times a day," he answered, his voice blurred with sleep. "It feels good."

"It does." I snuggled in closer. The cool, damp air played across my shoulders. It was warm and cozy under the covers. It felt like heaven; too bad it had to end so soon. "But I'm afraid you have to go. We're an all-girl clubhouse as soon as Sage wakes up."

Craig turned me on my side and spooned behind me. Damn, talk about unfair fighting. "It's not even light out. Not really."

"It will be soon." I turned to face him, our naked bodies brushing together. Big mistake. I kissed his chest. "Seriously, you have to go. It's the rule."

He kissed me on the forehead and said, "You have a lot of rules, Ms. Ginger. I'll call you later." He sat up and turned to put his feet on the floor. I traced the line of his spine down his back to the little wineglass-shaped birthmark just over his left butt cheek . . . the exact same spot where Sage had a wineglass-shaped birthmark.

I sat up, pulling the sheet up around me. "What the hell is that?"

"What?" Craig turned around and tried to peer where I was pointing. "Oh, that. It's an Esposito family thing. A bunch of us have it in that same spot."

"You can say that again." I scooted to the edge of the bed, getting as far away from him as possible. "What was this, some sick prank? Or are you one of those guys with a kinky thing for twins?" What was I saying? All guys had a kinky thing for twins. I'd seen the beer commercials. I'd walked the halls of a public high school.

Craig turned to face me. "What are you talking about?"

He was so cute, so handsome, so smart. And from such a different side of town than I was from. Why hadn't I listened to my mother?

"Don't play games with me." Tears stung my eyes. I had really liked this guy. Worse yet, I'd trusted him. What had I been thinking?

I kicked him as hard as I could right below the birthmark. "Get out. Now!"

He jumped off the bed. "Ginger! Tell me what's going on here."

"Tell *you* what's going on? That's rich. What were you hoping for? Or does getting to put a double notch on your bedpost pretty much sum it all up?" I scrambled off the bed, too, wrapping the sheet around myself.

Craig pulled his T-shirt over his head. "Notches? Have you lost your mind?"

I may not have lost my mind, but I had definitely lost my belief that things could be different for me. I pointed to the door. "Get out. Just get out."

"No problem. I am gone." He suited action to words.

"How *could* you?" I spat, shaking Cinnamon awake.

"What? Sleep with the racket you two were making? I put in earplugs. I'm just glad Sage's room is at the other end of the apartment." Cinnamon pulled herself into a sitting position. "What are you doing in here?"

"He's Sage's father, isn't he? That's why you turned so pale and nearly burned Ashley when you saw him. That's why you've been acting so weird. Craig is Sage's father and you let me sleep with him! It's . . . it's disgusting." I felt sick to my stomach. I had slept with my niece's father.

"He's not Sage's father," Cinnamon said quietly. "I thought he was when I first saw him, but it's not him."

Cinnamon often refused to answer questions, but she didn't lie. "He has Sage's birthmark—the little tilted wineglass over his butt cheek."

"He has it, too?" Cinnamon sat the rest of the way up. "Interesting."

"What do you mean, 'too'? Who else has it?"

Cinn pulled the blankets up over her shoulders against the morning dampness. "I don't *know* who he is. I thought he was . . ." Her voice trailed off.

"You thought he was who?"

She grimaced. "Not so much 'who,' as 'what.' I thought he was Poseidon."

It always amazes me how Cinnamon can yank the rug out from under me like an inept magician pulling the tablecloth from under a set of good china. I felt like I'd just crashed to the floor for the second time that morning. "You thought you had sex with a sea god?"

"When you say it like that, it sounds stupid." Cinn's jaw started to jut.

"Really," I said. I paced her bedroom. "Explain this to me."

"I was on the beach, the one with the good surf. It was late and I made a little fire."

"Why were you out there so late?"

"I was upset. I think Dad was back in town and everyone was talking about it. Everywhere I went all day, people would stop talking when I walked in. I was sick of it, so I went to the beach late because I knew I would be alone."

"Why didn't you come home?"

"Are you serious? With you stomping around with a major chip on your shoulder and Mom flitting around like everything was fine?"

She was right; whenever Dad showed up, it was exactly like that. I'd be pissed at Mom for letting him hang around since he was such a screw-up. Mom would be deeply invested in acting like things were totally normal, and Cinnamon would disappear. It had never occurred to me to figure out where she'd disappear to. I was too busy telegraphing my adolescent rage with much hair flipping, eye rolling, foot tapping, and the occasional slamming of a door.

"Okay. So you went to the beach and made yourself a little bonfire."

Cinnamon pulled her feet up to sit tailor-fashion on the bed. "So I'm just sitting there, drinking Boone's Farm apple wine."

Ooh, did that ever bring back memories! How many girls have lost their virginity due to Boone's Farm apple wine? I'm pretty sure it was a major lubricating factor when I decided to let Nick Pastis relieve me of my maidenhead in the backseat of his Mom's Buick.

"I'm beginning to understand," I said.

"Anyway, this guy came out of the sea. This beautiful boy with dark hair streaming with water swam out of the ocean and walked right up to my fire." Cinnamon's eyes went all dreamy.

"Did he tell you he was Poseidon?" Boy, was I ever going to ream this guy as soon as I figured out who he was. It had to be someone related to Craig. I remembered how Justin had looked at me at the wedding reception, and got a chill.

Cinnamon gave me a disgusted look. "Of course not! I would have known that he was just a guy if he'd said he was Poseidon. Do you really think I'm that naïve?"

I bit my tongue hard.

"He just said, 'Hey,' and sat down with me." Cinnamon wrapped her arms around her legs and cradled her cheek on her knees.

"And you threw yourself down on the sand and yelled 'Take me'?" While I well knew the power of Boone's Farm, I didn't think it was that powerful.

"I don't have to tell you all this. It's been eight years and I haven't tried to explain this to anyone, so a little patience, please?" Cinnamon glared at me, but her jaw wasn't jutting out.

I sat down on Cinn's bed and leaned against the wall. "Fine. What happened next?"

"I offered him wine and some of my food. We watched the stars and the fire and then he kissed me." Cinnamon's eyes were unfocused, as if she were watching the whole thing play out like a movie in front of her.

"And?" I prompted.

"Zing," she said.

Zing. I could well understand that. "But it wasn't Craig. You're *sure* about that."

"Yeah, I'm sure." Her chin trembled a little. "I'm really sure."

A wave of exhaustion washed over me. I wanted nothing more than to go back to bed. I had to ask, though.

"If you know who Sage's father is, don't you think you should tell her? Shouldn't a girl get to know her own father?"

"Like that did us any good?" Cinnamon snorted sarcastically.

Fine. At least I had some ideas about how to find out more. In fact, I was starting to think I knew exactly who Sage's father was. I shuttered my face and left her room.

My eyes had that gritty feeling that they get from keeping my contacts in too long, and my mouth felt coated in cotton wool. I went to the bathroom to splash water on my face and brush my teeth, shivering in the damp early-morning air. Crawling back under the cozy turquoise comforter on my bed seemed like a good idea—until I got there.

The sheets still smelled like Craig. Handsome, smart Craig, who I had literally kicked out of my bed less than an hour ago. What had I done? And how was I going to even begin to undo it? If only my life had an undo button like my laptop.

After tossing and turning for an hour, I got up, strapped on my running shoes, and headed for the coast trail. The fog felt good on my face as I ran along the path that threaded through hillsides covered with ice plants. I could hear the waves crashing on the shore down below and felt insulated inside the fog, protected. I reached the lighthouse and turned around. The fog burned off as I headed home, my own breathing my only company.

When I got back, Dad was in the front yard, Working on our screen door, which was propped against the porch railing.

"What are you doing?" I asked as I walked up.

"Planing your screen door." He ran a long metal tool down the length of the door, then squinted up at me and smiled. "No jokes about it being plain enough already, okay?"

"I wouldn't dream of it." Seeing Dad fixing something at our apartment had stunned me out of any desire to crack bad jokes. "Any particular reason?"

"I saw your sister bang the door to get it to release when I dropped her and Sage off the other night. I figured a door that opened without having to perform some sort of ritual might be nice for you guys."

He went back to planing. He looked like he knew what he was doing. Then again, Dad was one of those people who always looked like he knew what he was doing, even when he was shit-faced.

"I suppose. On the other hand, you know how Cinnamon feels about rituals." I started to head into the house.

"No," Dad said behind me, a touch of anxiety in his voice. "No, I don't know. Does she like them?"

Dad knew so little about us; the fact that he didn't know his daughter lit bonfires on the beach every solstice or that she made rune symbols on three-way intersections to honor Hecate really shouldn't have surprised me. "Yeah, she does." I turned around.

Dad's brow furrowed. "It would probably still stick if I stop now. Do you think I should put it back up?"

Are all fathers this clueless? Or am I just exceptionally lucky? "No, Dad. We'll be glad not to have it stick shut."

He looked so relieved, I felt a little guilty about teasing him. But only a little. "Where's Mom?" When Dad was in town, it was incredibly rare to see him without Mom attached to his hip. She is that gaga-crazy about him. Yet this was the second time I'd seen him without her hovering inches away.

"She's home. She had some things to take care of before she goes into the shop," Dad said, as if that was totally normal.

My friends in junior high and high school always tried to convince me that Cinnamon and I had it good. So many of their parents' marriages were coming apart. My friends talked about the constant sniping at each other, the tense meals where no one spoke, the unpleasant divvying of belongings as the fathers moved out of their family homes and in with new girlfriends, the horrors of divorce, and step- and half-siblings.

Cinnamon and I never experienced any of those things. Our parents never bothered to marry each other, making the whole divorce thing a moot point. Dad split on a pretty routine basis, but his stuff always lived at our house. I'm sure what my friends went through was hard, but they had no idea what it was like to live with an obsessive love that you were not a part of.

My mother's love for my father is so all-consuming that there's no room for anyone else at the party. Living with them was like constantly being the third wheel on a date—except when Dad was out on tour, when it was like living with Greta Garbo in *Grand Hotel,* with Mom tragically draping herself on the furniture.

When Dad came back to town, he didn't wander around doing chores at other people's houses. He was home. With Mom. Because while his bliss was playing guitar in the Surf Daddies, Mom was his passion. He used to refer to her as his muse, and probably still does.

One time when I was about nine, Dad had been gone for what seemed like a very, very long time. Anxious to see him, I watched for him from my bedroom window even though it was late and we were supposed to be asleep. I heard the van coming down the street, and Mom was on the front lawn before he was even out of it. I watched as he got out of the van, took two long strides, grabbed her in his arms, and pulled her to him. Then he rested his forehead against hers. They didn't kiss and neither said a word, but all the tension left his body.

I think for the rest of my life, my idea of homecoming is going to be the vision of them out on the front lawn, their foreheads resting against each other, bodies entwined and spirits soothed.

Unfortunately, it also sums up my feeling of being alone. There was no space between them for me. No little crack that I could wiggle into to get some of that love. There was no space between them at all.

"You girls have big plans for today?" Dad now asked.

"We have a wedding party to do this afternoon. And I heard Giovanni's doing *Fiddler on the Roof* at the diner today. Sage loves *Fiddler*."

He smiled. "She does? Seems like a funny pick for a kid."

"She prefers *Rent* but Giovanni won't do anything written after 1965 except *Grease*. Sage loves that one, too. I think she knows all the songs by heart. She only knows parts of *Fiddler*."

A shadow passed over Dad's face. "I didn't know that." Then he smiled. "Any chance there's room in your booth for the handyman?"

I may not have mentioned this, but my dad is really cute. Super cute, even. Think Kevin Costner portraying a slightly gone-to-seed baseball player. Winsome looks are somewhat his specialty as well. So while there was a huge part of me that wanted to tell him there was no more room in our booth for him than there'd been between him and Mom for me, I couldn't quite do it.

This may seem obvious, but it's not like my conversation with Cinnamon that morning was all that far from my mind either. Did a girl have a right to know her father? Did a father have a right to know his daughter? Did it make a difference?

I knew it did. I'd seen it too many times. I knew the girls who were so desperate for some kind of male attention that they'd do almost anything and anyone to get it. I'd felt that desperation more than a few times, too. Unfortunately, I'd also felt the pull of Dad's magnetism, which had always been followed by the emotional slap in the face when he turned it off and turned away. Maybe this time was different, though. Maybe he really was staying. He'd certainly been here longer and had been trying harder than he ever had before.

"Sure, Dad. I think we might be able to make room for the handyman."

I let myself in the front door and called out, "Hash browns and 'Sunrise, Sunset' anyone?"

The four of us walked the few blocks to the Coastside Diner. I asked Dad if he wanted to call Mom and invite her to join us. He hesitated but said no, he wanted to spend time just with us. He would see her later at the shop. Apparently, I'd stumbled into an alternate universe. I wondered if we should have brought an umbrella in case pigs started to fly soon.

Sage tugged on Dad's hand. "Faster, Grandpa. I don't mind if we miss the overture, but I need to be there for the beginning."

Grandpa. Sage was calling Dad Grandpa. Definitely flying pig time. Maybe monkeys, too.

"I hope they don't burn everything," Cinnamon said.

I looked over at her. "Giovanni hardly ever burns anything. Why would you worry about that?"

"I got Feoh as my rune card this morning," she said, looking pensive.

"And?"

"Well, it's a money card, which could be good. But it's also the fire card. You never know what can happen when you play with fire."

Fiddler was just starting as we walked in the door.

Every Sunday morning, Giovanni Solimeno puts on the soundtrack for one of his favorite musicals and he and his wife, Anjelica, sing along as they make omelets, hash browns, eggs over easy, and pancakes. This might be unappreciated if performed by any other diner owner in a forty-mile radius, but Giovanni and Anjelica are both retired from the Lyric Opera of Chicago. They decided to settle down with a career that seemed more stable, the restaurant business. Go figure. No one bothered to tell them how many restaurants don't make it, and apparently it didn't matter.

It's a treat to hear them sing, and they encourage the patrons to sing along. The rest of the week, they play opera. Cinnamon and Sage like to go if they're doing *La Bohème* or *Carmen*. Call me shallow, but I'm a Sunday-only kind of gal.

We opened the door as Giovanni started to belt out "Tradition" and he asked who scrambled for a living as we found a booth.

We slid in, Sage and Cinnamon on one side, Dad and me on the other.

Giovanni then asked who had the final word at home in his warm baritone.

Sage stood up on her seat and belted out, "The Papa!" She thrust her fist up over her head like she was proclaiming Jew Power.

She turned to beam at Dad and the funniest look crossed her

face. She sat back down. "Grandpa, are you the master of our house?"

Dad, who had been paying more attention to the menu than to Sage, looked up, surprised. "Am I the what, sweetheart?"

"The master of our house. Is that you? Do you scramble for a living? Do you feed us?" Sage looked very concerned. "Are we tradition?"

Jolene came over to our table with a notepad and pencil in her hand. Her face had filled out since that day that she'd plastered herself to the salon window, begging to be fixed before her wedding. Her color was better, too. Someone—Cinnamon, presumably—had highlighted her hair and given her a new cut. It wasn't quite the suburban mom bob, but it was close. "What can I get for you all?"

"Jolene! I didn't know you were working here." For some reason, I thought she was still stocking shelves at night at the IGA.

She beamed. "I started last week. Aren't they great? I love all the music. Although some of that German stuff is kinda spooky."

"I'm not a big Wagner fan myself," I said.

"I hear that," Jolene said. "But that Verdi guy? Now *he* has it going on."

"So do you, Jolene. You look great," Cinnamon said.

"Thanks to you guys. I probably wouldn't have got this job if it weren't for the work you've been doing on me." Her skin had lost the sallow tone it had had when we'd first met her. Her hair was neither dirty nor dry and strawlike. Her nails were even, smooth, and covered with a clear polish. "I'm like a real lady now. Ronnie says he don't hardly know me." She grinned. "Now Sage, sweetie, what do you want for breakfast?"

Sage was still staring at Dad. Anjelica had already sung the daughters' verse about preparing to marry whoever papa picks. Sage hadn't sung a word of it. "Mickey Mouse pancakes and a chocolate milk, please. Who scrambles for a living at our house?"

Anjelica was singing about who must know the way to make a proper kosher home.

"The Mama," Cinnamon sang. I wasn't sure if she was singing along or answering Sage's question. "I'll have the waffles with strawberries, hold the whipped cream."

"I'll have the Denver omelet with ham and cheese," I said, which earned me a glare from Cinnamon, who was against the bondage of chickens and pigs within the military-agricultural-industrial complex. I so did not care.

Then Jolene turned her attention to Dad. "And what can I get for this handsome gentleman?"

"Jolene, this is our dad," Cinnamon said.

Jolene set her pad down on the table and squeezed in beside Sage. "Well, drop my drawers and spank my fanny. You all have a daddy?"

I felt a headache starting right in the middle of my forehead. "Everyone has a daddy, Jolene."

"But I didn't know you had a daddy that you knew." Jolene reached across and patted Dad's arm. "Where you been?"

Dad shifted uncomfortably. Come to think of it, I wondered where Dad had been recently, too. I turned to look at him.

"Around," he said.

Jolene nodded, her eyes narrowed. "Around. I know how that is. I been around a bit, too. You want an omelet or something?"

"How about eggs and hash browns?" Dad said, not looking at Jolene.

Jolene stood. "Eggs and hash browns it is."

"So where have you been, Grandpa?" Sage asked, her little face serious. "Why aren't we tradition?"

Nobody answered.

I sang "Matchmaker" with Sage, but I don't think her heart was in it.

CHAPTER TEN

Tanya Mitchell and Scott Bernheim were married at 4:30 P.M. on Sunday, April 30, at the Church of the Light of the Open Door in Santa Bonita. The bride wore an ivory floor-length strapless gown with satin ribbon detailing and a cathedral-length veil. She carried a bouquet of apricot and white hydrangeas.

Today's wedding was blessedly simple. Tanya Mitchell didn't want to be a Vulcan princess, wasn't a movie star, and wasn't hiding a pregnancy. She did want a Courtney, but it wasn't life or death. She was just a normal happy bride having normal happy bridal stress. Would the humidity make her hair frizz? Would the string quartet show up on time? Would Uncle Greg get drunk and sing "That's Amore"?

It felt like an ocean of sanity to do her and her bridesmaids, one of whom was her older sister, Valerie.

I'd finished Valerie's hair and makeup. Natalie had just finished their cousin Beth's nails, so we were about to swap bridesmaids. Valerie told Natalie she'd be there in just a second and fished a little box out of her purse. "I have something for you to use as your something old, Tanya."

"Oh, thanks, but I've got something. I found some earrings

at the antiques mall," Tanya said, not looking around since Cinnamon was still doing her hair.

"I think you're going to want these instead," Valerie said softly.

Cinnamon let go of Tanya's head and let her turn and watch as Valerie extended the box out to her. She made no move to take it though. "What is it?" she asked, her hands bunched under the purple cape.

"Mom's diamond earrings," Valerie said. She shoved the box closer to Tanya.

Tanya still made no move to take the box, but she didn't take her eyes off it, either. "They're yours."

"So they can be your something borrowed and your something old." Her laugh sounded nervous. "Two birds with one stone."

"Beth's veil is my something borrowed." Tanya's lips pursed.

Valerie's shoulders slumped and the box wavered a little. "Tanya, don't do this. This is supposed to be a happy day."

"It is a happy day. I just don't want your Pity Earrings." Tanya tore her gaze away from the jewelry box and back to the mirror. Cinnamon went back to curling ringlets.

"They're not Pity Earrings. They're Love Earrings. Take them," Valerie urged, the box still extended.

"Whose love?" Tanya asked. "Hers?"

Valerie's gaze dropped. "Mine. Take them because I love you."

Tanya turned to look at Valerie and that's when the waterworks started.

"Nooooo!" Cinnamon, Natalie, and I all yelled at once, running at them with tissues. Natalie and Cinnamon got there first. Beth, who had settled in my chair for her French twist and makeup, looked back at me and rolled her eyes.

"I never wanted them," Valerie said. "I didn't, but I had to take them. She would have given them to Patti Jo instead. You know she would have."

"It wasn't your fault," Tanya babbled back. "I knew it wasn't. I just wanted them so much."

Beth shook her head this time.

"They were yours to start with. She should never have taken them." Valerie's whole body had started to shake. I sighed and pulled out the cold cream and a bunch of cotton balls. I had no idea what was going on, but I knew it wasn't going to be done until an ocean of tears had been shed.

I sighed as tears puddled up in Beth's eyes, too.

Even the happiest of weddings have some sort of drama to them. Someone always wound up in tears, tears that I ended up having to dry up and cover up.

And Cinnamon wondered why I didn't believe in weddings.

"So it turns out the earrings belonged to their mother, who died when the girls were little. The mother had given the earrings to Tanya, but the grandmother took them. She said she only wanted them for safekeeping, but she wore them all the time. Then when the grandmother was dying, she gave the earrings to Valerie." I recounted the whole thing to Brian, who was sitting at the dining room table, eating an apple and leafing through his microbiology notes.

"The grandmother sounds like a bitch," Natalie said from the computer, where she was ostensibly looking up something our professor had posted on the course website, but I suspected she was actually cruising dating sites.

"Ix-nay on the itch-bay alk-tay," I hissed. Sage was in her room, and the walls weren't that thick. The last thing we needed was calls from Santa Bonita Elementary about Sage's use of epithets.

"Are you speaking pig Latin?" Brian looked up at me, a smile playing at the corners of his mouth.

"Or are you suggesting that the grandmother wasn't an itch-bay?" Natalie asked.

"Don't mind her," Cinnamon said, walking through the living room with a bowl of popcorn. She and Sage were going to watch DVDs in Sage's bedroom while we studied. "She's been cranky all day."

I stared at her. Since part of the reason I had been cranky all day had to do with the bomb I'd had dropped on me this morning about Sage's father, it seemed rude to mention it.

Then I realized that I was not the only person staring at Cinnamon. Brian was looking at her, too, and not at her face. I took another look at Cinnamon. Was she wearing panties under those yoga pants? Oh, hell, she was wearing a thong. You could see its outlines through the yoga pants. She definitely wasn't wearing a bra under the tank top, and the sway-and-bounce motion clearly mesmerized Brian.

"What about the dad?" Natalie asked.

"What about him?" I didn't know much about him; dads tend to recede into the background during weddings unless you need a check signed.

"Did he remarry?" Natalie asked.

I thought for a moment. "Yeah, there was a stepmom mentioned. I don't know how close they are. She wasn't at the bridal salon, but some moms aren't."

"Oh, too bad." Natalie started tapping on the keyboard again.

"Sometimes a mom at the beauty salon just makes more trouble." We've had plenty of moms that I would have liked to duct-tape in a closet. There's the Critical Mom, or C.M. The C.M. marches around saying things like "You're wearing your hair like that?" or "Why would you want people to think your eyelids are that color?" Many of Critical Mom's conversations start with the phrase "I'm only telling you this for your own good."

There is also Panic Mom, who reminds me of Chicken Little, making the smallest glitches—like a broken curling iron—into total disasters. "The curling iron is broken? Completely broken? How will we ever get everyone's hair done in time with only three functioning curling irons? It can't be done! We'll all be late! The wedding will have to be postponed! We'll have to forfeit the caterer's fee!" I often fantasize about having a bottle of spray Valium to spritz in their faces and drop them in their tracks. Sort of like pepper spray, without the inconvenient tears that would mess up their makeup.

There is also Disapproving Mom. The difference between Disapproving Mom and Critical Mom may seem too slight to call at first, but while both will second-guess, cut-down, and/or belittle every decision made by the bride, Critical Mom usually has an agenda. Critical Mom wants things *her* way. Disapproving Mom has no agenda. There is no possible way to please Disapproving Mom. No matter what you choose, it will be wrong. If you wear your hair up, it's too formal. If you wear it down, it looks like you're not trying. If you have been cursed with Disapproving Mom, you might as well shave your head bald and have "Please help me" tattooed on your naked skull.

In some ways, Tanya and Valerie's Dead Mom was the best mom to have during wedding preparations. Dead Mom can do no wrong. Dead Mom wishes she could be there. Dead Mom would be so proud of you and would have loved your dress/flowers/music choice/groom.

"That's not what I meant about it being too bad," Natalie said. "I meant it was too bad their father remarried. It means he's not on the market."

"Natalie!" I turned to Brian for support, but he was looking at the DVD Cinnamon had been taking into Sage's room.

"How is this one?" he asked, smiling down at Cinnamon. "After seeing *Doogal*, I've been leery of trying another animated movie with a huge all-star cast."

"We haven't watched it yet. I'll have to let you know." Cinnamon twirled a ringlet around her finger. "I know what you mean about *Doogal*, though. I may never forgive Jon Stewart for that one."

My mouth dropped open. Was Brian flirting with my sister? Was she flirting back? The nerve!

I looked down. I was wearing a cute outfit. I had on jeans and a white lacy shirt with a camisole beneath it. My panties were not visible and I had on a bra, but it was still a cute outfit. Plus, I'm pretty sure the yoga pants Cinnamon was wearing were mine.

"Yeah, I think a widower might be a nice thing," Natalie said. "Especially one with grown daughters—I don't want to raise any more kids. This is about me now."

"Isn't everything?" Brian asked, handing the DVD back to Cinnamon. Did their fingers touch as he handed it back to her, or was that just my imagination? I was definitely not imagining the sashay in Cinnamon's hips as she went to Sage's room.

"Bugles, anyone?" Brian asked. "Ginger, what's up with your jaw. Are you grinding your teeth?"

We'd progressed past the aorta and moved on to capillary beds when I heard Cinnamon's cell phone go off in the other room. I heard the murmur of her voice through the door.

"Glomerular filtration pressure?" Natalie asked.

"Distal convoluted tubule. Water's reabsorbed. Sodium's excreted," Brian responded.

Cinnamon burst into the room. "We've got to go. Tanya Mitchell is in trouble. She set herself on fire."

"On purpose?" Brian asked.

"Of course not!" Cinnamon said, grabbing her jacket from the coat tree by the front door. "They did that thing with the unity candle. You know, where she has one candle and he has the other and they use those to light one, big one, and it's a symbol of how they're making their two lives into one? Anyway, the big candle flared up when they lit it and her hair caught on fire. Now she's hysterical and I've got to go. Are you coming with or not?" She grabbed my jacket off the tree and stood with it in front of her.

My notes on the kidney would still be here when I got back. A self-immolating bride was something you don't see every day.

I stood up. "I'm in."

We wound up the hilly streets to the church perched on the hill, the air chilling around us. Brian had agreed to stay with Sage. Cinnamon had praised him lavishly for his willingness to help, going on and on about how he was putting himself out and about how grateful she was until I nearly gagged. Especially since she kept twirling that ringlet around her finger as she did it.

Brian seemed to eat it up with a spoon. Personally, I think he originally offered because he wanted to watch *Hoodwinked!* Then something definitely shifted. When Cinnamon said she'd have to do something nice for him later, I wasn't crazy about the look on his face.

There was no time to worry about that now, though. We let ourselves in the side door of the church, headed downstairs, and shoved our way through the crowd outside the ladies' room.

"Where is she?" Cinnamon asked, sounding like a doctor looking for a patient.

Valerie, the maid of honor, said, "Right this way. She's in here."

We pushed the door open and Cinnamon and I slipped in as Valerie kept everyone else out. "Damn rubberneckers," Cinn cursed under her breath.

The smell of burnt hair was strong enough to choke me. Cinnamon rushed immediately to Tanya's side. All the ringlets on the right side of Tanya's head were burned off, and I do mean *all*. Singed strands stuck out at odd angles among the few long strands that were still there.

"I don't understand." Cinnamon examined the strands. "How could it have burned so quickly? I didn't use anything flammable on it."

Tanya's eyes closed and her lips trembled. "I sprayed on some of *that* right before we went up. You know, just to keep it in place through the ceremony."

We all looked to where Tanya was pointing. My jaw dropped in disbelief.

"Aqua Net?" Cinnamon grabbed the can from the counter. "You put Aqua Net on your hair? What possessed you?"

"It was there!" Tanya wailed. "It was only a spritz or two!"

Cinnamon knelt before her, gently running her fingers through the singed hair. She took a deep breath and sat back on her heels. "I can fix it, Tanya, but it's going to be drastic."

Tanya began to weep. "I knew I should have taken the pictures first. I didn't want him to see me in my dress until I came down the aisle. I wanted to see his face when he saw me. I wanted it to be like it is in the movies, when the groom turns and sees the bride, and looks like he never saw anyone so beautiful in all his life."

"And was it?" Cinnamon asked, her voice kind again.

Tanya nodded, head still in her hands.

"Was it good?"

"Yes!" she wailed.

"So it was all worth it. The pictures are just pictures. Your memory of the day is what counts." Cinnamon began unpacking scissors and combs from her bag. "I'm going to need an extension cord and some towels."

They didn't have much in the way of towels, but I found a stack of worn tablecloths that would have to do. Extension cords were tucked in the storeroom by the baby Jesus in his cradle. I hustled back to the restroom with my booty.

Cinnamon stood next to Tanya, eyes closed, hands hovering mere centimeters away from her hair. She made a small humming noise.

Tanya looked like a deer in headlights. A very lopsided deer with seriously bad hair.

"Yes," Cinnamon said finally. "Yes. I can see it. Ginger, hand me the scissors."

As I handed them to her, she turned Tanya's chair away from the mirror. "I don't think you should watch this," she told her. "You're going to have to trust me."

Tanya nodded.

"Are you ready?" Cinnamon asked.

"I am," Tanya said in a small voice.

With the first cut, the crowd gasped, and I thought Tanya was going to come right up out of her seat. Cinnamon turned on the mob, brandishing her scissors. "Do you think you're helping? This is an emergency here. If you're not going to be one hundred percent supportive of Tanya and Ginger and me, there is no place for you here in this room."

Amazingly, several women ran out, choking back sobs. While

part of me applauded their empathy, a bigger part of me wanted to bop them on their heads. It was just hair.

There was no time for more thought though. Cinnamon's scissors were flying with an almost Edward Scissorhands kind of frenzy. At first I couldn't see where she was going besides making Tanya look like a badly shorn sheep; then I started seeing the cut take shape.

Still, her scissors flew. More women left the room, some with hands clasped over their mouths.

Finally, Cinnamon stuck out her hand to me. "Blow-dryer. With the diffuser attachment."

I snapped it into her hand. She leaned Tanya gently forward. Using her left hand, she began to blow-dry Tanya's hair.

She held out a hand to me, palm up. "Mousse," she demanded.

Feeling like Sally Kellerman in *M*A*S*H**, I shot a dollop of foamy goo into Cinnamon's hand. She scrunched it into the roots of Tanya's now very, very short hair. It only took a few seconds for it to dry, now that there wasn't much of it. "Sit up," Cinnamon commanded.

Tanya obeyed, her movements slow and dreamlike, as if she were a volunteer at a hypnotist's show.

"More mousse," Cinnamon said, hand outstretched. I shot more into her palm. She moved around Tanya to finish her styling, blocking our view of what she was doing. Cinnamon always was a heck of a show-woman.

Then, just like that, she was done. The blow-dryer snapped off. Cinnamon lifted Tanya's chin to look directly into her eyes. "Yes," she said quietly. "That's what we should have done all along anyway." And then she stepped away.

There was a communal gasp from the assembled women.

"Sharon Stone," someone whispered. "But without that rode-hard, put-away-wet look."

"Meg Ryan before the unfortunate collagen lip thing," someone else said.

It was Tanya's perfect haircut. Her eyes looked huge. Her cheekbones arched gracefully upward.

"Give me the veil," Cinnamon said, hand outstretched. Someone snapped it into her hand. She turned it around, lips pursed, then grabbed her scissors and cut off a yard of foofy tulle. She placed it gently on Tanya's head, then turned her so she could see herself in the mirror.

"What do you think?" Cinnamon asked.

"It's perfect," Tanya breathed. "Thank goodness you got here before I had my pictures taken. It's like it was fate." She stood up from her chair and walked through the crowd as if she was in a trance. They parted before her, like the Red Sea before Moses, then, as she passed, turned and followed her out of the room, leaving Cinnamon and me alone again.

Cinnamon sank down in the chair where Tanya had been sitting.

"That was amazing," I told her as I started to pack up her supplies.

"Thank you." Her face was pale and a little drawn.

I found a broom in the corner and swept up as much of the hair as I could. "Seriously, where did you come up with that haircut?"

"I always thought Tanya would look good with short hair," Cinnamon said, as if it was that simple.

"You're a genius. You know that, don't you?" I said, sitting down on the chair next to her. I was exhausted just from having watched her.

"I'm not a genius," Cinnamon said. "I have a knack. That's all. Like you do for school."

School. That thing I needed to study for. With Brian, who

was still waiting back at the apartment. Who had been watching the outline of my sister's thong through her yoga pants with more attention than he had paid to our dissection of the sheep heart—and he had been really fascinated by the sheep heart.

"You can't have Brian," I blurted out.

"Who says I wanted Brian in the first place?" Cinnamon said, slamming the door of the Mustang as she got in.

"You didn't have to say anything. I saw the way you were twirling your hair." I shut my door much more gently. It felt like it gave me a sort of moral high ground.

She started the engine and shot me a look as the Mustang grumbled to life. "I was not twirling my hair."

I rolled my eyes.

"You didn't even want him until he started flirting with me," she said.

"I do, too," I said. "I want him to be my study buddy. You'll flirt with him for a couple of weeks and then you'll get tired of him, and I won't have anyone to quiz me on body parts for the rest of the semester."

"*That's* not why you want me to leave him alone." Cinnamon skidded a little on the damp street at the bottom of the hill.

"Stop driving like a maniac; you're going to hit something. Besides, it's not like you really want him, either. You'll toy with him, go out with him a few times, then slam the door in his face. It never goes farther than that."

"I don't toy."

"You *so* toy. All you do is toy. You're the toying queen."

Cinn glared at me. "You are so selfish. You have everything, and you won't let me have one simple boy that you're not even using."

"I am too using him. I'm studying with him. And what is this about me having everything? You're the one with everything!"

"Me! I don't have anything!"

I started ticking things off on my fingers. "You're the one with the career that you're totally suited for. You're the one with the daughter. You're the one with all the talent. What have I got?"

"You're the one with the brains who could get out of here," Cinnamon said, staring at the road ahead of her. "You're the one who could leave if she wanted to."

By the, time we got home, Brian and Sage had finished watching *Hoodwinked!* and were playing Chutes and Ladders.

"Help me," Brian mouthed over Sage's head.

"Hey, Chutes and Ladders!" Cinn said enthusiastically. Cinnamon thinks Chutes and Ladders is hysterical. Plus she loves that even though it may look like you're going to win, at the very very end, you can try to steal cookies from the jar on the high shelf and go skidding down a chute practically to the beginning. "Any chance I can play?"

"You can take my place." Brian got up so fast, he almost knocked his chair over.

"Where'd Natalie go?" I asked.

Sage frowned. "She had a date. She didn't want to watch the movie with us or anything." Her tone implied exactly what she thought of Natalie's priorities.

"What happened with your self-immolating bride?" Brian asked.

"Cinnamon was amazing, as usual," I said. "She gave her a whole new haircut, altered her veil, and sent her off to have her picture taken. She saved the wedding."

"Awesome," Brian said, flipping his blond hair and smiling at Cinnamon.

"Thanks," she said, smiling back. Her hand went up toward that damn side ringlet, but she caught my look and dropped it.

I looked up at the clock; fixing Tanya's hair had taken longer than I'd realized. "Do you still have time to work on kidney functions?" I asked. "Those equations are driving me nuts."

"Sure," he said. "For you, anything."

There was no way we were going to be able to study with Cinnamon and Sage in the room, and the kitchen was way too small. "Let's go to my room," I said. "We can study there."

"Are you sure this is okay?" he asked, glancing over his shoulder.

What? He could practically drool down the front of his shirt while watching my sister's ass, but he couldn't sit in a room alone with me?

"Do you need to get permission from your mom?" I snarked.

Brian stiffened. "I'm just asking if this is a good idea with Sage right down the hall."

"What exactly do you think I'm inviting you to do, Brian? To examine my personal anatomy and physiology?"

"No," he said, his face flushing.

"How 'bout we keep the door open and I keep one foot on the floor?" I pulled my legs into the lotus position (Cinnamon makes me do yoga with her at least three times a week, and I am nothing if not flexible) and braced my hands behind my back, which I knew popped my cleavage a little.

Okay, maybe more than a little.

I'm not stupid. I do know that Brian has a little bit of a crush on me. Not a huge, soul-thrashing crush, but a crush nonetheless. Until now, I hadn't really been interested. I'm not even sure I was interested now. I just knew that *I* was the person whose thong he was supposed to be admiring, not my sister.

"Did I do something to piss you off?" he asked, his eyes narrowed now.

Oh, lord, save me from sensitive men. Yes, clearly I was pissed. Unfortunately, I wasn't sure why.

"Just get in here and help me figure out the equations for the filtration pressures. Please?" I slumped forward. How come other women were able to use their breasts to get things and I was completely incapable of it? I'd seen Natalie lean forward to look at the lettuce at Subway and end up with a free bag of chips. My own mother had a way of stretching her back that had men leaping over parking meters to help her carry boxes. Me? I couldn't even get a guy who already had a crush on me to come into my room and study.

He took a tentative step in. "Okay."

"How was the movie?" I asked as I flipped open my textbook.

He sat down next to me. "It was funny. Everybody in the movie was telling the truth, but it looked like they were lying. Very clever."

"Sounds great." Just great.

Brian, my useless breasts, and I spent the next hour and a half working our way through the kidney; then I walked him to the front door.

"See you tomorrow," I said.

"Yeah," he said, hesitating; then he turned tail and left.

I woke to the sound of music and rolled over to look at the clock. Two A.M.? I stumbled out of bed and down the hall to the living room to see what was going on. Cinnamon and Sage were kneeling on the couch, elbows braced on its back, looking out the window. Sage had on Hello Kitty pajamas. Cinnamon had on a tank top and boxer shorts. I looked down at my tank top and boxer shorts. "We should talk before we go to bed," I told her.

She rolled her eyes. "We have bigger problems than matching outfits."

"What's going on?" I asked as I clambered onto the couch next to them.

"The man whose mama and auntie don't teach him manners is playing music for us," Sage said.

I groaned. Sure enough, there was Lamont with his iPod iHome held over his head à la John Cusack in *Say Anything*. It was playing Neil Young's "Cinnamon Girl."

"Go home, Lamont," I yelled out the window, over the sound of Neil singing how he could be happy with his cinnamon girl.

Lamont didn't answer.

"I'll call the police, Lamont," I called.

He still didn't say anything, but his lips tightened as if he was fighting the impulse. He held the iHome higher. Neil sang about running in the night.

"Lamont, you've got the wrong sister. She's Cinnamon," I said, gesturing at her. "I'm Ginger. You should at least keep track of whom you're stalking."

That was apparently more than Lamont could resist. "I couldn't find any songs with 'ginger' in them. This was the best I could do," he called over Neil singing about chasing the moonlight.

"It's not good enough, Lamont. Plus, John Cusack had a boom box, not an iHome," I pointed out.

"I know that." Lamont's voice held a trace of irritation, like who was I to question his stalking techniques. "Who has a boom box anymore? This was the closest I could come."

Oh, lovely. I had a lazy stalker who couldn't be bothered to put a real effort into it. "It's not close enough, Lamont. Now go home before I call Troy."

Lamont turned the music off. "Okay." His shoulders slumped and for a second I felt bad for him. Then he looked up again. "Do I at least get points for trying?"

"No," Cinnamon and I said in unison and shut the window.

"I think it's your turn to make the hot chocolate," I told her.

CHAPTER ELEVEN

Over Frosted Flakes the next morning, Sage asked me, "Does everybody have a daddy, Auntie Ginger?"

It was Monday and Cinnamon was sleeping in. I wanted to get an early start on studying, so I'd told her I'd get Sage off to school and then start my day.

I'd been wondering how long it would take for this particular topic to come up. For a long time, kids assume that whatever happens in their own house is normal. It takes a while to realize that other people do things differently.

I actually remember when I realized our family wasn't entirely "normal." I was at Lauren Hasselbaum's house. I asked why they had pictures of her mom and dad and grandma and grandpa dressed in funny clothes up on the wall.

Lauren had told me those were wedding pictures. Didn't my mommy and daddy have pictures of their wedding up, too? Didn't everyone?

Of course, my mommy and daddy didn't have framed pictures of their wedding up on the wall; they hadn't had a wedding. Grandma Rosemary had had a wedding, but it didn't really count since it wasn't actually legal, what with Grandpa Basil being married to someone else and all. She might have had a picture somewhere, but it wasn't something we were likely to put up on a wall. We did have quite a few framed Surf Daddies posters, though.

Cinnamon and I had at least had some sort of daddy we could point to. All Sage had was a big fat secret and a long line of single mothers.

"Yep, everybody has a daddy. It takes a mommy and a daddy to make a baby." I could at least be biologically honest with her.

Sage set down her spoon. "Can either of them be a unicorn, ever?"

"Not unless we're talking baby unicorns." I was sad to burst her bubble, but the unicorn thing had to stop.

"Where's mine?" Sage folded her arms across her nearly concave little chest.

"Your unicorn?" Perhaps we were indulging her princess tendencies too much. "At the special unicorn stable, obviously."

Sage's jaw jutted forward. I knew that facial expression far too well. "I meant my daddy. Where's my daddy?"

"I'm not sure," I told her, which was technically true, although I had a suspicion. It seemed too big a step into the cold ugly world to tell Sage that I was pretty sure her daddy was on his honeymoon with his newly knocked-up wife.

"Does Mama know where my daddy is?"

"I think so," I said.

"Why won't she tell?"

"I've been trying to figure that out for a long time, honey. You know how your mama is, though. She'll tell us when she's good and ready."

The jaw receded. I took our cereal bowls to the sink and rinsed them out. Sage stuffed the lunch I'd packed for her (a peanut-butter-and-grape-jelly sandwich with the crusts cut off and sliced diagonally, a bag of Fritos, an apple, and two humongus chocolate-chip cookies) in her *Dora the Explorer* lunch box and then into her Tinkerbell backpack. I stuffed my lunch (a peanut-butter-and-raspberry-jam sandwich with the crusts still on and sliced in half, a bag of Fritos, an apple, and two huge oatmeal raisin cookies) into the wool-tapestry-and-ostrich-hide bag I'd scored from Pass It On last spring.

"Ready to go?" I asked as we headed for the door.

Sage nodded. "Yep. Auntie G?"

"Yes, pumpkin?"

"I'm good and ready to know who my daddy is."

Sage did not particularly like being walked to school. She felt that, at seven, she was more than capable of walking by herself. "You can stop at the corner of Second and Juniper, okay?" she said.

I shook my head. "Nope. I can't see the front door of the school from there. How about in front of Esperanza's Mercado?" I could see the front door from there, and I could check out what Esperanza had on special this week. You never know when you're going to need some chile-and-lime-spiced peanuts; they made my lips feel poutier than Sephora's lip plumper.

Sage marched on for a few steps, her pink Converse hightops slapping on the sidewalk like the exclamation marks of her indignation. "Fine, then," she said at last. "But no waving and yelling stuff about making good choices, okay?"

I sighed. "Are we that embarrassing already?"

She nodded.

I sighed again. It was like my life was one big detour around having any kind of fun.

I couldn't even seduce men who had crushes on me. I had useless breasts and no knack for hair. I decided I would treat myself to the Café Ole! specialty to pick myself up before I hit the books. Plus, I really needed the caffeine.

I headed in that direction as soon as I saw Sage make it safely through the double doors of Santa Bonita Elementary and also ascertained that Esperanza was featuring tamarind candies this week. I'm not a tamarind fan, even in Jolly Rancher form.

Café Ole! makes Mocha de Mexico, a mix of Mexican hot chocolate and coffee. It's hot and sweet and a little bit spicy. In short, it was everything I apparently wasn't. Nope. I was cold and mean and evidently as bland and uninteresting as yogurt with no fruit.

I came around the corner and saw Craig across the street. He had on running shorts and a hooded sweatshirt, and was limping. Clearly, he needed my help. That was the *only* reason I crossed the street—not the breathless hope that I would be able to explain to him why I'd kicked him out of my bed and called him names after a night of doing the horizontal samba.

"Hey," I said, a little breathless from sprinting down the street after him.

"What are you doing here?" Craig asked.

"I kind of live here. How about you?" I looked up at him, trying to give him my most engaging smile.

"Me too." He crossed his arms in front of his chest.

I couldn't look up at him anymore. For one thing, it strained my neck. "I owe you an apology," I said to my shoes.

"Ya think?" He let his arms drop to his sides. "You accuse me of—I'm not even sure *what* you accused me of—because I have a birthmark above my ass and throw me out of your house without any explanation, and you think that just maybe you owe me an apology?"

"And a drink! I could buy you a drink and explain it." Ouch. A touch too eager, maybe.

"I don't think so. Halfway through my margarita, you'd probably notice that my second toe is longer than my big toe and call me an insensitive bastard and throw me out of the bar."

"It's called Morton's Toe," I said.

"Excuse me?"

"The second-toe-longer-than-the-big-toe thing is called Morton's Toe. You should be careful when you buy sneakers; it's probably why you're limping."

Craig straightened up. "Seriously? That's why the bottom of my foot hurts? Because of my toe?"

I nodded. "Yep. It has to do with the way you transfer your weight as you walk or run. You can get metatarsal pads, but you'll probably do better buying sneakers with a high, wide toe box. So can I buy you a coffee?"

He nodded.

We went back across the street to Café Ole! and ordered. "Have you heard from Justin and Ashley?" I asked over the whirring of the milk being frothed.

He nodded.

"Are they having a fabulous time and wishing we all were there?" I pressed.

He shook his head. "Not so much. In fact, they're coming home today. Ashley got some kind of flu and has been puking the whole time. Justin sounded like . . . well, like some guy whose new wife has been puking through their whole honeymoon in scenic, expensive Hawaii."

I resisted the urge to ask if she'd been barfing mainly in the morning. Either way, it was one more point in Cinnamon's hunch's favor. "That's too bad."

"Yeah. Not exactly a good omen, is it?" He shook his head

and took his coffee from the girl behind the counter. She handed me mine and we found a table to sit at between the guy with the long gray ponytail wearing a suit jacket, jeans, and Birkenstocks with socks who was reading *The Wall Street Journal,* and the spiky-haired guy who was either talking into the freaky clip-on earpiece of his cell phone or was seriously delusional and making stock trades with his imaginary broker. Sometimes it's hard to tell in Santa Bonita.

"So I'm really, really sorry about the other morning," I said.

Craig looked at me and waited. "Go on," he said, finally.

What? Did he expect me to tap-dance or something? "That's it. I'm sorry."

He leaned back in his chair and crossed his arms in front of his chest again. "How about giving me a hint as to why you suddenly went crazy, kicked me, called me names, and threw me out of your bed?"

My face got warm thinking about Craig in my bed. He'd done a nice job while he was there. "I can't."

He brought his chair down with a thump. "Then I can't accept your apology."

I gasped. "You have to accept it. It was totally sincere and it came with coffee." Plus, I couldn't tell him anything. They weren't my secrets to tell.

"How am I supposed to judge its sincerity when I have no idea why you did what you did, much less if you mean it now when you apologize for it? The act was totally irrational."

I sighed. "I had reasons. I just can't tell you what they were." There was no way I could tell Craig about Cinnamon and the sea god. I especially couldn't tell him that I suspected his newly wedded cousin was my sister's Poseidon.

He stood up. "Thanks for the coffee, Ginger. I'll see you around."

I put my head down on the table so I wouldn't have to see him walk out.

After anatomy class, I headed home and flung myself on my bed. Through the open closet doors, the Audrey Hepburn *Sabrina* dress mocked me. That hadn't worked out at all like I'd planned. I stuffed it into a bag to take back to Mom. I hadn't spilled anything on it; she could still sell it.

When I walked into the shop, Dad was sitting behind the counter, feet propped up on a footstool, eating sunflower seeds, and reading an ancient-looking copy of *The Big Sleep*.

"Hey, Ginger," he said, setting down the book when I walked in. "What can I do for you?"

He seemed positively chipper. Chipper was not what I was looking for. My clothing was mocking me, and I hadn't gotten much sleep. "Where's Mom?"

"Out." He popped another sunflower seed into his mouth.

"Out where?"

"Just out." He spit the seed husk into a napkin. "Can I help you?"

Well, wasn't he the informative one? Two can play that game, though. "No, I don't think so. I'll come back later."

I turned on my heel, and walked out of the store face-first into Craig. This time, he was wearing jeans and an untucked dress shirt with the sleeves cuffed—and Kendra draped over him like a cheap pashmina.

I froze. Total deer in the headlights.

He froze, too.

Kendra didn't freeze. "Ginger! How are you?" She did not disentangle herself from Craig. In fact, I think she snuggled a little bit closer.

"Hi, Kendra. Hey, Craig," I said, without meeting his eyes.

If I could have sunk down into the cracks in the sidewalk and seeped away, I would have. I thought about turning and running, but I seemed to be rooted to the ground.

"We're just going to meet Ashley and Justin for lunch. What are you up to?" Kendra cocked her head and pointed to the bag slung over my shoulder. "Hey! Isn't that the dress you wore to the wedding? It is, isn't it? Taking it back to your mother's shop?" She shook her head. "Why bother? No one else in Santa Bonita will be able to wear it, now that everyone's seen you in it."

From another woman's mouth that might have sounded like a compliment. Not from Kendra's, though. "You never know," I said.

Kendra simpered up at Craig. "Besides, you don't want to be too hasty. You could have another wedding to wear it to soon."

I wanted to gag. Craig looked like he did, too. "I'll take my chances."

"Come on, sweetie, we don't want to be late," Kendra said, smiling up at Craig, who looked like he was made out of wood. "Ta!"

I watched them walk on down the sidewalk. "I'll show you 'ta,'" I muttered under my breath.

"What exactly is 'ta'?" a deep voice said behind me.

I squealed and whirled around. Troy. "You have got to stop doing that," I told him.

"I know," he said, sounding miserable. There were dark shadows under his eyes and his lips looked dry. His glorious hair even looked a little brittle.

"Why are you lurking here, anyway?" I asked.

"I'm not lurking." He crossed his arms over his chest.

"Are too."

"Maybe a little." Across the street, Justin and Ashley got out of a BMW convertible. Troy sighed.

Then his cell phone rang. He checked the caller I.D. and scowled. "I have to take this. See you later, Ginger." Then he answered the phone, "I told you no. I meant no. Stop calling me. Those photos are mine and they're staying that way."

When the doorbell rang at eight o'clock, Cinnamon and I looked at each other. "Are you expecting someone?" I asked.

She shook her head. "Is your stalker coming by tonight?"

I checked my watch. "He usually opts for a later hour."

"I noticed," she said. "Do you think you could talk to him about that? I don't think it's good for Sage to have her sleep interrupted like that."

The doorbell rang again. Sage skipped out of her room and headed to the door to answer it. "Are you two going to just sit there? Do I have to do everything around here?"

"Hold on to your horses there, pony," I said, and climbed onto the couch to peer out the window. It was Brian. I banged my fist against my forehead. We were supposed to study for the quiz tonight. I gave Sage the all-clear sign to open the door.

"Hey, tiger," Brian said to Sage as he kicked the door closed behind him. I took the grocery bags he held from his arms.

"I'm not a tiger," Sage said, her mouth pursed in disapproval.

"Oh, then what are you?" Brian asked.

I set the bags down on the table and started pulling out our study aids. Apples? Snap peas? I dug deeper. There must be chocolate here somewhere.

Sage appeared to be taking Brian's question very seriously. "Can I be a unicorn?"

Brian tossed his jacket over the back of the papasan chair. "This is California, kid. In the privacy of your own home, you can be anything you want."

Sage looked over at me, clearly confused. "That means yes, right?"

"Yes, it does," I confirmed.

She pranced out of the living room like a prize pony in a dressage competition.

"If she gallops everywhere she goes for the next month, it's your fault," Cinnamon said, following her.

I hit pay dirt at the bottom of the grocery bag.

"Hey!" Brian grabbed the candy from my hand. "Those are for rewards later. Two M&M's for every correct answer." He put a jicama stick in my hand.

"Where's Natalie?" I asked, flipping my anatomy book open.

"Spendin' some quality time with her kids." Brian opened his book and pulled a spiral-bound notebook from his backpack.

"She brings better snacks."

"I bring healthier snacks."

"Same difference," I said.

"Name the segments of the small intestine."

"Duodenum, jejunum, ileum."

He tossed me two M&M's. "Stop whining and study."

I sighed, opened my own notebook, and asked, "Where is the majority of food absorbed?"

After class the next day, Brian walked me to my car.

"What did you think about question four?" he asked.

"Was that the one about net filtration pressure or the one about kwashiorkor?" I unlocked the Mustang and got in.

"Kwashiorkor."

"I thought that only an evil soul- sucking bitch would put that on a quiz," I said. "How 'bout you?"

"I was going to say I thought it was challenging, but you

might be right about the evil soul-sucking bitch thing." He shut my car door for me, waved, and started to walk away.

I turned the key in the ignition and the Mustang sputtered. I turned the key to Off, waited a second, and then tried it again. More sputtering.

In my rearview mirror, I saw Brian turn around and head back toward me. "Problem?" he asked.

"Yeah. I think I know what to do, though. My dad did something with a screwdriver the other day when it wouldn't start." I popped the hood and went to get the tools out of the back.

A moment later, Brian said, "So explain to me again what your dad did with the screwdriver." The hood of the Mustang was up and we were peering into her inner workings together.

I pointed to various metal bits. "He put it from there to there, and then I turned the key and she started."

Brian ducked in, his blond hair flopping down over his forehead. He touched one metal bit and then another. "He put it between these two pieces?"

"Mmm hmm." I braced my elbows on the Mustang and leaned my chin on my hands.

Brian wore a black snap-front shirt untucked over jeans. He'd rolled the sleeves up, but he wasn't going to stay clean. "You're going to get all greasy," I said.

He smiled up at me. "It's a good thing I wore black, then."

As he peered up at me through that floppy blond hair, his head deep inside my engine, it hit me that Brian was cute. Seriously cute.

"What?" he asked.

"N-n-nothing," I stammered, feeling my face flush.

"You're looking at me funny." He straightened up. His shoulders looked broader than I remembered, and I wondered if he'd been working out. "Do I have something hanging from my nose?"

I stood up, too, suddenly aware of the fact that I'd had Mexican food for lunch and that my breath might smell like a taco. "No. Nothing like that."

He leaned against the front of the car and wiped his hands on a towel he'd grabbed from his toolbox. "I think it's your alternator."

I leaned, too. "What exactly does that mean?" He smelled nice. Soapy. Why hadn't I noticed that before?

"Are you sure there's nothing hanging from my nose?" he asked again.

"I'm sure. The alternator?"

"I think I can replace it for you, but I'd like to talk to your dad first. If he's replaced it before, he might have a trick or two." He shoved his hair off his forehead. "Any chance of that?"

"Sure," I said. "How about coming with me to their house for dinner tonight?"

Brian and I figured out the screwdriver thing, though he looked like he seriously didn't approve of it. As I headed back to Santa Bonita for this afternoon's customers, a little pit of dread settled in my stomach. Another day of sticking my hands into other people's hair. Another day of combing and snipping and plucking. My skin began to itch.

To distract myself, I called Pass It On as I drove.

"You're coming for dinner and you're bringing a date?" Mom asked. "Is this some kind of joke?"

"No, Mom." Had I really been that difficult? "But Brian isn't a date. He's just a friend."

"I'll tell your father. He'll bake a pie!"

"He doesn't have to bake a pie. He just has to talk to Brian about what's wrong with the Mustang's alternator."

"He can do both. Your father is nothing if not multitalented," Mom said, her voice reverberating with pride.

She'd gotten that right. He'd managed to work his way back into my life, despite the fact that I'd sworn I'd never let him do it again. It definitely took multiple talents to achieve that.

CHAPTER TWELVE

I tried to forget about Brian's clean scent and floppy blond hair as I finished doing Jean Snyder's cut and color, but his cuteness battled with the fact that if Jean didn't start taking Rogaine soon we'd have to paint her scalp. I listened with half an ear as Jean expounded on her son's latest problems at school, which were undoubtedly partially responsible for her thinning hair.

"I wouldn't let them put that thing back in me for ten thousand dollars. Not even fifty thousand dollars," Mira Wexler was telling Cinnamon. The thing she was referring to was her uterus. "Seriously, who wants the bother?"

"You certainly seem perkier," Cinn said.

"Perkier, happier, healthier. They even shored up my bladder. I can hold it for hours on end. I'm like a camel."

"That would be handy." Cinnamon twirled her around to show her the back of her new haircut. Mira cooed and clapped her hands like a baby.

"Would you let them put it back in you for a hundred thousand?" Jean asked.

"Can I use part of the hundred thousand to have it taken back out again?"

"I think that begs the question," Jean said.

"I just wanted to establish the parameters." Mira thought for a second. "A hundred thousand would be hard to turn down."

The doorbell chimed and Laura walked in, without Monroe for once. Cinnamon ran over and threw her arms around her. Laura winced. I wondered if she was getting a little sick of being the miracle girl who survived the big crash, or if Cinn was just squeezing too hard.

Laura smiled. "I wanted to talk about my hair for the wedding, if you guys have a minute."

"We're both finishing right now, so we do." Cinnamon smiled back. "But I thought we'd worked all that out, back before . . ."

"Before the accident?" Laura asked.

Cinnamon nodded.

"That's the thing. I don't remember exactly what we decided back then."

"She should get one of those Courtneys," Jean said, over the noise of the blow-dryer.

"That's a nice updo," Mira said. "I thought it looked real pretty on Tanya before she lit herself on fire."

"Oh, it did," Jean said. "It looked nice on Philippa, too."

Laura looked back and forth between everyone and nodded. "The Courtney," she said slowly. "What exactly did that look like again?"

"It's one of the beauties of the Courtney," Cinnamon said. "It looks a little different on each person. Here, let me show you."

She fished the album of Courtney brides from under the counter and opened it in front of Laura, while I rung up Jean and Mira.

"Here's what it looks like on a blonde like you," she said, pointing to a picture of Ashley.

"She's got a lot more hair than I do," Laura said, her hand rising falteringly to her still-short hair.

"You have another month to grow it, but it doesn't really matter," Cinnamon said.

"Show her Chloe's picture." Jolene peered over Cinnamon's shoulder, leaning on her broom. "That'll give her an idea of what she'd look like with it short."

Cinnamon nodded and flipped to Chloe's picture. "She's not blonde like you, but her hair was the same length yours is now. See how nice it came out?"

Laura leaned forward and studied the photo. Mira and Jean leaned with her. Laura's hand shook a little as she tapped on the picture. She gnawed on her lower lip as she inspected the photo. "That does look nice. It's the same?"

Cinnamon sat back in her chair. "It's the same, but a little bit different. That's what makes the Courtney so special. I can make it look good on anyone."

Jean patted Laura on the back. "Go for it, honey. You'll look great. You know Cinnamon wouldn't steer you wrong."

Jean and Mira signed their credit card slips and grabbed their jackets. Laura wrung her hands. As the door closed behind the two older women, I heard Mira say, "Maybe Laura should get rid of her uterus. Something's making that girl a nervous wreck."

Laura took a deep breath and sat back in her chair. "Okay, the Courtney it is. Mom will say it's one more thing I'm changing, but she'll have to live with it."

Cinnamon covered Laura's hand with hers. "Why, Laura? Why are you changing everything?"

For a long second, Laura just looked at Cinnamon. "I feel like I'm a different person than the one who chose all those other things. I want the wedding to be about the me I am now, not the me I was then."

"How does Monroe feel about all the changes?" I asked.

Laura smiled, and it was like the sun came out. It spread to her entire face. I hadn't seen her look like that since the accident and it made my heart glad. I know, I'm such a sap. "At first he was a little confused, like he couldn't understand how I could change my mind about so much stuff, but it turns out he likes the changes I'm making. He even likes the new plans better than the old ones."

"That's lucky," I said.

Laura's mouth continued to smile, but something left her eyes. "Yeah, that's me. Lucky."

The shop slowed down around two thirty and had completely emptied out by about three. Cinnamon left to walk Sage home from school, something Sage disliked as much as being walked to school.

I opened up my notebook, but my heart wasn't in it. When I looked out the window, I could see Cinnamon about a block and a half down the street. The wind tossed her curls and she lifted her head. The breeze must have been coming from one of the flower farms; she looked like she was smelling something really good. She wrapped her arms around herself, so it must have been a little chilly outside.

Then I got goosebumps as a tall, dark-haired man slid out from behind the Coastside Diner and shadowed Cinnamon down the street. For just a second, I thought it was Craig—but there was something different about how he walked.

I slammed my book shut and rushed out the door. I took the stairs down two at a time, but they had already disappeared around the corner. I took off down the street, cursing the fact that I'd worn flip-flops. They're crap to run in. I took them off and ran barefoot, but when I got to the corner, the man had disappeared. I could see Cinnamon, alone, walking to the school.

Great. I was actually starting to hallucinate men.

The phone was ringing as I came back into the shop. I leapt across the desk to grab it. "Do It Up. How can I help you?"

"Oh, thank goodness you answered, I didn't know what I was going to do if you weren't there," a breathless voice said.

Okaayyy. "Well, we are here. What can I do for you?"

"Everything. I need everything redone," the breathy voice said. "And I need it right away. Can I come now?"

I looked around at the empty shop. Why not? Cinnamon wouldn't be back for a little while, but surely I could handle the salon for a bit on my own. "No problem. May I have your name?"

There was silence now on the other end of the line. "It is Ashley, Ginger. I can't believe you didn't recognize my voice."

I can't believe she *did* recognize mine. "Sorry. There must be static on the line."

"Well, okay then," she said, sounding somewhat mollified. "I'll be there in half an hour."

I hung up and called Cinnamon's cell. I could handle a regular salon customer on my own, but I didn't think I could handle Ashley.

"Good tidings," Cinnamon sang into the cell phone.

"It's just me," I said.

"I know," she said. "What's up?"

"Ashley's home," I said. "And I think I need backup."

Ashley crashed open the door of the salon, flung the door shut, and locked it behind her. "Hide me," she gasped. "He's right behind me."

Cinnamon dropped her scissors right on the floor as I dropped my pen, and we both rushed to her. "Who?" I asked. "Who is right behind you?"

Footsteps pounded up the stairs. Before Ashley could catch her breath and say a word, Troy Patu was banging on the door.

I took a deep breath of relief. "It's okay now. Whoever it was won't get through Troy."

I started toward the door but Ashley grabbed me. "No! Troy is him. I mean, he is Troy." Tears filled her round blue eyes. "Please. Don't let him in."

"You're running from Troy?" I asked.

Ashley nodded.

Troy pounded on the door again. "Cinnamon. Ginger. Let me in. I need to talk to Ashley."

"Well, Ashley doesn't want to talk to you," Ashley yelled back.

Troy stopped pounding and rested his forehead against the door. "Ashley, I only want to talk. Please let me in. I'm worried about you."

"Don't be. I can take care of myself," Ashley said, pulling herself up straighter.

"I know that," Troy said through the door. "I only want to help. Please, Ashley. I know something's wrong. I saw you just now."

"So?" Ashley said.

"So it's not normal to be throw up into trash cans on the street."

"Is it illegal?" Ashley gnawed on her pinkie finger.

Troy's voice dropped another octave, which I hadn't thought possible. "I'm not trying to arrest you. I'm trying to help."

"Stop, then. I don't want your help." Ashley stopped gnawing on her finger and dropped her hands to her sides, clenching and unclenching them into little adorable fists.

"Ashley, we need to talk." Troy's voice was soft now. "I think I know what's going on."

"We don't need to talk," Ashley said firmly. "There is nothing going on. Stop stalking me."

"I'm not stalking you. I'm a police officer."

"That doesn't mean you're not stalking," Cinnamon said.

Troy's head fell. "Oh, man. Forget it then. I'm going home." He started to turn away from the salon door and then turned back. "Ashley," he said quietly. "Please." The heartache in his voice nearly broke my heart.

I looked over at Ashley, who was stuffing food in her mouth. She shook her head.

Troy shut his eyes for a second and then turned away again. This time, he didn't turn back.

"What are you eating?" I backed away from Ashley. Surely no one in their right mind would eat—

"A steak burrito dipped in caramel sauce." She took another huge bite. "The jalapeño-cheddar bagels with peanut butter stopped working. This is the only thing that settles my stomach."

Just the thought of it made my stomach roll. Cinnamon remained serene as she gathered up the supplies to highlight Ashley's hair. "For me it was pink grapefruit. I had to have it every morning, right through to the final trimester."

Ashley stiffened. "What do you mean by that? By 'trimester'?"

"It's okay, Ashley. We know."

Ashley turned as white as a bleached mustache hair. "What do you know? Who told you?"

Cinnamon laughed a little. "No one had to tell me anything. I kept my pregnancy with Sage secret from everyone for months. I know the signs of a newly pregnant woman who isn't saying anything to anyone about it."

Ashley sat down in Cinnamon's chair. "Oh," she said. "What else do you know?"

Cinnamon shrugged. "What else is there to know? Have you told Justin yet?"

Tears welled up in her eyes. "No. He can't know. Not yet, at least."

"They're all going to figure it out eventually, Ashley." Cinnamon began to comb through Ashley's hair.

"I know that; I need time to figure out how to tell him, how to explain it."

"I'm guessing he knows how it happened," I offered. If the night I spent with his cousin was any indication, the Esposito boys had no problem figuring out how to make that part work.

"No. No, he doesn't," Ashley said, putting her hands over her face. "He doesn't have the slightest idea."

"Whether or not he knows, it's important you take care of yourself," Cinnamon said, combing Ashley's hair. Some of the tension left Ashley's face. "To take care of the baby, you need to take care of *you*. You look tired. You need to make sure you get enough rest."

"I am tired," Ashley said. "All the time."

"Then you should sleep more. You need it. You're building a human being. Plus, you should eat right. Maybe buy some prenatal vitamins to take." Cinnamon began to lather shampoo into Ashley's hair, and the worry lines in Ashley's forehead began to disappear.

Then her eyes flew open. Ashley looked up at us both. "You won't tell, will you? Please say you won't tell."

Cinnamon said, "We only have a few rules here at Do It Up, but the first one is . . .

"What happens at Do It Up, stays at Do It Up," we said in unison.

Brian picked me up at five and we headed over to my mom's house. Surf music pounded out of the windows of the house as we walked up. "I probably should have told you to bring ear-plugs. It can get a little loud," I said.

He gave me a curious look. "Is that Dick Dale?"

I gave him credit for being close. "Nope. That would be the Surf Daddies."

Brian laughed. "Your parents play Surf Daddies music?"

"My dad *is* the Surf Daddies."

Brian stopped dead on the sidewalk. "You're joking, right?"

"No." He had no idea how unfunny I found the fact that my father was the lead guitarist.

"Your father is one of the Surf Daddies." Brian stated it like a fact, but his facial expression clearly made it a question.

"Well, he was. Apparently they're disbanding, and he's teaching guitar now. And he wasn't just one of the Daddies, he was the main Daddy."

"They're disbanding? Oh, man, that's a shame! I caught them once in this totally gnarly dive bar in Santa Cruz. They rocked the place. Why are they breaking up?" Brian still wasn't walking.

I grabbed his hand and started to tug. "Uh, because he's a grown man?" I suggested.

Brian shook his head. "That makes no sense. Seriously, why? They've been around forever. Why are they doing this now?"

It occurred to me that I didn't really know. When he'd first come back, I hadn't really cared. Dad had "come back for good" more than once, but it had never lasted as long as this time, and I was beginning to think he really meant it. Now that I was taking him somewhat seriously, I supposed I could ask why.

If it was to spend more time with his family, it was a little late for that. Seeking other opportunities? Playing music had always been Dad's bliss; I sincerely doubted he harbored secret ambitions to be anything else. As little as we'd spoken during the past few years, though, he might have had a yen to be an astronaut and I wouldn't have known it.

I pulled open the screen door and ushered Brian in. The living room furniture was pushed up against the walls and Sage and Mom were doing the twist in the middle of the room. Over to the left, in the kitchen, Cinnamon and Dad were bopping to the music while they made spinach casserole.

I went into the kitchen to further explore. Hurray! It looked like there would be roast chicken, too. "I brought bread," I said, setting it on the counter.

Dad looked at the wrapper. "The Little Flower Bakery—great!"

Sage came up behind me. "Is there a cookie for me? Is it pink?"

"Like Fatima would let me out of the bakery without a pink cookie for you. Pffft." I waved my hand at her.

Sage clasped her hands in front of her, her eyes huge. "What shape is it?"

I couldn't wait to see her face. I drew the cookie out of the package with great care and set it in her hands.

"Ohhhh," she breathed when she saw the pink-and-white unicorn. "I think I'll eat the eye first. Then I'll eat the tail."

The unicorn had a Skittle eye and the tail and mane had tons of sprinkles.

"Only the eye," Cinnamon warned her. "I don't want you to spoil your dinner."

"Spoil whose dinner?" a raspy voice asked from the door. "Is this where the party is?"

Grandma had arrived. I looked over at Brian, whose sweet, open face was wide-eyed, and felt like I'd brought a lamb to a wolf-pack dinner.

* * *

"I should have probably warned you," I said as I walked him to his car afterward. The night had gotten cold and I shivered a little. "They're nuts."

"Everybody's family is nuts," he said, shoving his hands in his jean pockets.

"Is your family?" He seemed so . . . well, normal. He couldn't possibly be the product of the kind of chaos that we'd just left inside.

"My father drinks directly from the kitchen faucet." He leaned against the side of his car.

I shook my head. "That's distressingly normal, not crazy."

"Every morning, he reads the celebrity birthdays in the newspaper out loud and my mother either says how interesting it is that people so dissimilar have the same birthday, or she says how interesting it is that people who are so alike have the same birthday." He cocked his head. "Every morning. Without fail."

"Still not crazy." I took a step closer to him. Only for the body heat, really. It had nothing to do with the electric hum that seemed to be vibrating my entire body. "Although I can see it becoming irritating after a while."

"My older sister and her ex-husband share custody of their cat. He moved to Nevada, so once a month she puts Fluffy on a plane to go visit his dad, and the next month he puts Fluffy on a plane to fly back to her. It costs close to two hundred dollars each time." Brian arched both brows at me.

"*That's* crazy."

"Thank you, I appreciate the validation." Then he said, "It makes sense in its own way."

"I don't think so. Can't one of them just get a new cat?"

"I meant your family, not the cat."

"How could my family possibly make sense to anyone? They don't even make sense to me."

"I just knew that someone as special as you couldn't have come from a normal family. I was right."

Brian thought I was special! Though I'm well aware that this is an anatomical impossibility, my heart felt like it was prancing like a unicorn.

"Listen, Ginger, I really like the time we spend together," he said.

Uh oh. The prancing stopped.

"And you are the best study buddy I've ever had," he went on. "You're always prepared. You never flake out and you bring good snacks."

My heart gave a physically impossible clutch. I was clearly about to get bad news and didn't think I could take much more rejection this week.

"I really don't want to mess any of that up," he continued.

He just wanted to be friends. I couldn't bear to hear any more. "It's okay, Brian. I totally understand. You don't have to explain."

"Yes, I do."

He grabbed me by the waist, pulled me to him, and kissed me.

I felt like I was melting. I felt like I was flying. I felt like my feet were no longer on the ground, and my whole body tingled.

He pulled away. "I don't want to lose any of the other stuff," he said. "But I couldn't not do that anymore."

Then he got into his beat-up Dodge Charger and drove away.

I straightened my shirt and went back into the house. Dad was washing the dishes, Cinnamon was drying, and Mom was putting the dishes away. Grandma sat at the counter, drinking a cup of coffee. Everyone looked extremely nonchalant. Too nonchalant.

"You all were watching, weren't you?"

"He seems nice," Mom said.

"He is nice. And you all were spying on me. Admit it." I sat on the kitchen counter across from the sink.

"I like him, too," Dad said. He looked over at Mom and smiled. "He seems like he has a good head on his shoulders."

What kind of judge Dad was of anyone's head was a mystery to me, but for once, I decided to keep that to myself.

"He has a nice, strong chin," Grandma rasped. "I like a strong chin on a man. It denotes good character."

"I've always liked him," Sage said. "Even before he kissed Auntie Ginger. He doesn't talk too much during movies and he smells okay for a boy."

"Aha! You *were* spying!"

"It's not spying if someone happens to walk by a window and look out and see something and comment on it to the rest of the group." Mom started to lift the glass casserole, frowned, and then looked over at Dad. Without a word between them, he came over, picked up the casserole, and put it in the cupboard next to the stove. She rubbed at her left eye and grimaced. Dad came up behind Mom, wrapped his arms around her waist, and pulled her to him. She stopped rubbing her eye and he kissed her neck. They both smiled.

I rolled my eyes. "I think I'm going to walk home." I wasn't really bent out of shape about them spying on Brian and me; I totally would have done the same thing. I just needed to clear my head. I felt like I was reeling and I hadn't even been drinking.

CHAPTER THIRTEEN

Tuesday evening in Santa Bonita after seven is beyond quiet. The streets have emptied out. The stores have closed. A couple of the nicer restaurants are still open, but Tuesday nights are slow. People are at home, helping kids with homework and folding their laundry while they watch TV.

It might be the time I like Santa Bonita best. I wrapped my jacket around myself a little tighter against the chill of the evening and breathed in the scent of the bougainvillea that wrapped around the fences of my mother's neighbors.

I got to the corner of Spruce and Elm. Just as I was about to cross against the light, a Jeep hurled down the empty street. I jumped back onto the curb. Idiot! She probably didn't even realize that she still had on sunglasses. I managed to keep myself from giving the driver the one-finger salute. It's a small town and the stranger you flip off today may be your niece's third-grade teacher tomorrow. Plus, she did have the right of way. As she turned the corner onto Oak, the white-blonde ponytail pulled through the back of her baseball cap registered with me.

What on earth was Courtney Day doing back in Santa Bonita? And why was she driving south? The only thing in that direction is the Santa Bonita Trailer Park. I shrugged. Someone would know, and eventually that someone would need to have their hair highlighted or cut at Do It Up.

No one else tried to run me over as I walked the rest of the way home. When I arrived, the front door wasn't locked. Damn, Cinnamon must have forgotten to lock it again.

I walked in, marveling at how nice it was not to have to bang the screen door to get it to open.

What I found in the living room, however, was not so nice. Lamont Gilman was draped across our wicker sofa. Naked.

"Lamont!" I squealed. "Cover yourself up."

"No," he said, his voice deep and sonorous. "I will not cover myself up. I will strip myself bare to show my love for you." He gestured with his free hand, the one that was not holding the part that was demonstrating its love for me.

A soul-deep "Ewwwww" wheezed its way out of my body. "That's it, Lamont. I'm calling the police."

Lamont looked sorrowful. "Don't do that, Ginger. You'll regret it."

"I sincerely doubt that." I grabbed the phone and dialed.

Letisha, our police dispatcher, answered on the fourth ring. "Santa Bonita Police, how may I be of assistance?"

"Letisha, it's Ginger Zimmerman. Lamont Gilman is naked in my living room and he won't leave."

Letisha snorted. "Seriously?"

"Serious as a heart attack."

Lamont began to sing how he could be happy for the rest of his life with his Cinnamon girl.

"Is he drunk?" Letisha asked.

"I don't know, and I'm not getting close enough to smell his breath. Are you sending someone?"

Lamont sang that he wanted to live with his cinnamon girl.

There was a pause. "Does he know you're not Cinnamon?"

"Yeah, he knows." I sighed. "He can't find a song with Ginger in it and thinks this is close enough."

Letisha snorted again. "I'll send Troy over. Since he's still our newest guy, he gets all the naked calls."

"We have frequent naked calls in Santa Bonita?" I was shocked. Maybe there still were a few secrets in this town.

"You'd be amazed," Letisha said. "Troy's on his way."

Lamont sang that he wanted to run in the moonlight.

I sat back to wait for Troy. "Can I ask you something, Lamont?"

He finally stopped singing. "Ask anything you want, princess."

"Why me?"

Lamont blinked a few times and appeared to be considering the question for the first time. "Because you said no?"

I'm not sure when I've ever felt more honored.

I woke up Wednesday morning feeling like my whole body was tingling. Maybe it was the prospect of seeing Brian at school with the memory of that kiss still fresh on my lips. Maybe it was due to a full night's sleep uninterrupted by Lamont. Maybe it was because Cinnamon's rune card for the day was Sol, which boded excellence, the attainment of goals, and big things happening.

I got up and headed to Do It Up after breakfast. Jolene showed up about fifteen minutes later, with Natalie right on her heels. "Hey, Jolene, what's shaking?" I asked.

"I signed up for beauty school." Jolene her grabbed me and pulled me to her bosom. "I'm gonna be a beautician, just like you and Cinnamon!"

"You did?" I said into Jolene's cleavage, which had become more substantial since she'd been eating regular food on a routine basis and steering clear of ye olde crack pipe.

"Yep," she said, releasing me. "I thought and thought and thought about what I wanted to do. I decided I want to help people, like you guys do."

I sat down. "Jolene, I'm not sure how much real help we provide. We cut hair. We don't heal."

Jolene sat down next to me. "You don't think it healed something when you fixed me up so I wouldn't have to go to my own wedding looking like the Bride of Frankenstein?" she asked. "Look at me now. Look at my skin and my nails and my hair. You don't think it does something good for me to look this way?"

I know that people feel better about themselves if they like the way they look. I also know that the best manicure in the world can't get a couple to start talking to each other about their problems, or fix a leaky roof, or cure cancer.

Natalie shot me a look. "It would free you up if Jolene was helping Cinnamon here at the salon."

She had quite a point there. Jolene could easily take my place as a stylist. I wasn't the best hairdresser on the planet, after all.

"Does Cinnamon know you're going to beauty school?" I asked her.

"You bet!" Jolene smiled. Had she whitened her teeth, too? "She's the one who suggested it in the first place. She says she thinks I have a knack for it. She says I have a good eye. And Ronnie? Well, he's so damn proud he's just about to burst. He says I'm like a fairy-tale princess."

A princess whose plans my sister had known about and kept secret from me.

My cell phone vibrated in my pocket, and I checked the caller I.D. Brian. Heat rushed to my face and I felt the tingle grow. Either I really liked him or I should set my phone to vibrate more often because it was a lot more thrilling than I realized.

I slipped outside the door of the salon to answer it. "Hey," I said.

"Hey, yourself," he replied, his voice creating more tingles. How could it have taken me so long to realize what he had to offer? What was I, an idiot?

Apparently so.

"What's up?" I asked. The chill of the air outside felt good against my flushed cheeks.

"Nothing," he said. "I was just thinking about you and about last night, and thought I'd call. Are you already at the salon?"

"Yeah, I'm just opening up. Natalie and Jolene are here."

"I'll make it quick, then. I was thinking about what your dad said last night about your alternator."

"My what?"

"Your alternator. That thing that's been keeping your car from starting. The reason you're carrying screwdrivers around in your purse."

"Yeah, I got it."

"It's not a huge job, but it's not a little one, either. I think I should wait until this weekend to do it, in case it takes longer than I expect."

"This weekend?"

"Yeah, like maybe Saturday I could work on the car, and then maybe Saturday night I could work on you a little."

"Sounds intriguing," I said. Plus, it was only Wednesday! I felt so respected.

"How about dinner and a movie?" he said.

On the romantic date scale, it was no balloon ride over wine country, but still, he was asking on Wednesday. Besides, I didn't think Brian's budget ran to last-minute balloon rides. I was actually surprised it ran to dinner and a movie. "I think I'd be up for that."

"In the meantime, you're going to have to keep starting the car with the screwdriver. I'm not so crazy about that."

Oooh, he worried about me. I kind of liked that. "It'll be okay. I've been doing it off and on for a while now."

"Just don't electrocute yourself."

"Maybe you should hang around when I start the car, just in case I need mouth-to-mouth." I smiled.

There was a groan from the other end of the phone. "You're killing me here, Ginger."

I laughed. "See you in class."

"Who were you talking to?" Natalie asked when I came back in.

"Brian," I said nonchalantly, trailing my finger along the edge of my desk as I went around to sit at the computer.

"And you needed to go outside to talk to him?" Natalie narrowed her eyes at me. "Are you two planning a study session?"

"Uh-uh," I said, hoping my voice didn't sound as dreamy as it felt.

"Does discussing the ankle bones suddenly require privacy?" Natalie pressed.

"Maybe," I said coyly. I could imagine Brian taking some time with my ankle. It could be good.

Natalie's lips became a straight line. "You slept with him," she said flatly.

"Nope," I said. "At least, not yet."

"I hope you hold out for at least one date." She shook her head. "Poor guy. You'll probably kill him."

"You have a new beau?" Jolene asked, stirring the wax as it melted. "Is Brian the one who's been so in love with you for so long?"

I raised my eyebrows.

"Yep," Natalie said. "She finally took pity on him."

Had I? Or had I finally taken a little pity on myself?

"What happened with the Esposito boy?" Jolene put the lid back on the wax and started straightening the clips in Cinnamon's drawers.

"It didn't work out," I said.

"A shame. He's yummy." She swept the already clean floor.

I felt a little wobble in my chest. Craig had been yummy, in more ways than one. He'd been charming and funny and dynamite in bed. It didn't hurt that his family had more money than God, either.

But Brian was no consolation prize. He was charming and funny, too, in a totally different way. I'm not sure how I felt about the fact that my family seemed to approve of him. Generally, Dad's seal of approval would make any guy instant anathema to me. This time, however, it didn't feel that way. It felt . . . cozy.

"Why?" Natalie demanded as she started taking the nail equipment out of the centrifuge.

"Why what?"

"Why didn't the Esposito boy work out?"

I sighed, remembering my misplaced rage. "I made a mistake."

"So tell him and apologize."

"I tried. He didn't go for it."

"What kind of mistake?" Jolene asked, leaning against the counter.

"It's complicated."

Natalie looked at her watch. "I got time."

Luckily, our first customer was coming up the stairs. "No, you don't," I said.

"Did you hear?" Marci asked, eyes agog.

"Hear what?" I've learned never to start guessing; you wind

up giving away way more than you mean to. Ignorance may be bliss, but feigned ignorance gets you the really good stuff.

"Someone broke into Troy Patu's mobile home last night," she breathed.

"That took some nerve," Cinnamon said.

She had that right. "What did they take?" I asked.

"He says nothing," she said in a hushed voice.

"Why would someone bother to break into a cop's house and then not take anything?" Jolene asked.

"Maybe they planted something, instead," Natalie said, pausing with the nail polish brush suspended over Marci's hand. "And they're going to frame him for drugs or a murder or something."

"Except we already know that Troy's house was broken into. If someone says they found a murder weapon or a bunch of drugs in his house now, we'll all say it was planted. It would never work," I pointed out.

"I didn't say they were smart people, whoever they are," Natalie replied.

That got me thinking. I wasn't sure what was going on between Troy and Ashley, but I had my suspicions. She wouldn't have tried something that hare-brained to get rid of him, would she?

Marci looked back and forth between us. "What if he broke into his own house so that whatever it was would look planted? What about that?"

I blinked a few times. "Why wouldn't he throw whatever it was into the ocean and just forget about it, if he had something he didn't want anyone to see?"

Marci frowned. "Because that would make really boring gossip."

Good lord.

The phone rang. I picked it up. "Do It Up. How can we help make you beautiful?"

"Um, er," a male voice mumbled. Men never know how to answer that question.

"May I help you?" I said, taking pity on whoever it was.

"May I speak to Ginger Zimmerman?"

"This is she."

"Ms. Zimmerman, this is Lamont Gilman Senior."

Oh, great. Were all the Gilmans going to start stalking me now? "Yes?" I said with a faint edge to my tone.

"I was hoping we could talk about last night's unfortunate events."

"By unfortunate events, do you mean when your son broke into my home, took off all his clothes, and laid in wait for me?" I asked, trying to sound a little sweeter this time.

Marci whipped around to look at me. "Really?" she mouthed.

I nodded. "Really," I mouthed back.

"Yes, er, well, without stipulating anything, I believe that is what I wanted to discuss," Lamont Sr. said.

"There's not much to discuss," I said. "Maybe you should talk to the police about it."

"Funny you should say that, Ms. Zimmerman. I have been chatting with Police Chief Schulte. We play golf every Wednesday morning. Have for years."

"Super." I couldn't have cared less.

"According to Hal—that's Police Chief Schulte to you, I suppose—if you would drop the charges, this whole thing could just fade away."

"Why would I do that, Mr. Gilman?"

"Well, my boy is occasionally a little too dogged in his determination to get what he's after, but there's no need to besmirch his reputation with something of this sort."

"What about *my* reputation, Mr. Gilman? What do you think my neighbors might be saying about a naked man sitting in front of an open window, playing slap the salami in my living room?"

"Your reputation?" He sounded like I'd asked about my winged elephant. What, my reputation was already so bad that it didn't matter that naked men were pleasuring themselves in my living room? Jerk. I wasn't the only one living in that apartment. "And what about my seven-year-old niece, Mr. Gilman? What if she had been the first one through the door last night? Exactly how much therapy do you think it would take for her to get over seeing your son in that state?"

"I'm sure Lamont never intended . . . ." he blustered.

"Mr. Gilman, I don't care what Lamont intended. I just want him to stop."

"I'll make sure of that," he said.

"I appreciate that."

"On one condition. That you drop the charges against my son."

"No deal," I said, and hung up.

Natalie agreed to give me a ride to school and back, so I didn't have to risk electrocuting myself starting the Mustang. Her little Camry suited her. It was clean, reliable, and looked great even after a lot of mileage.

As much as I grumbled about the Mustang and how unreliable it was, I liked the rumble it made as it started, and the way heads turned when it cruised down the street. Nobody stops to stare at a white Camry. It's just not that kind of car.

Good lord, maybe I was more like my mother and grandmother than I realized. That was an unpleasant little realization.

Natalie broke into my reverie. "I'm seeing the oil-change guy again."

"Tom?" I asked.

"No, the other oil-change guy," she said sarcastically.

I smiled. "So you like him."

A smile twitched at the corners of her mouth. "Maybe." Then she frowned. "I'm not crazy about his fingernails. They're dirty all the time."

"He's an oil-change guy; what do you expect? Besides, you're a manicurist. Don't you think you can do something about his nails?"

"Possibly. And what are you going to do about *him*?" She pointed as we pulled into the science building lot at Foster City State. Brian was standing by his Charger, clearly watching for us.

I looked over at Natalie, suddenly serious. "I'm not entirely sure."

Brian walked over to where we parked and opened my car door. "No Mustang today?" he asked, as he helped me out.

"It seemed smarter to let Natalie drive me," I said as he took my book bag from me.

"And here I was looking forward to an opportunity to fine-tune my mouth-to-mouth technique."

Don't worry, it doesn't need any refinement. Besides, I'm sure opportunity will knock." I smiled.

Natalie slammed her door. "Will you two get a room or something?"

We all walked into class together.

Cinnamon had appointments booked all afternoon, so I picked Sage up from school and offered to do the grocery shopping and make dinner. I don't do it often enough that it becomes expected of me, just often enough to make everyone a little grateful.

We decided on chili, cornbread, and salad for dinner. I considered sneaking a little meat into the cart for my own bowl of chili, but Cinnamon would probably smell it and have a fit. If I ever got my own place, I would eat meat every night. Possibly raw.

When we rolled our cart out to the Mustang and unloaded, Sage pointed over my shoulder. "Look, Auntie Ginger, it's that man again."

"That's nice," I said absently, stowing the groceries in the backseat.

"That's not what Ms. Brooks said at school, when she told him to get away from the playground or she'd call the police," Sage said.

I straightened up fast, clocking my head on the door frame as I did so. "What man? Where?" I asked, holding the top of my head.

"That man. There." Sage pointed.

Justin Esposito stood at the edge of the parking lot, staring at us. I'd expected some horrible trenchcoated pedophile, not a remarkably handsome man who looked like a Ralph Lauren ad. "Ms. Brooks shooed that man away from your school?" I asked Sage. "That man there?"

Sage nodded. "I'm sure. Annabelle thought he was looking at us, so I waved to him and he waved back."

A sick feeling began to twist in my stomach. I was pretty sure I knew why Justin Esposito was stalking my niece.

Adding up the wineglass-shaped birthmark that I'd seen on Justin's cousin, who said it was a family thing; that same birthmark on my niece; the way Justin almost fainted at his wedding reception when he saw me, then inquired about my identical twin; and the look on Cinnamon's face when she first saw Craig

Esposito, who looks almost exactly like his cousin—it didn't take a rocket scientist to complete the equation.

Still, it's pretty damn stunning when you discover your sister's sea god in the supermarket parking lot, looking like he's just fallen in love with his own daughter.

CHAPTER FOURTEEN

"You had Lamont Gilman arrested?" Mom stared at me as if I'd told her I'd dropped a hair dryer in a sink full of water on purpose. "What were you thinking?"

"I was thinking that he'd broken into my apartment and was lying naked on my couch." I left out the part where he was using his right hand to demonstrate his love, wishing I could delete it from my brain as easily.

Mom sank down behind the counter of the store and put her head in her hands. I could swear her hair looked thin. That was weird. Mom has great hair. At least, she always used to. And the ends were brittle. She needed to come by the shop for a quick trim. "Couldn't you have just thrown an afghan over him?"

"Mom! You can't mean that. What if Sage had come home and found him like that? Besides, he has no right to break into my apartment! It was bad enough when he was hanging around outside of it."

"Seriously, Ginger, this could mean big trouble. His father insures all of our businesses: the salon, the shop, Grandma's restaurant." Mom rubbed at her eye again as if she had a headache. She definitely needed to come to the shop; Cinnamon could shampoo that headache away in seconds.

"So we'll go someplace else for insurance. It isn't the end of the world."

"How long have you lived in this town?" Mom asked, shaking her head. "Have you noticed any other insurance agencies here?"

"So we'll go to someplace in Pacifica or Half Moon Bay. Or we'll get it online." How often did you need to interact with your insurance guy, anyway?

"You really don't understand how this town works, do you?" Mom looked at me as if I were some kind of idiot child who'd been dumped on her doorstep. "I'm not sure even your grandmother will be able to straighten this out for us."

Dad strolled in from the back room with a big black trash bag slung over his shoulder. "What doesn't Ginger understand about how this town works?" He opened the bag up and dumped the contents onto the counter in front of Mom, then planted a kiss on her head.

"She had Lamont Gilman arrested." Mom began to sort through the clothes. They looked nice, if a tad on the matronly side, and brand new.

"What'd you have him arrested for?" Dad asked, pulling a pair of trousers out of the tangle of clothes and folding them over a hanger.

"Breaking and entering, and indecent exposure. Troy's checking into the stalking laws for me." I untangled a blouse from the pile. It felt nice; I checked the label. One hundred percent silk. Plus, it still had the tag from Lord & Taylor on it. "Who dumps a silk blouse that they've never even worn? This stuff is expensive."

Mom shrugged. "It happens all the time. At least once a month I get a big black hefty bag full of brand-new clothes like this. Always different sizes, different stores. Some people have more than they need, I guess."

"Who leaves them?" I asked, pulling a sweater set out of the pile.

"Who cares?" Dad asked. "Tell me about Lamont."

I told him, and he laughed until he nearly choked. "Naked? Singing 'Cinnamon Girl'? He knows you're Ginger, right?"

"Yep."

Mom gave sort of a strangled half-giggle.

"It's not funny, Mom."

"It is a little." Then she straightened her face. "But you still have to drop the charges. If you don't, there'll be big trouble. I guarantee it."

"You have to tell Sage who her father is." I'd waited patiently until Sage was done with her homework, dinner, and bath, and was sound asleep. The apartment was quiet and Cinnamon had settled down on the couch with a copy of *Vogue*.

"No," Cinnamon said. "I don't."

"If you don't, I will."

Cinnamon looked at me as if I'd said I was going to start selling state secrets to Arab terrorists. "What?"

"I know who he is, Cinnamon. I know it's Justin Esposito."

She gasped. Her hand went to her throat. "How did you know?"

"That's not the point. The point is that you have to tell Sage."

"Why?"

"Because it's her right to know." I was pretty sure of that one. I was also pretty sure that my recent conversations with Sage were only the tip of her daddy-interest iceberg.

"We knew who our father was. What huge favor did that do us?" Cinnamon pulled the afghan around her shoulders.

She had a point, but she was missing another one. "Our

father is an alcoholic guitar player of small fame. Sage's father is a lawyer from a wealthy family who could make her life a million times easier."

"Dad is an *ex*-alcoholic, and exactly how would Justin make Sage's life easier?" Cinnamon asked.

"There is no such thing as an ex-alcoholic; that's why they refer to themselves as recovering alcoholics. And Justin could make Sage's life easier with financial and emotional support."

Cinnamon shook her head. "Do you really think this is the time, Ginger? When he's just gotten married? Right when he's about to find out that his new wife is pregnant?"

"He knows about Sage, Cinnamon. I'm not talking about telling him. I'm talking about telling Sage." I sat down next to her and pulled part of the afghan around my own shoulders. The apartment was drafty and the cold air seeped in through all the cracks.

Cinnamon sat up straight on the couch. "What do you mean 'he knows'?"

"I saw him following you the other day, and this afternoon he was following Sage. Apparently he's been hanging around her school, too. He knows. Don't you think Sage deserves to know, too?"

"No," Cinnamon said, shaking her head vehemently. "I don't think she needs to know. I don't think anybody needs to know. I don't think I even like *you* knowing."

"Thanks a lot."

Cinnamon's chin began to jut out again. "You're welcome."

We'd gone to bed with the matter unresolved. It's not like Cinnamon and I never fight. We fight all the time. We fight about eating meat and what to do with people's hair, and who gets to wear the purple sweater that we both like and refuse to buy two of. We'd just never fought about anything this important before. On the big stuff, we'd always been united.

The result for me was a very restless night. I know I slept some, but it sure didn't feel like it. At six thirty, I gave up and decided to go for a run to clear my head.

It was still dark out when I slipped out the door of the apartment. I could head down to the ocean walk and run along the cliffs, but it would take fifteen minutes just to get there and I wasn't sure I wanted to run that far. Plus, it would be uphill on the way home. I decided to turn in the other direction and head up into the hills on the other side of town. It would be tough going at first, but it would be a breeze on the return.

I headed through the quiet streets with only the slap of my feet and my own thoughts to keep me company. The air smelled like eucalyptus trees and roses. I turned onto Palo Verde Street just in time to see a white Cadillac with a big gold wheel on the back stop in front of Pass It On. A woman who looked to be in her seventies got out. She looked familiar, but I couldn't place her. She pulled a big bundle out of the trunk and tossed it in the doorway of Mom's store. I ducked into the doorway of Luna's Jewelry and waited while the woman got back in her car and drove away, then I checked it out.

It was a big black garbage bag, full of brand-new clothes from Saks. They still had the price tags on them. I shoved them back inside and trotted down the street where the Cadillac had gone.

When I went around the corner, I smelled Linda Johnson's cigarette before I saw her. She was hanging out her window with a cup of coffee. "Hey, Ginger, you're out early."

"Couldn't sleep," I said.

"That's a drag."

"Yeah." I hesitated for a second. "Did you see a white Cadillac come by here a few minutes ago?"

Linda nodded.

"Do you know who that was?"

"Nope," she said. "But she must have a lot of extra clothes. I've seen her before. She must come by your mom's place at least once a month with a big bag full of stuff."

Cinnamon didn't look like she'd gotten any more sleep than I had. She had dark circles under her eyes and she was dragging around the apartment like a *Shaun of the Dead* version of herself.

"Hey," I said. "Do we know anybody who drives a big white Cadillac with one of those gold wheel thingies on the back?"

"I hope not. Those are so tacky." She stretched and yawned.

"I like them," Sage said. "They're shiny."

"They are indeed," I said. "And expensive."

"Annabelle says she has very expensive taste. Do I have expensive taste?" Sage asked.

I considered for a moment. Sage's taste still ran toward plastic Hello Kitty items. On the other hand, she only liked Jelly Belly jelly beans, which were gourmet items. She wouldn't even accept the factory-second Belly Flops. "Sometimes."

She frowned at me. "That's not a real answer. Everyone must have expensive taste sometimes. I want to know if I usually have expensive taste. Annabelle says she usually has expensive taste."

"It doesn't matter," Cinnamon snapped. "Sometimes you like things that cost too much. Sometimes you're perfectly happy with whatever we can afford. Drop it, okay?"

Sage and I both stared at her in stunned silence. Cinn never talked to Sage that way, even when she was totally PMS-ing. I was the snippy twin, with or without PMS. What the hell was she doing co-opting my role?

Sage's lower lip protruded and began to tremble. She pushed

her cereal bowl away. "I'm not hungry," she said, and slid her chair back from the table.

"Come back here and eat your breakfast," Cinnamon said. "Now."

"Cinn," I said quietly.

"Keep out of this, Ginger," Cinnamon snapped at me.

"No," Sage said.

"What?" Cinnamon and I said in unison.

"I don't want it. I won't eat it. You can't make me." She put her fists on her skinny little hips and glared at us both.

Sage can be a handful, but her style runs more toward subtle manipulation or ignoring requests rather than open defiance.

"Go get dressed then," Cinnamon snarled.

"Fine. I will."

"Fine," Cinnamon said.

Apparently the two of them had been possessed by demons, because they both turned on their heels and marched to their rooms, almost simultaneously slamming their doors.

My stomach growled. I hadn't eaten before I ran, and it seemed wrong to let a perfectly good breakfast go to waste.

I sat down and ate Sage's Cheerios.

I offered to walk Sage to school since she and Cinnamon still weren't speaking to each other when I got out of the shower. I wondered which one of them would crack first. My money was on Cinnamon; she's soft and sentimental and always has been. Sage is more like me. There's a hard-headed side beneath all the unicorns and rainbows and butterflies.

I might have been wrong this time, though. Cinnamon refused my offer, saying, "She's my daughter. I can walk her to school. I can decide what's best for her."

She couldn't have surprised me more if she had slapped me

with a white glove. For seven years, we had been co-parents. For seven years, I had put my plans second, or sometimes third or fourth. For seven years, I had stood by her. Suddenly, I wasn't good enough to walk Sage to school.

"Fine," I said. "Decide away."

Then I slammed the door to *my* bedroom. I threw on a pair of jeans, a tank top, and an off-the-shoulder cotton sweater. Then I flung open the front door and went downstairs to see if the mail had come.

I always pick up our mail. Cinnamon doesn't believe in rushing to pick it up. She feels that if someone had something important to say to her, they'd call. Everything else she pretty much counts on me to relay to her.

Sometimes I resented this. It's not like it was hard to open the mailbox, pull the stuff out, and carry it upstairs, and it did get me first dibs on the *Entertainment Weekly* and *People*. But it would have been nice if someone else dealt with it once in a while. It was one more thing that made me wonder what would happen if I left. I had visions of returning at Thanksgiving break from school to find mail spilling out of the box onto the street and Cinnamon looking at me, all sweetness and light, saying, "Mail? What mail?"

Today, any thought of resentment faded the instant I saw the envelope from San José State University. It was a big, fat envelope and I knew immediately it was good news. Bad news came in skinny little envelopes, because how much room did you really need to say "Dear Loser, thank you so much for your interest in our school, but we don't want you"? But it took an entire eleven-by-thirteen-inch envelope to tell you everything you needed to know about housing and tuition reimbursement and all the other stuff that was involved now that you'd been accepted to the physican assistant degree program. I was going to be a physician assistant! And even better, I was going to leave this podunk town behind me forever.

I ran up the stairs to our apartment and flung open the door that no longer needed to be banged once in the top right corner to unstick it. I dumped the gas bill and the *PB Teen* catalog on the dining room table and clutched my envelope to my chest.

It was all mine. Mine, mine, mine. It wasn't anybody's legacy or path but my own, and I loved it! Now I just had to figure out how to tell everybody else about it, and when. Until then, I figured I could keep this under my hat, even though I felt like dancing down the stairs and out onto the street.

But for now my beautiful envelope needed a good hiding place. I took it to my room and slid it inside my silk pashmina, which I knew Cinnamon wouldn't touch because she's against the enslavement of silkworms.

My decision was made.

Let Cinnamon go ahead and decide everything else for herself and Sage.

"What is with you two?" Natalie whispered to me.

"I don't know what you're talking about," I said, intent on getting all of our books up to date. I was going to have to figure out how to tell Cinn I was leaving. I didn't have to figure out what shape I intended to leave her in.

"You're barely speaking. You're scaring the customers."

I looked around. The salon was particularly quiet, but it wasn't exactly crowded. Cinnamon was just finishing up Josie Bernard, who was explaining about her migraines. "I kept hearing this high-pitched whining sound."

"Sure it wasn't little Josie?" Stacy asked from the nail dryer.

She had a point. Little Josie couldn't even ask for a drink of water without it sounding like a whine. Just knowing the kid was coming in for a haircut was enough to give the hairs on the back of my neck the fingernails-on-a-blackboard feeling.

"It's nothing," I said to Natalie. "Ignore it."

"How am I supposed to ignore it when Cinnamon is breezing through here like the Ice Queen, and you're so intent on ignoring her that Josie stood in front of you for close to five minutes before you looked up and saw her?"

I looked at Natalie. "Deal with it."

"Fine," she said, and stomped back to her nail station.

I went back to my books until the door to the salon opened again.

"Hi, Ginger." Laura stood in the doorway to the salon. "I wanted to give you these." She thrust three ivory envelopes into my hand. One was addressed to me and "guest," the next to Cinnamon and "guest," and the last to Natalie and "guest."

"Laura, you don't have to invite us to the wedding." It was incredibly sweet, but after Ashley's wedding, I was feeling a little gun-shy.

Cinnamon came over and I silently handed her her envelope. "Ginger's right, Laura," she said. "We're happy to do your hair. You don't have to invite us."

"Please, Ginger. I want you guys to be there. You've been . . ." Laura's lower lip trembled. "You've been amazing. You've been real friends. Please, come. Monroe and I would be honored to have you there."

I hesitated. It could be fun. "Okay. I mean, we'll be there anyway to do your hair, right? We'll just stay and party with you when we're done." And ditch the second things turned dicey.

Laura threw her arms around me. "Thank you, Ginger. Thank you so much."

If anything, Laura felt even thinner than she had when she'd first come in here after her accident. The circles under her eyes were darker, too. It was going to take a lot of concealer to cover those up. I made a mental note to put an extra tube of it in my traveling makeup bag.

Laura left and I rang up Josie and Stacy. Natalie headed out with them as they left, leaving Cinnamon and me alone in the shop. We were just settling down in our spots again when Ken Liu came to the door. Ken is one of the city inspectors who come through on a regular basis.

"Ken, we weren't expecting you!" I glanced around the salon. Everything seemed like it was in order, and I sure hoped it was. I could have sworn Ken had been through just a month or so before.

Ken gulped. "Well, yes, if you always know when I'm coming, it isn't really an accurate picture of the salon, is it? A surprise inspection now and then is good for everyone."

If it was good for everyone, why was Ken sweating right now? "You know where everything is. Help yourself," I said, and went back to my studying. It was tempting to follow Ken around as he made his inspection, but we followed all the health and safety guidelines carefully and there was nothing to hide.

Which made it all the more shocking when he came back five minutes later with a list of violations.

"The Barbicide isn't cloudy," I said, grabbing his clipboard and looking over it. "We change it every Sunday evening. It's practically brand new."

Ken's lips pursed and he took the clipboard back. "It looked cloudy to me, and that's all that matters."

I opened my mouth to argue, but Cinnamon put her hand on my arm and shook her head. "We'll change the Barbicide again right now, Ken."

"That's fine, but it still goes on the record. I'll be back later in the week to check all of these items." He ripped the sheet off his clipboard and handed it to Cinnamon.

I grabbed it from her hands. "This is ridiculous, Ken. You're writing us up because the lid of the garbage can was askew? You can't be serious."

Ken gulped a few more times. "I can be and I am. Get your salon in order or I'll have to close you down."

My heart damn near stopped. Close us down? Over an askew garbage can and some so not cloudy Barbicide? What the hell was going on? I started to stand up, but once again Cinnamon put her hand on my arm and shook her head. I sank back into my seat, seething.

"It will all be in order when you get here, Ken. I promise." Cinnamon opened the door for him.

"What the hell is that about?" I burst out as soon as the door shut.

"I don't know," Cinnamon said, gnawing at her lower lip. "There is definitely something wrong there."

"No joke. I changed that Barbicide myself, Cinnamon. There's no way it's cloudy."

"I don't mean with the Barbicide, Ginger. I mean with Ken. Did you see how he kept gulping? How he wouldn't look us in the eye and kept shifting from foot to foot?"

"Maybe. So?"

"So this wasn't his own idea. Someone's making him do this; he didn't want to. I know he's fussy, but that's his job. This was totally different." Cinnamon chewed her lower lip. "We don't have much else scheduled today. You can take off."

Fine. I wasn't needed at home, or at the salon. That suited me fine. "I'm gonna fly then." I might be able to catch Brian having lunch before class. I packed up my books and flash cards and was just getting ready to step out the door when someone knocked.

I opened the door to Justin Esposito, who looked at me with his brows furrowed. "Ginger, right?"

I gave him full points; people who don't know us well usually can't tell us apart. Granted, he'd known Cinnamon in the biblical sense, but that had been quite a few years ago and in the dark. "Right," I said.

"Is your sister here?" he asked, sounding unsure of himself.

"I am," Cinnamon said from behind me.

Justin's face twisted. "You're real," he said. "You're actually real."

"I am," she said.

"I had to see for myself," Justin said. "I more than half convinced myself you were a dream."

They really were a pair—Cinnamon bopping around convincing herself she'd had sex with a sea god, and Justin claiming he thought it was all a dream.

"I would have thought it was all a dream, too, if it hadn't been for Sage." Cinnamon took his hands in hers.

"Sage? Is that her name?" Justin took Cinnamon's hands to his lips and kissed them. Cinn looked like her knees might give out. "Can I see her?"

Cinnamon's brows drew down. "I don't know if that's a good idea, Justin. It might be better for her to have no father at all, than to have a father who can't publicly acknowledge her."

"Who says I can't publicly acknowledge her?" Justin looked stormy.

"You're married, Justin. That changes everything. If we'd figured this out a year ago, it would be different. It's complicated now." Cinnamon backed into the interior of the shop.

"I didn't say it wouldn't be complicated. But I won't deny her. I honor my commitments, Cinnamon." Justin took a step toward her.

I stood there, gaping. It was like watching a soap opera come to life.

"No one's asking you to make any kind of commitment to us, Justin." Cinnamon shook her head.

"You don't have to." He crossed the salon and pulled Cinnamon to him. "Tell me I can see you again. Please."

"I can't see you. Not like that." Cinnamon bowed her head until it touched his shoulder.

"Why?" he demanded.

Cinnamon pushed him away. "Because you're married, Justin."

And your wife is pregnant.

Justin bowed his head, too. He turned to leave, then stopped. "I may be married, Cinnamon, but that doesn't mean that I'm in love."

He left, closing the door softly behind him.

Tears streamed down Cinnamon's cheeks.

"I told you he knew," I said.

She nodded in acknowledgment.

"You really love him, don't you?" I asked.

"I always have," she said. "Always and forever."

What kind of crazy genes did we have? "He's married," I said. Zimmerman women may do a lot of things, but we don't mess with married men. Well, except for Grandma Rosemary, but that was an accident. Basil had lied to her, and as soon as she found out, she took steps to correct it. I'm not sure shooting him was the right thing to do, but a jury of her peers decided it was okay.

"He doesn't love her and you know she doesn't love him." Cinnamon still hadn't moved from where Justin had left her standing. Just like he'd left her standing and holding the bag eight years before.

"Ashley may not love him, but she's pregnant. She's having a baby." I got up from behind the counter and walked toward her.

"The baby's not his."

I stopped in my tracks. *What?*

"Ginger, are you blind?" she asked. "The baby is Troy's."

"No," I said, but felt in my gut that she was right. "It doesn't change anything, though. He's still married. Ashley's still pregnant."

"It changes everything," Cinnamon said. "Knowing the truth changes everything."

"What happened to swearing to Ashley that we wouldn't tell?" I asked.

"We don't have to. The truth will tell itself when Ashley gives birth to a half-Samoan baby."

She had a point there. "But that's still months away. You have to wait and let it work out on its own."

"I've waited long enough. I'm going after him," she said, drying her tears.

"Don't do this, Cinn."

"I have to," she said, and ran out the door after him.

My head began to hurt. But it wasn't my problem anymore, was it? Cinnamon had made it manifestly clear that she didn't want me interfering. And I had that big fat envelope hidden in my desk drawer, the magic envelope that would get me out of here.

Sage had a father who sounded like he'd help financially. Jolene was going to beauty school and could take my place at the salon. Mom and Dad were behaving strangely responsibly and could be reliable backup.

It was beginning to look like I could leave for P.A. school in the fall with a clear conscience.

CHAPTER FIFTEEN

Brian and Natalie were waiting for me outside our classroom, their eyes bright. Natalie was bouncing on her toes. "Did you check your mail? I went home before I came here and checked my mail. Did you check yours?"

"Maybe," I said, unable to contain my grin anymore.

"You got in! Hurray!" Natalie leapt up and chest-bumped me. She was just going to have to stop watching WWE Wrestling—I don't care how hunky John Cena is.

Brian picked me up and swung me around. I felt dizzy and tingly and wonderful.

"I'm still not sure how I'm going to pay for everything," I said, once he set me down.

Natalie blinked. "Oh. They didn't offer you anything?"

I bit my lip. "They offered me two parts of a teaching assistantship and one part of a research assistantship. That will cover tuition, but there's no way I can commute from here."

"I know. I talked to my boys last night. I'm selling my house and buying a condo. Between downsizing and going inland, I should be able to cover my living expenses if I'm careful." Natalie grabbed her backpack and started into the classroom. "I could use a roommate to help pay the mortgage and stuff. I'd want someone clean and polite, who kept the same hours as me." She smiled.

"Are you serious?" My heart felt like it was going to burst.

"Dead serious," she said. "Please? It would make my life so much easier."

"Stop pretending like I'm doing you a favor," I said. "Then maybe I'll say yes."

"How about you, Brian?" Brian said in a high, squeaky voice. "Why, thanks for asking," he answered himself in his normal voice. "I believe I've got it covered between savings, scholarships, and a loan."

I smiled up at him and said in high, squeaky voice, "I'm so glad."

My cell phone vibrated in my pocket. I slid it out and glanced at the caller I.D. Santa Bonita Elementary? Why on earth were they calling me in the middle of the afternoon? I slid out of the classroom. "Hello?"

"Auntie G?" Sage's voice sounded so much younger over the phone. "Can you come get me?"

Why wasn't Cinnamon there to pick her up? "Where's your mama, honey?"

"I don't know." The quaver that shook her little voice told me everything I needed to know.

"I'll be there as fast as I can." I slipped back into class and grabbed my bag and notebook. Brian gave me a questioning glance. I grabbed his pen from his hand and scribbled "Sage needs to be picked up" on his open notebook. He nodded and started packing his stuff up, too.

Once we were outside, I said, "It's not an emergency. At least I don't think it is. Cinn didn't show up to pick her up."

"You were just an excuse to get out of that classroom. Have you ever heard a worse speaker?"

We walked out to the parking lot together. Brian was parked

a few rows away from me in the lot. I got in the Mustang, turned the key, and nothing. I dropped my head onto the steering wheel and whispered, "You can do this, girl. I need you."

I turned the key again. Still nothing. "Sage needs you," I told the Mustang. "Now start."

I turned the key so hard, I'm surprised it didn't bend. In return, the Mustang gave me nothing. I popped the hood and did the screwdriver thing. Nothing.

I didn't have the foggiest idea of what to do next.

Brian pulled up next to me. "Are you okay? Do you need help?"

"It's not starting. Even the screwdriver thing isn't working."

"I was afraid of that." Brian shook his head. "You need a new car, Ginger."

"You're one to talk," I said, eyeing his old Dodge Charger. A new alternator? Probably. A new car? Certainly not.

"Mine starts." He leaned over, unlocked the passenger door, and opened it. "Get in. I'll take you to Sage."

I shut the Mustang's hood and grabbed my bags.

Sage was taut with tension when we got to the principal's office. "Where were you?" she cried into my shoulder as I threw my arms around her.

"I'm so sorry, baby. It takes a while to drive here from my school. I left as soon as you called. I promise I did."

"It's true. She did," Brian said from behind me.

Sage peeked around my shoulder. "Hi, Brian. Why are you here?"

"I came with your Auntie G so I wouldn't have to sit through class without her. The only thing that keeps me awake in that class is the snarky notes she writes about the speakers."

Sage pushed me away and looked into my eyes with horror.

"You write notes in class, Auntie G? Miss Krocher makes you sit in the naughty chair for passing notes."

"There is no naughty chair in college. It's one of the perks." I stood up.

"Can I go to Annabelle's? She invited me."

"Sure, baby. We'll call on the way."

I gave Melinda, the school secretary, a tense smile. The fact that Cinnamon hadn't picked up Sage from school was undoubtedly spread halfway around the town already. By nightfall, it would be everywhere. Damn Cinnamon anyway. Did she have to give them more to gossip about?

Sage went to Annabelle's and Brian had to go to work, so I came home to an empty apartment. I went to my room and pulled my Envelope of Freedom out from under the pashmina.

I heard the clack of Grandma's pumps on our stairs and she rapped imperiously upon our door.

"Coming," I yelled, and opened the door to the apartment.

"I won't have it." Grandma Rosemary stood in our doorway in her spotless Chanel suit.

"What won't you have?" I asked. She was in full drama mode; what had set her off?

"Cinnamon running around with that Esposito whelp." She said "Esposito" as if she were spitting.

Ah, apparently Justin and Cinnamon hadn't been too discreet. Well, it wasn't my problem. "What happened to 'I hear you've gone and snagged yourself an Esposito boy,' making it sound like I'd bagged a prize buck?"

"You had. Lord knows what you did to foul it up afterward, but that's another topic altogether."

Not in my book. "You've seen Craig?"

"I'm not discussing that now, though he's been moping about town like a lovesick moose since you threw him over. It doesn't help that that horrid Lewis girl is all over him like ugly on an ape. Anyway, I'm discussing your sister and that other one, Justin." Grandma stamped her well-shod foot.

I sighed. If I played along, I might find out what I wanted to know later. "What's so bad about Justin?"

"He's not worthy of her. He's weak." She crossed her arms over her chest.

"He looks pretty strong to me," I said. "Maybe he just hasn't had a chance to prove that he's strong yet."

"He's had plenty of chances, missy," Grandma said. "He squanders them. He's a squanderer."

"There's nothing I can do about it," I said. "The situation is a mess."

"You don't know the half of it," she rasped. "Do you have any alcohol? I could use a drink."

I was about to offer the table wine that Vanessa gives us from her winery in exchange for hair care, but then I remembered the cases of champagne Lamont had left for me. "As a matter of fact, I do. I have champagne. And I have something to celebrate, too, if you think you can keep a secret."

Grandma cocked her head and gave me a look. "I've kept more secrets than you'll know in ten lifetimes."

"Ha!" I said. "I doubt that."

"Fine," Grandma said. "So dish."

"You first," I said, leading the way into the kitchen.

"Ha!" she said. "You'd like that, wouldn't you?"

I pulled out a bottle of champagne and popped the cork.

Grandma rifled through our cupboard. "Where the hell are your champagne flutes?"

"Your granddaughters are not leading champagne-flute kinds of lives." I plucked two juice glasses out of the drying rack. "Hello Kitty, or My Little Pony?"

"Pony," Grandma said, her disgust apparent. "For Hanukkah I'm getting you girls proper stemware."

"Don't bother," I said. "By Hanukkah I'll be long gone, and I'd just as soon travel light."

"Is that so? You got into that physician assistant school, did you?" Grandma poured champagne into both the glasses. We clinked glasses and drank. "Good stuff, darling. Very good. Don't waste your time on the cheap stuff. It's beneath you."

"Thanks. So how'd you know about P.A. school?"

Grandma leaned against the kitchen counter. "Information is very powerful in this town. I like to stay informed."

"Did Wallace tell you that I got a big, fat envelope?" I asked. Wallace is my postal person.

"Of course. But I should get some credit for knowing when to ask," Grandma observed.

We clinked glasses again and drained them. I refilled both of our glasses.

"I always thought that you'd be the one who finally successfully flew the coop. You were always more like me. Sensible. Not flighty, like Cinnamon and your mother."

"I'm getting a little tired of being the sensible one, Grandma. I'm ready to get out of here and just be myself."

She set her cup down and inspected her stockings. "It does wear after a while. Still, there are good things about living here and knowing what to expect from people. A small town is like a family."

"Grandma, you, of all people, know better than to believe that bullshit about how we're all here to support each other."

Grandma raised an expertly shaped eyebrow at me. Jolene

really was getting good with the waxing. "While I am well aware that there are people in this town who wouldn't cross the street to piss on me if I was on fire, I will also point out that a restaurant is a highly risky business venture, and Rosemary's has never been anything but profitable. Support comes in all different varieties, Ginger. Your little salon does quite well for a small-town business."

I made a disgusted noise in the back of my throat.

"What I meant was that everyone in a family has a role to play, and that's true in a small town, as well. We all contribute somehow. We Zimmermans contribute a bit of allure, some spice. And I'm not just talking about our names, sweetie." Grandma winked.

"What if I'm sick of playing my role? What if I think I was miscast?"

Grandma shrugged and took another sip of champagne. "Some of the best actresses were cast against type. Vivien Leigh was a brown-eyed Englishwoman. But can you even hear the name Scarlett O'Hara without seeing her saying 'fiddle-dee-dee'?"

Grandma weaved out of the apartment at about six, promising not to drive. Sage had called from Annabelle's and was spending the night. Annabelle's mother said she'd keep her until we were done with Therese the next day.

Cinnamon and Justin showed up around nine.

"Nice of you to call," I said, looking up from my books when they came in.

Cinnamon blushed. "I'm sorry. We had so much to say to each other. I lost track of time."

"You lost track of your daughter, too," I said.

Cinn spun around. "Where is she? Is she okay?"

I let her stew for a second. "She's at Annabelle's. We can pick her up tomorrow after we're done at the salon." I turned back to my books. "I had to leave class to come and get her at school."

"Ginger, I said I was sorry." Cinnamon walked over to the table and put her hand on my shoulder.

I looked up at her. "That doesn't change anything."

Cinnamon looked stricken, then stubborn. "I did what I did, Ginger. I wouldn't change it, either. I'm sorry you don't approve."

"You're acting just like Mom, Cinnamon. Don't do this," I said.

She turned away from me. "Do you want some tea, Justin? I'll put the water on to boil."

She left the room and Justin sat down on the couch.

"You're still married, you know," I said.

"I know," he said. "But once I knew who she was, I had to see her. I don't know what it is about her. The second she touches me, it's like everything is better."

I thought of all the times I'd seen clients at the salon relax the second Cinn's fingers met their scalp. "She's special," I said. "She always has been."

"I know. I knew it that first night I met her. You don't know how many times I thought about her over the years." Justin rubbed his face. He looked older somehow, like the lines of his jaw had finally settled.

"You sure didn't spend much time looking for her," I pointed out.

He stared directly into my eyes. "I know. I should have. I don't know exactly what stopped me. I was scared, I guess. She seemed so . . . magical. Somehow I convinced myself that she was really a dream—but I think I was just frightened that if I found her, I would never be able to walk away again."

"*She* didn't walk away. She stayed right here, holding the bag." A bubble of anger rose in my chest. I thought of all the times we'd eaten lentils and rice for a week because we couldn't afford anything else. I thought of how we'd juggled our schedules to make sure there was always someone with Sage. For the amount of money that Justin probably spent on gasoline for his sports car each month, our lives could have been so much easier. *My* life could have been so much easier. My life could have been mine.

I took my books and papers and went to my room, shutting the door behind me.

I spent the night reassuring myself that this business with Cinnamon not showing up to pick up Sage didn't have to stop me from going to P.A. school. Mom and Dad were here, after all. They could be Cinn's backup. Maybe it would make up for all the times they'd blown us off, like things coming full circle. I convinced myself that I even liked the idea. Later that morning at the salon, Roger Simpson showed up to check if we were in compliance with code. "What are you doing here on a Saturday?" I asked.

He looked uncomfortable. "Just getting in some overtime."

I looked at Cinnamon, who was pinning up Therese Millian's hair into a Courtney. "Have at it," I told Roger, and went over to start her makeup.

Roger came out from the utility room a few minutes later. I wondered if it was warmer in there than in the rest of the salon, because his face was red and there was a fine sheen of sweat on his forehead. "You don't got your water heater attached by an earthquake restraint, Ginger. I'm gonna have to cite you."

"You're kidding." I set down my pen.

"Wish I was, Ginger." Roger kept his eyes down on his clipboard. "I really wish I was."

I held my hand out for the citation and Roger ripped it out of the form and handed it to me, his Adam's apple bobbing convulsively.

"What's really going on here, Roger?"

"I don't know what you're talking about, Ginger. Names come up at random for these inspections and I drew yours this morning. Now, you need to get someone out here to put one of them metal restraints on your heater."

I threw myself back in my chair, knowing I was acting like a sulky teenager and not really caring. "Fine, Roger. Just go."

He paused in the doorway. "I'm sorry, Ginger. Really, I am."

"That's the last time his wife gets a break on the cost of her perm," I muttered as the door closed.

After Therese was ready, we watched her walk down to her car, studiously not looking at each other.

"Well, that was somewhere between no fun and torture," I said dryly. I had a bad feeling that that was how most of our customers had been feeling this week. Cinn and I had kept the atmosphere in the shop pretty frosty.

"I know," Cinnamon said, her voice wobbling.

I can't stand it when Cinnamon cries. Watching her cry is worse than crying myself. "I'm so sorry," I said, hearing my own voice wobble.

"Don't cry," Cinnamon said. "I hate it when you cry."

We hugged, and while part of me felt better, part of me knew that nothing about our situation had changed, but that something inside me had changed irrevocably.

Brian had managed to get the Mustang running again and had driven it to Santa Bonita to pick me up. You can't have a dinner-

and-a-movie date in Santa Bonita; we have no movie theater. We headed up the coast to Palo Alto.

"So you still haven't told your sister you're leaving?" he asked. "Why not?"

"There hasn't been a good time." I picked at the meatloaf I'd ordered. There were flowers in the center and I wasn't sure if I was supposed to eat them or not. We were at one of those places where they serve French fries with peach ketchup. Nothing like turning comfort food into something weird and challenging.

"Oh." He took a big bite of his macaroni-and-cheese, which was made with Gruyère and white sauce. Seriously, what do these people have against the orange stuff? "Do you think there will be a good time? To tell her, I mean?"

"Of course there will."

"Good," he said. "Because it would be a shame if you didn't take this opportunity, Ginger."

I looked up at his wide-open face. He was so sweet. "Yeah," I said. "A real shame."

We ended up not going to a movie. Nothing appealed to me. I didn't feel like laughing, so a comedy was out. But I wasn't in the mood for endless car chases and explosions. Nothing with tons of CGI effects really appealed, either, so we ended up just walking around Palo Alto and talking.

We held hands and I felt like I was back in high school.

Since his car was still back at the college lot, where he'd fixed the Mustang, we drove back there at the end of the night.

"I had a nice time tonight, Ginger," he said.

"Me too," I said.

"See you Monday."

"Yeah," I said. "Monday."

Then he leaned forward and kissed me. Definite tingle.

"Hey," I said. "Do you want to go to a wedding with me next week?"

"You got way too many appliances plugged into that outlet, Ginger. It's a fire hazard." Jordan pointed at my station.

"No problem. I'll unplug the straightener and the curling iron. I can plug those in when I need them." I started across the salon to do just that.

"That'd be fine, but I still have to cite you," he said, writing on the form on his clipboard.

I swore that I'd make one of these men eat his damn clipboard. Jordan had been a year behind me in high school and it still didn't seem right that he could even drive, much less show up at my place of business and tell me I had to pay a fine. "Why do you have to cite me? I'll unplug stuff and everything will be fine."

That's not the way it works, Ginger." Jordan wasn't meeting my eyes.

"And what happens if I don't want to be fined? What happens if I don't accept the fine?" I stood in front of him, hands on my hips. I was sick of all these picky fines and the men who were imposing them.

Jordan ripped the familiar yellow sheet out of the triplicate form. "Then we close you down, Ginger. Too many more fines and citations, and they'll close you down whether you pay them or not," he said, his voice quiet and a little bit sad.

I was shocked into immobility as he left. Close us down? For chicken-shit violations like this? This couldn't be happening.

"You know what this reminds me of?" Jolene asked. "It reminds me of in prison when someone wouldn't cooperate with one of the guards, and all of a sudden they'd be getting written up on every little thing."

"What are you suggesting, Jolene?"

"I'm suggesting that there's somebody you didn't cooperate with, and now you're paying the price."

"Who haven't I cooperated with? I'm the most cooperative person in the world."

Jolene snorted. "Yeah, and I'm the queen of frickin' England."

"Well, your majesty, I'm leaving for class now. Enjoy yourself," I said, picking up my bag.

"Hey, will you drop this conditioner off for Mom on your way?" Cinnamon asked.

"Sure." So I wasn't the only one who'd noticed that Mom's hair had been looking too dry lately.

The Mustang turned over without a hitch, and I gave her a little pat on the dashboard. I cruised the three blocks, parked in front of Mom's shop, and went in.

"Ginger, I'm glad you're here," Dad said, gathering up Mom's purse and her favorite poncho. "Can you close up the shop for us?"

I looked at my watch. It was only two o'clock. Mom usually keeps Pass It On open until at least seven. "Sure, but why are you closing now?"

Dad looked at me and then at Mom. Mom gave a tiny shrug. "Your Mom's not well. I need to take her to the emergency room."

"What's wrong?" I rushed over to Mom, who looked a little pale.

Mom patted my arm. "It's nothing, really. I just can't seem to move my legs."

"You can't move your *legs*? That doesn't sound like nothing.

How long has this been going on? Did it just start? Did you get any warning signs?"

Dad moved me aside. "We don't have time for this now, Ginger. I'm taking your mom to the hospital. Close the shop. We'll talk later." Then he swooped her up in his arms and carried her out of the shop. I ran after them and opened the door to his van.

"I'll be there as soon as I can, Mom. I'll call Grandma and Cinnamon and let them know what's going on."

Mom grabbed my arm. "No! Don't call them. Don't tell them."

"Why?" We had always rushed to each other's side when something went wrong, or when something went right. We had all been there together in the hospital when Sage was born. We had all been there together when I'd tripped on the stairs down to the beach and broke my arm. Why not now?

"Please, Ginger. Promise you won't call them. I'll explain later." Mom looked desperate. Of course, that could be because she couldn't move her legs. That would make me feel pretty desperate. And scared. Which she also looked.

"I promise," I said. "I'll follow you as soon as I get the shop closed."

Tight-lipped, Mom nodded. I closed her door and Dad pulled out of the parking space with a squeal of rubber.

CHAPTER SIXTEEN

They were already wheeling Mom back into the emergency room when I got there. The middle of the afternoon on a Thursday isn't exactly a busy time in the E.R., so we were getting fast service. I trooped behind the nurse as she went to get us settled in our little curtained-off room.

"Can you get onto the gurney, Mrs. Zimmerman?" she asked.

"Ms.," Mom corrected. "I don't think so. I can't move my legs at all."

The nurse frowned as if she'd never faced this before. Surely they'd had wheelchair-bound patients before. Surely they, of all people, would know how to get a patient from a chair to a bed.

Surely this was all some kind of bad joke or weird dream and I'd wake up any second.

"I can lift her," Dad said, and started to suit action to words.

"Wait," Mom said.

We all looked at her. She blushed. "I need to use the ladies' room first."

If the nurse couldn't figure out how to get my mother onto a bed, how in the world was she going to get her on a toilet? "Let's go," Dad said, and started wheeling her down the hall. I trailed after them uncertainly.

They disappeared behind the heavy wooden door. Standing outside, I could hear the murmur of their voices. I'd stood outside a lot of doors and heard the two of them murmur to each other. This time, it didn't have the familiar cadence that their voices usually had. They'd always had that sweet bill and coo. This time, I could hear tension underneath the murmurs.

A few minutes later, following a flush that sounded like it could have sucked Mom down and out into the ocean, Dad wheeled Mom back out. Mom's eyes looked a little pink and Dad was clenching his jaw so hard that I could see a vein bulging in his neck. We went back down the hall to where we'd left the nurse. Without a word, Dad lifted Mom into the hospital bed. She clung for a second to his arms before she let him go.

He patted her hand, then turned to me. "I need to go out and make a couple calls. I'll be right back. Can you stay here with your mother, Ginger?"

"Of course," I said.

"Be right back," Dad said and left.

"So what precisely is going on, Mom?" I asked, sitting down in the chair next to her bedside.

"Oh, look," she said, pointing over to the counter where there were some magazines. "Is that an *Us Weekly*?"

I glanced. "Yeah. Now, will you tell me what's going on here? What were you doing when you suddenly couldn't feel your legs?"

"I love that magazine. I like that thing where they show two celebrities wearing the same outfit and talk about who wore it better. People just don't know what looks good on them. Don't you think?"

"Mom," I said. "Stop it."

Her lower lip trembled and I felt like a total shit. My mother was in a hospital bed, unable to move her legs, obviously scared out of her wits, and I was yelling at her. Clearly, I was going to hell.

I reached for the magazine and glanced at the date. It was nearly two weeks old. Why hadn't it shown up at the shop yet? *Us* must have the worst subscription department ever.

I flipped the magazine open. "I think J Lo wore it better." I handed it to Mom.

She took one glance before handing it back. "No contest. That Kate Bosworth is too skinny."

The curtain twitched open and the doctor came in. "So what seems to be the problem here, Ms. Zimmerman?" he asked, barely looking up from the papers he was flipping through. His eyes were bloodshot and his chin was stubbled. It looked like he hadn't slept, but in a cute Clive Owen–at-the-end-of-*Inside Man* kind of way.

"Oh, it's probably nothing," Mom said.

I stared at her. "How is not being able to move your legs probably nothing?" I asked.

Dr. Clive ran his hand over his face. "I know it's alarming, but you have to expect a few things like this with your mother's condition."

I swiveled my chair to stare at him. "Her condition?" What the hell was he talking about?

"Her M.S.," the doctor said, examining my mother's legs.

I laughed. "Wow, do you ever have the wrong chart. My mother doesn't have M.S."

My mother blushed and put her hand on my arm. "I didn't want to worry you, Ginger."

It felt like my blood literally ran cold. Ice water was flowing through my veins and chilling me in places that the cold should never be able to penetrate. I stood up. "You have *what*?"

Mom looked over at Dr. Clive. He shut Mom's chart and held it against his chest. "Your mother has relapsing and remitting multiple sclerosis. It is nearly inevitable that she will have what we call exacerbations, like this one, from time to time. In all likelihood, she will recover full use of her legs relatively quickly. I can't give you a specific timetable, though."

"How long have you known?" I asked Mom.

Her fingers plucked at the threadbare sheet. "Almost a year."

"Who else knows?"

"Your father."

My father. My father who had suddenly given up the band that had been his passion for three decades and returned to live with my mother on a permanent basis. At least *that* now made sense.

Dr. Clive was speaking and I tried to tune back in over the static that had suddenly filled my head. "I'm going to start the paperwork to admit your mother. I think we should keep her at least overnight."

I nodded. "Do you want me to go get some of your things?" I asked Mom.

"There's a case in your father's van," she said.

"I'll go get it."

I walked past the nurses' station and out of the emergency room. A young Latina sat in one of molded chairs, holding her stomach and moaning softly. A little boy with the same dark chocolate eyes and thick black hair pushed wooden beads up and down a green plastic wire attached to a board. The static in my head got louder.

The double doors opened in front of me with a whoosh and the damp air slapped me in the face. I stood on the sidewalk and took in deep lungfuls of chilly air and exhaust fumes from the ambulances. Slowly, the noise in my head subsided enough to let me navigate my way to the parking lot where Dad's van was parked.

It was gone.

I managed to force myself to walk back into the hospital. It wasn't easy. Every step I took toward my mother felt like a battle. I wanted nothing more than to simply turn tail and run as fast as I could. Problem was, there was no place to run to escape this.

I told Mom that Dad had left a note on my windshield, that he'd had a student he couldn't cancel, that he would be back tonight.

I smoothed my mother's hair after the orderlies transferred her from the gurney to the hospital bed. I figured out how to make the T.V. remote work and got her a magazine from the gift shop. I left, promising to come back with Mom's toothbrush and a book. I left, promising not to tell. There was no point in worrying Grandma Rosemary or Cinnamon, was there? It was best to keep this to ourselves. It was best not to tell. It would be easy, too. After all, not telling was my specialty.

I turned my cell phone back on as I left the hospital. It buzzed in my hand like an angry bee. There were messages from Brian and Natalie. I'd missed two classes. Was everything all right? They'd taken excellent notes. Brian would stop by with them tonight and check on me.

It was sweet of them. Too bad it didn't matter. My final grades wouldn't matter. Neither did that big bulky envelope. None of it mattered, because I wasn't going anywhere.

Ever.

I can't say that I was shocked to see Dad's van outside of Mom's house. Where else would he go, after all? Nor was I all that surprised to hear the music pounding from the house. It was only four o'clock in the afternoon. Chances of the neighbors calling the police with a noise complaint were small, but he was still pushing it. And finally, it really, really didn't surprise me to find Dad inside the house with his guitar in his hand and an open bottle of tequila by his side.

Dad has had many bouts of sobriety that ended abruptly; why should this one have been any different? Seriously, I wanted to know why—because for some reason I had thought this time was different. Maybe it was the A.A. attendance thing. Maybe it was how he'd fixed stuff around our apartment. Aw, hell. I didn't know what it was; I just knew that I'd let him in again, and that he had once again reverted to form.

"You're drunk," I said, sitting down next to him on the couch.

"It's too hard, Ginger." Dad looked down at his guitar.

"I know, Dad." I started to get up off the couch, but he grabbed my arm.

"No, Ginger, you don't know." His bleary eyes searched mine. I'm not sure what they were searching for. If it was forgiveness, they could have searched forever. I was not in a forgiving frame of mind.

"I don't want to hear it, Dad. Whose fault is it going to be this time? Mom's, for being sick? A record producer? A bouncer at a bar? Me?" We'd all made the list at one time or another. Besides, it didn't really matter what the reason was. Drunk was drunk.

"Give me credit for having come at least this far, Ginger. I know it's my fault." Dad let go of my arm.

"So why, Dad? She really needs you now. We *all* really need you. Why dive back into the bottle?"

"The booze smooths things over. All those little details that can trip a guy up, they're not there. I don't have to worry about them because they don't even register." He ran a hand over his face, which suddenly looked much older.

I knew how that felt. It didn't take more than a mojito to have me missing a hell of a lot of details—like, oh, how to button my blouse properly or where my purse might be.

"Without the booze, there's all this little shit bombarding me every minute of every day. There are so many little nuances to decipher. Stuff I never saw or cared about, because . . ." His voice trailed off.

"Because you were drunk or hungover." The words sounded harsh. I'd wanted them to. I felt duped. Again. I'd sworn he wouldn't suck me in, and I'd let him, and he'd let me down. I couldn't seem to learn to stop trusting my dad. Until now.

This time when I stood up to walk away, he didn't try to stop me.

"Hey," Brian said when I opened the door to him. He looked a little confused. I can't entirely blame him.

I had decided to be true to all my roots, Dad's and Mom's. I'd cranked up the music and was drinking an appletini, or whatever you want to call it when you mix green apple vodka with green apple rum.

"Hey, yourself," I replied.

"Are you okay?"

"I'm fine. Just peachy."

He looked around. "Are Cinnamon and Sage here?"

"Cinn and Sage are not here. They are, in their ignorant bliss, over at my grandmother's restaurant for dinner. I'm all alone. Alone. Alone. Alone. Poor little me," I sang. Wow. Where had that come from?

He took the glass from my hand and sniffed it. "What are you drinking?"

"Stuff," I said. "Want some?"

"I think I'll pass." He handed the glass back. "What's going on?"

"Nothin'," I said. "Nothin' at all."

"Where were you today? Were you sick? Is Sage okay?"

Lord, he was sweet. I reached up and patted his cheek. "I'm fine. Sage is fine. I am not at liberty to say anything else."

"What does that mean?" He steered me to the couch, which, surprisingly, was difficult to get to. When had the path between the armchair and the coffee table become that treacherous?

"No comment," I said, trying to summon as much dignity as I could after having bounced off my own furniture.

"How drunk are you?" he asked, sitting down next to me on the wicker couch.

"Reasonably drunk," I said. "Considering."

"I take it you had a bad day." He dragged the afghan off the back of the couch and tucked it around me.

"You would take it correctly." I, on the other hand, had been taking it straight up, shaken and not stirred.

"I also take it you don't want to talk about it."

I shook my head. "Don't want to. Not one bit."

"Okay, then." He put his arm around me and pulled me close.

Something inside me unspooled, like a spring suddenly relaxing. My insides felt warm and melty, and I knew exactly why.

I love that feeling when a guy looks into my eyes and it's like I'm the only person there, like all he sees is me. I realize that that look is often caused by the fact that all the blood has left his brain and has rushed to another extremity, but it's hard to care about that when the world seems to contract and whirl around us.

When you're riding that wave of sensation, there is no other place but right there and then. There is no tomorrow. No yesterday. No next week. There's just you and him and the moment.

I needed that right now. I needed to not think about my future sliding away from me.

So my heart did that anatomically impossible flip flop. Brian looked at me like I was a magical creature and told me I was special, and . . . well, I jumped him.

"Where did you ever learn to do that?" I moaned.

He blushed. Fifteen minutes with his head between my legs, five of which I spent with my hands twisted in his hair while yelling "Oh, God, oh, God, oh, God," and the boy could still blush. I didn't know if I felt dirty or lucky. Both, probably.

"It helps to have studied anatomy."

"I should say so."

Too bad he'd be gone in the fall, and I'd still be here in Santa Bonita washing people's hair.

Brian left in the pre-dawn hours.

Despite a crashing hangover when I awoke, I showered and headed out to the hospital to check on Mom.

A bleary-eyed Dad sat at her bedside. "Hey, Ginger," he said. "How are you?"

"I'm okay. How's Mom?"

"I'm much better, dear," Mom said. "Look!" She wiggled her toes.

"That's great," I said, relief washing through me. "That's really great."

"I know. The doctor says I might be able to go home this afternoon."

"That's wonderful! I can be back here by one o'clock to help," I said.

"There's no need," Dad said. "I'm here. I can take care of it."

I shot him a look.

"I'm fine, Ginger. I can do it," he insisted.

"Go to class, honey. You don't have much longer to go. You've worked so hard. Finish strong," Mom said.

"Okay, I will," I said, knowing that it didn't matter anymore.

"I'll walk you out," Dad said.

We rode the elevator downstairs in silence. As we walked out into the parking lot, I said, "This is why you came back home, isn't it?"

"Yep," Dad said, shoving his hands in the back pockets of his jeans.

"It's why the band is breaking up and you're staying, right?"

"Uh-huh," he said.

"It's harder than you thought, isn't it?" I asked.

"Absolutely," he said. "Look, I'm sorry about yesterday. I can't crawl back into the bottle every time things here get hard. Your mom needs me now."

Like we hadn't needed him before?

"I'll get used to it. I'm just not accustomed to these things. Your mom and I went a different route than most people. I followed my bliss and she followed hers. Whenever we could intersect, we did."

"Your bliss was the Surf Daddies, right?" I picked at my nail polish where it was starting to peel.

"Yep," Dad said.

"What was Mom's bliss?" I asked, still studying my fingernails.

He yawned a little. "Her shop. And you guys."

I shook my head and looked up at Dad. "No, we weren't. You were Mom's bliss."

He leaned forward. "You're wrong, Ginger. Her bliss was here. That's why she stayed here instead of coming on the road with me."

I stood up. "No, Dad. *You're* wrong. She stayed here because it was what a grown-up would do."

Speaking of grown-up, the activities Cinnamon and Justin were engaged in back in her room were definitely of the adult variety. She'd snuck him in after Sage had gone to bed and I assumed she'd have him out before Sage got up tomorrow morning. We'd never made a "No sleeping with your baby-daddy" rule, although apparently I should have thought of that.

I should also probably have thought to study in my own room. Watching the two of them come stumbling out of Cinnamon's bedroom turned my stomach.

I apparently inspired a similar reaction, because the two of them stopped slobbering all over each other. "Hey, Ginger," Justin said, running his hands through his hair to finger-comb it.

"Hey," I said, trying to keep any emotion out of my voice.

"I'm just leaving," he said.

"Good night," I said, and looked back down at my book.

"Ginger," Cinnamon said, her tone an admonition.

I didn't bother to look up. The two of them went out on the porch to say good-bye. The door swung shut behind them.

I still didn't bother to look up. Not until I heard Sage's door creak open. I looked up to see her looking out the window at the porch.

"Is he my daddy?" Sage asked, her voice a hushed whisper.

Oh, shit. I weighed my options.

I could tell her the truth, but it wasn't my secret to tell.

On the other hand, in some ways, it was Sage's secret. Was it so wrong to give her possession of her own secret?

I opened my mouth and it felt like Cinnamon's voice came out. "Yes, Sage, he's your daddy."

I whirled around. Cinnamon was standing behind me.

"He's really my daddy?" Sage took a couple steps toward Cinnamon, but didn't come within arm's reach.

"Yes. He's really your daddy. He even has the exact same birthmark you have on your lower back," Cinnamon said.

I turned and looked at her, brows arched in a silent question.

She gave me a wistful smile and shrugged her shoulders. "Apparently it's like curly hair in our family. It's genetic and very dominant. They all have it. That's why Craig had it, too."

Sage was twisted around, trying to look at her own bottom, a difficult proposition even when you're seven and have rubber bones.

"But that man is married already. He's married to that blonde lady." Sage turned back around to face us.

"How did you know that?" I asked.

"Because Mommy and me went and looked in the windows of the hotel the night they got married."

I looked over at Cinnamon again.

"When I saw Craig, I knew he had to be a relative. We took a walk over by the reception to just take a look. That's when I realized that Sage's father was Ashley's new husband." She looked down at her feet.

"And that's why you were watching *Sandcastles* that night." I had been right; it *had* been a dark night of the soul for Cinnamon. I couldn't imagine what that would have felt like, to have finally found the man you had loved and wished for on the very day that he married someone else.

"And she's going to have a baby." Sage crossed her arms in front of her chest and her jaw began to jut out. "I heard you say that."

"Yes," Cinnamon said, holding her arms out for Sage. "She is."

Sage didn't budge. "Then even though I have a daddy now, we're still not tradition, are we?"

Cinnamon looked over at me, her brow creased in confusion. "Tradition?"

"Fiddler on the Roof," I said.

I watched understanding dawn on Cinnamon's face, followed by sorrow. "No, baby, we're not tradition. We're Zimmerman women. We're never tradition."

"Then I'm not so sure I want to be a Zimmerman woman." Sage marched back to her room and closed the door.

I knew exactly how she felt. I experienced a huge pang of it later that night as I took my Envelope of Freedom out of its hiding place and dumped it in the trash.

CHAPTER SEVENTEEN

Business was slooowwww at the salon. We'd had three cancellations today and two for tomorrow. Cinnamon was teaching Jolene to give a facial and using Natalie as a guinea pig. I fanned my flash cards out in front of me, but what was the point? I had decided to finish out the school year, but my heart wasn't in it anymore.

"I'm going to get some coffee," I told them. "Anyone want anything?"

Natalie wanted a white mocha; Cinnamon wanted green tea with honey. Jolene asked if anyone ever drank a good old-fashioned cup of joe anymore.

I headed downstairs to Café Ole!

I almost didn't recognize the woman in front of me in line, even though she was a regular client. In fact, she'd been one of our morning cancellations.

She now had hair like a mudflap on a truck. What the hell had happened to her? She must have gone to Trudy at ExcellaCuts. Why on earth would a self-respecting woman do such a thing to herself? I gave a mental shrug. She'd certainly paid the price, and based on how short her bangs were, she'd be paying it for several months until her hair grew back in. "Trying something new, Nancy?" I asked.

She turned scarlet red, mumbled something about needing a change, then took her coffee and practically ran from Café Ole!

Back at Do It Up, the phone rang minutes after I sat back down behind the counter. It was Lamont Gilman Sr.

"So I hear you've been having a little problem with your licensing," Lamont Sr. said.

"Where did you hear that?" I asked.

"Oh," he said nonchalantly. "You know how small towns are. Things get around."

"I don't suppose you have anything to do with that, do you, Mr. Gilman?"

"Of course not, Ginger. But I could use my considerable connections to help you clear this all up—if so much of my time wasn't being taken up with my son's legal difficulties."

I yearned to wrap my hands around his throat and squeeze it. until his big fat pumpkin head popped off.

"Are you saying that if I drop the charges against Lamont Junior, these inspections and fines will stop?" I put my head down on the counter. I felt so tired. What was the point of fighting this man? What had I thought I could possibly gain? "What about all the cancellations? Would those stop, too?"

"I'm saying that things could definitely get easier on you if they got easier on my son." I could practically hear his crocodile smile. "In addition, no city inspectors would being paying visits to your mother's or grandmother's places of business."

"And will you get Lamont to leave me and my family alone?"

"I was thinking of sending Lamont to work for a friend in New York for a while. Would that do?"

"You have yourself a deal, Mr. Gilman. I'll call Troy right now."

"Thank you, Ms. Zimmerman. It's been a pleasure doing business with you."

"I wish I could say the same." I hung up the phone.

"You're dropping the charges?" Cinnamon asked. "What about Sage? What about protecting her?"

"I am protecting her," I said. "I'm protecting her and you and Mom and Grandma Rosemary. That man has his fingers too deep into too many pies."

Jolene came over and patted me on the shoulder. "I know it feels bad, honey, but trust me, you can't fight the man."

"That's not true," Cinnamon said, raring up for a fight as surely as if we'd suggested having veal for dinner. "We could fight him. We can do something. Together we could."

Jolene shook her head. "No, honey, let it go. You'd just end up like those guys at the end of *Fargo,* and there'd be poor Troy asking you if that was Ginger in the wood-chipper."

"Hey! Why would it be me in the chipper?" I protested.

Jolene gave me a "duh" look. "Because you would have been the one who started it."

"You don't have to do this, Ginger," Troy said. The circles under his eyes had gotten deeper and darker.

"Just tell me what to sign and let me get this over with."

Troy had offered to come to Do It Up with the paperwork for dropping the charges against Lamont Jr. I'd been happy to accept. I wanted to stay inside the salon, where it was safe.

"Take some time to think about it," he said.

"Thanks, but there really isn't much to think about. I'd like my grandmother, my mother, and my sister all to stay in business. This is the only way to do that."

Troy glanced around. "Let me talk to you about this," he said in a hushed tone.

"Fine," I said. "It's not going to make any difference."

"Just hear me out, okay? Can we talk someplace private?"

Cinnamon, Natalie, and Jolene had pretty much been staring at me with their mouths pursed up into little O's ever since I'd gotten off the phone with Lamont Sr. The silent Greek chorus thing was clearly starting to unnerve Troy.

"Fine," I sighed. "I'll trim your ends for you. They look brittle."

Why not hear him out? I had plenty of time. In fact, it looked like I had the rest of my life to hang around Santa Bonita and listen to other people talk while I stuck my hands in their hair.

I led him back to the shampoo room.

"Do you think you're the first people Gilman and Esposito have pulled this kind of crap on?" Troy asked, his head back in the basin.

I ran water through his hair and started to shampoo him. "Honestly, I hadn't thought about it. I'm guessing not though."

"Absolutely not." Troy said. "Have you ever wondered why Gilman and Associates is the only insurance agency in this town?"

"Because we're a tiny little town?" I suggested.

"No, because they don't allow competition here. If you don't get your insurance from Gilman and Associates, Mayor Esposito starts sending out city inspectors. Pretty soon, you're up to your ass in fines. Purchase your insurance from Gilman and Associates and suddenly those fines all go away."

"So?" This wasn't a total news flash, since I had just lived through something similar.

"The corruption in this town goes deep, Ginger. Let's say you had a little illegal card game going. Maybe that was how you kept your legitimate business afloat. Maybe if you paid a certain amount into the mayor's reelection fund, the police would be told to leave your card game alone."

"Once again, what does it have to do with me?"

"Connect the dots, Ginger. Between Gilman pulling all this

crap on you to get you to drop the charges against Lamont, and the kickbacks Mayor Esposito takes from your grandmother, you're perfectly placed to bring them all down."

I froze, my hands deep in Troy's hair. "Why is my grandmother paying kickbacks to the mayor?"

"For her card game," he said impatiently. "She's got to pay a kickback. Either that or she's got something juicy on him, because we've been told in no uncertain terms to stay away from her restaurant after hours."

"My grandmother is running an illegal card game? *My* grandmother? The one who favors Chanel suits and slingbacks?"

"You don't think she's been supporting herself and subsidizing all of you with what she makes on the restaurant, do you?"

"Subsidizing all of us?"

Troy closed his eyes. "How could you not know? Everyone in town knows."

It all started to make sense. Grandma's restaurant was never crowded, yet she never seemed to have a cash flow problem. It was all a front. "I guess I didn't want to know," I said.

"So, wouldn't you like to put an end to this crap?"

I squirted conditioner into my hands. "How exactly would we do that?"

"Expose them. Drag all their secrets out into the daylight for all the world to see."

"Forget it, Troy. There's no point."

What did it matter where I bought my insurance? What did it matter if I took my final exams? What did anything matter?

Regardless of what happened with the Espositos or the Gilmans, the Zimmermans were all stuck right here.

I had always thought I knew most of the secrets in Santa Bonita. Troy had pulled the blinders off me: I didn't have a clue what was going on, and that needed to change. Grandma R had been right when she said that knowledge was power, and I was all about getting a little more power.

And I'd start with Grandma herself.

After Cinnamon and Sage went to bed, I bundled up in my warmest jeans and faux-Ugg boots and headed out. I parked the Mustang down the street from Rosemary's, poured myself a cup of hot chocolate from the thermos I'd brought with me, and settled down to watch what happened after the last diners left at ten o'clock.

It didn't take long. The first man came strolling down the street at about ten thirty. He wore a dark windbreaker, dark pants, and a baseball cap pulled low over his eyes. He walked briskly, hands stuffed in his pockets. He glanced over his shoulder and down the street before turning and going through the archway that led into the courtyard of Rosemary's.

Two more men ambled down the street and I stared hard as they walked under the streetlight, but I didn't recognize either of them. It felt strange not to recognize someone strolling that confidently down what I considered to be my streets, but really, we're only half an hour from San Francisco and San José.

Then Justin Esposito wandered up the sidewalk and, after doing the same over-the-shoulder check that the other three men had done, turned and walked into my grandmother's restaurant. I'd seen enough. I started the Mustang (thank goodness for Brian!) and started home through the deserted streets. The only other car I saw was a Jeep that passed me on Willow Street. I blinked. Were my eyes fooling me or had Courtney Day just passed me again?

I walked into Rosemary's at around two o'clock the next afternoon. While our schedule at Do It Up was starting to fill up again, it was still pretty quiet. And two was usually a good time to talk to Grandma R; the lunch rush was over and dinner hadn't begun.

"Ginger," Grandma said from behind the bar. She had on a bouclé suit in a shade of chartreuse that most women could not pull off. "What a lovely surprise! What can I do for you?"

"I thought maybe I could do something for you," I said. "I forgot that you had asked me to come by and fix your computer. I'm so sorry."

She waved a hand in the air. "Not to worry. It's all taken care of."

"Oh?"

"Yes, your father stopped by and sorted it out." She straightened a stack of menus that was already straight. "He knows quite a bit about computers."

"Dad? And computers?" I sat down on a bar stool across from her. "What a surprise. But that seems to be a constant state for me these days. Maybe you could fill me in on something else, too."

"What's that, dear?" Grandma's beautifully manicured fingernails tapped the stack of menus.

"Exactly how much money does Justin Esposito owe you?"

Her fingers froze in mid-tap and I felt a surge of pleasure. I'd guessed right. That was her objection to Justin Esposito and the reason she'd said he wasn't good enough for Cinnamon. He must owe her a lot. That would explain the hold she had over Mayor Esposito, as well.

"I don't know what you're talking about."

"And I'm the queen of freakin' England," I said.

CHAPTER EIGHTEEN

Laura Jenkins and Monroe Flaherty will wed at the Coastside Country Club on May 10 at 4:30 in the afternoon.
Laura, who survived a devastating car accident last year,
will be wearing a vintage Lazaro gown of silk satin fabric
with brilliant beadwork. More than two hundred and fifty
guests will be there to wish the lucky bride and her groom
a life of joy and unity.

It was finally Laura's big day. We were doing her hair at the
country club, along with her mother's hair, her sister's hair, and
her grandmother's hair. I got grandma duty.

I didn't mind; I like to watch old ladies and decide which kind
I'll be. Will I be like that old lady at the bakery counter quoting Os-
car Wilde? Or will I be the one who thinks everybody cut in line in
front of her and gives people's shoes flat tires with her quad cane?

Old ladies are also full of a lot of useful information. They
know how to get chewing gum out of a five-year-old's very curly
hair. They know where you can cut corners on a recipe and where
you can't. They know which cuts are likely to scar, and the best
way to bring down a fever.

I approached Laura's grandmother, who sat to one side of the
room in her wheelchair. "Hi, Mrs. Jenkins," I said.

"Hello, young lady, what can I do for you?"

"It's what I can do for you, Mrs. Jenkins. I'm going to do your hair."

"Do my hair? Whatever for?" Her wrinkled hand rose to pat her lavender-rinsed bob.

"For your granddaughter's wedding," I said, smiling. Laura had warned me that her grandmother got a little confused now and then.

"My granddaughter?" the tiny little lady said, looking around her. "She's here?"

"Right there," I said, pointing to Laura. Laura waved.

"Oh, her. Such a pretty girl." Mrs. Jenkins smiled and waved back to Laura.

"She is, isn't she?" I said, pulling some combs and pins from my case.

"She's not my granddaughter, though."

"Of course she is. And she's getting married today. So let's make you extra pretty." I started combing Mrs. Jenkins's hair, and she relaxed a little under my hands. Maybe I did have a bit of magic, after all.

"Oh, I like to be pretty. That sounds nice," Mrs. Jenkins murmured, her eyelids beginning to droop.

"Super," I said.

It was more of a mob scene than most weddings we do. Crowds of people came in and out to wish Laura well. I could understand. She was, after all, the miracle girl. Plus, it seemed as if the whole town had been invited. Even Mom and Dad were there. Apparently, Laura had been overcome with gratitude when Mom helped her score her vintage gown.

Even the mother of the girl who didn't get the miracle came through to wish Laura well.

"It was so nice of you to invite us," Mrs. Reeve said. "So good to see all of Jamie's friends again."

"I'm so glad you could find the time to come," Laura said.

Something in her voice made me turn. The pitch was wrong—too high or too loud, I wasn't sure. Cinnamon was staring, too.

"Oh, it was our pleasure. It makes us feel like we're a little closer to Jamie to be here with you today."

"Oh, it does? Like it makes you feel closer to her when you visit her grave?" Laura smiled. Well, I think it was supposed to be a smile, but it didn't look like one. It looked more like a grimace.

"I'm not sure . . . ," Mrs. Reeve stammered.

"Not sure? Not sure of what? Maybe of where Jamie is buried? Is that why you haven't been to visit her grave in six months? Because you forgot where it is?"

"No! Of course not! Of course I remember where Jamie is buried."

"Oh, then maybe you've been too busy to visit your daughter's grave. Is that it? Have you just been too busy to grieve for your daughter?"

"What do you mean by that? Of course we're grieving for our daughter."

Laura shook her head. "You sure have a funny way of showing it. Do you even miss her? Does anyone miss her?"

"Absolutely. You should have seen her funeral. Hundreds of people came to pay their respects."

"But I couldn't see her funeral, could I? I was in a coma still. Did you make a video? Could I see that?"

Mrs. Reeve looked horrified. "A video? Of our daughter's funeral? It's not like it was a ballet recital."

"Oh? Did you tape many of those? Because I seem to remember you missing quite a few of those."

Mrs. Reeve stared at Laura. "How do you know who might have missed Jamie's ballet recitals?"

Cinnamon let out a loud laugh. "Ha ha ha! Bridal nerves. Aren't they funny?" She gave me a little head toss.

I grabbed Mrs. Reeve and shepherded her from the room. "So did you have a long drive?"

"What did she mean by all that?" She seemed near tears. Her breath came very fast and I could feel her tremble.

"I doubt she even knows. It's a big wedding. I think it's been very stressful for her. She has no idea what she's saying." Something told me that Laura had known exactly what she was saying. I hadn't realized that she and Jamie had been that close.

Mrs. Reeve, mollified but definitely confused, went up to the ballroom.

When I got back down to the basement where the girls were getting ready, Laura looked and acted as if nothing had happened.

"People don't believe in miracles these days," Mr. Jenkins said, his glass of champagne in his hand for the toast at the reception. "It's a shame, because I think miracles happen around us all the time."

I looked over at Laura, who I expected to finally have that serene bridal look on her face, but she looked even tenser than before.

"The fact that my daughter is with us today is a miracle," Mr. Jenkins said. Laura's jaw clenched. "I'm made even more aware of that right now because of others among us who did not receive that miracle."

Mr. Reeve put his hand on his wife's back. She gave him a tremulous smile, but I could see the tears shining in her eyes. How painful it must be to watch someone who looked so much like your daughter go through this important rite of passage, knowing your daughter had been cheated from ever experiencing it.

Cinnamon might be right. I might not believe in fairy-tale endings, but I did understand the importance of these ceremonies and what they represented. I understood why a woman and a man would feel compelled to stand in front of their friends, their family, and their community and declare themselves a united front against the world.

I looked over at my mother and father, sitting across the table from me. My mother leaned gently against my father's shoulder, and his hand covered hers on the table. I understood that it also might not mean anything when a man and a woman didn't make that declaration in front of everyone; sometimes what passed between two people was enough.

I looked over to where Justin and Ashley sat, a few tables away, and understood that making that public commitment meant nothing without the private commitment.

Maybe what I didn't believe was that a man and a woman could drop all the pretense between them, could strip themselves naked enough that they could truly be everything to each other.

I looked over at Brian and thought about our shared ambitions and dreams, and our newfound shared passion for each other. Would that be enough? Could it withstand the fact that he was moving on and I was going to remain stuck right where I was? I leaned toward him to kiss him.

Boom!

I jumped, and it took me a few seconds to figure out that Laura had shot a gun. Plaster dust coated her Courtneyed hair, from the large hole in the ceiling above her that had been caused by the shiny gun in her hand.

"Shut up!!!" she screamed. *"Just shut the fuck up!!!!!"*

Okay. That was another hint.

"Laura!" Her father stared at her, clearly horrified.

"You think I don't know what you're doing? You think I don't see your little plan?" Laura waved the gun at him and the guests collectively gasped.

Brian shifted his chair slightly, blocking my view. I peered around him and he whispered, "Stay back. Please."

Like hell.

"I d-d-don't know what you're talking about, Laura. What plan?" Mr. Jenkins said.

"The plan to out me. Don't think you've been fooling me with all that lovey-dovey father-daughter crap." Laura backed toward the wall behind her, the gun still pointing toward her father.

"Is she gay?" Mom whispered to Cinnamon.

All the guests were turning to each other, murmuring questions. A wave of shrugs and head shakes went through the room.

"Quiet!!!!" Laura screamed, waving the gun at all the guests. "Shut up, all of you!"

Mom drew back in her chair. Dad put his arm protectively around her. Brian pushed me more firmly behind him. It was sweet, but he was totally blocking my view.

Once the room quieted down, Laura nodded. "That's better." She took a deep breath.

Monroe stood up. "Honey, don't do this."

Laura turned. "Oh, Monroe, you don't know how much I wish I didn't have to, but he was going to tell. Then he'd ruin everything."

"Tell what?" Mr. Jenkins asked.

Laura turned to point the gun back at her father. "That I'm not her," she said, her voice thick with tears. "I know that you know. You've been trying to catch me out all these weeks. All those little father-daughter talks, all those 'remember when' discussions. You were trying to trip me up."

"Trip you . . . ? What the hell are you talking about, Laura? I demand to know what's going on right now." Her father put his hands on his hips as if he were reprimanding her for coming home after curfew, rather than pulling a gun on all her wedding guests.

Laura's face went pale under her lovely bronzing makeup, and the gun drooped in her hand. "Are you serious? You don't know? You *really* don't know?"

"Know what?" Mrs. Jenkins rose to stand next to her husband. "Laura, what are you saying?"

"I'm not Laura!" she screamed. "I'm Jamie Reeve!"

The entire room gasped. How was that possible? Jamie was dead. All around the room, people's mouths were open in big O shapes.

"I went to sleep in the back of the van, and when I woke up Monroe was sitting next to my hospital bed, calling me Laura and telling me how happy he was I survived and how much he loved me."

I'm not sure what had us more spellbound now, what she was saying or the gun in her hand.

Mrs. Reeve stood tentatively, her legs shaking. "Jamie?" she said, her voice breaking. "Baby, is that you?"

Jamie pointed the gun directly at her mother. "Don't give me that 'baby' crap," she said, her voice harsh. "I know the truth now. When was the last time you went to my grave? You couldn't even stop by with some fucking daisies once in a while?"

"It . . . it hurt so much to see your name there." Mrs. Reeve stretched her hands out to her daughter, pleading.

"Blah, blah, blah." Jamie covered her ears with her hands. "You've always got an excuse, don't you?"

"Wh-wh-what do you mean? Jamie, if that's you, baby, put down the gun. Come to me." Mrs. Reeve's arms opened wide.

"What do I *mean?* I mean things like how you spent all the money sending my brother to college so there wasn't any left for me, so I had to work two jobs and go part-time while he was partying until he puked every night. Like how I couldn't go out for the cheerleading squad because my sister had already done that, and you needed me to help at home. Things like that."

"But, honey, all that was true. We did need—"

"I said shut up!" Jamie screamed. She pulled the trigger, and the ice sculpture by the champagne fountain exploded.

In the distance, I heard the faint sound of sirens. Apparently Jamie did, too, because she trained the gun on the doorway to the ballroom.

Cinnamon stood up. "Jamie, stop this. We can help."

Jamie swung her gaze and her gun toward our table. Brian tried to pull me toward him, but I was grabbing for Sage. Dad turned and covered Mom with his body.

"Oh, for Pete's sake, Cinnamon. With what? Some of your stupid crystals? Laura's dead. I stole Laura's identity! Do you get it yet?"

"I understand that you're in pain and that we can help you," Cinnamon said in her shampoo voice.

"Do not patronize me!" Jamie screamed.

Watching her pull the trigger felt like a slow-motion nightmare. I threw my body over Sage's and felt Brian's cover mine. Out of the corner of my eye, I saw Justin leap from his seat at the adjacent table and fling himself toward Cinnamon. I heard something explode at our table.

"You do not know what it's like to carry around the weight of a secret like this!" Jamie shrieked. "Every move I make I'm sure is going to betray me. Every word out of my mouth is stressful. Every facial expression, every decision. It's been hell!"

I lifted my head slowly. Our centerpiece was blown to smithereens, and from the cut on Cinnamon's cheek, a chunk of it had hit her. Who knows how much worse it would have been if Justin hadn't flung himself on her?

"But why, Jamie, why?" Mr. Reeve stood now. "Why would you put us through this?"

Jamie rolled her eyes in disbelief. "Laura had it so much better than me. Why wouldn't I want to change places with her? Look around you." Jamie gestured around the hall with her gun. "Would you have thrown me a wedding like this? Would you have bought me this dress? Plus, Laura had Monroe."

Monroe stood up now, visibly shaking. "She doesn't have me anymore, Jamie. You do."

Jamie stared at him. "You knew?"

"Not at first." Monroe ran his hands through his hair, ruffling it back into spikiness. "Too many things had changed, though. Too much was different. Plus, there was your obsession with going to her grave . . . your grave."

"And you married me anyway?" Jamie took a step toward him.

"Put the gun down Jamie," a bass voice rumbled from the doorway.

Troy stood there, his gun drawn.

Jamie whirled toward him. "No. You put yours down."

"You know I can't do that," Troy said. "You need to calm down."

"Calm down? How am I supposed to calm down? My life is a nightmare. I can't keep this secret anymore; it's *killing* me."

I looked around our table. I certainly knew what she was talking about; our family's secrets had pretty much flattened me.

The truth of that hit me a like a truck. That was it. I'd had it.

"Oh, wah, wah, wah," I said, pushing to my feet. "Call the wahmbulance. Listen, Jamie," I said. "We all have secrets."

"Oh, yeah, like what?" The gun turned waveringly toward me. Funny, the barrel hadn't seemed that large until it was giving me its one-eyed stare.

"Well, Linda Johnson is smoking again and lying to her husband about it."

"Ginger, no!" Linda cried.

Ed turned and looked at her sadly. "It's not like I didn't already know. Do you think I'm stupid? How much time does anyone need to spend in the bathroom with the fan on?"

"Oh, no, honey, I didn't think you were stupid. I just didn't want to disappoint you, after we spent all that money on the hypnosis and everything." Linda put her hand on Ed's shoulder.

"Whatever," Ed said, shrugging her hand off.

Linda glared at me, then stood up. "Well, that woman back there is the one who's always dumping bags of stuff at your mother's shop. What's that all about?" She pointed to the older woman I'd recognized toward the back.

"You, back there. Stand up," Jamie demanded.

The woman stood up.

"What's your name?" Jamie asked.

"I'm Rose Vitelli," the woman said.

Vitelli? I knew that name! "As in the widow of Basil Vitelli?" I asked.

She nodded. "One and the same."

"And you give those bags of clothing to my mother?" Why on earth would my grandfather's widow be helping the daughter of the woman who had killed him?

"Cassia is the only piece of Basil I have left. I've always

smoothed what paths I could. You didn't make that easy, though, dear," Mrs. Vitelli said with a quiet sort of dignity.

Mom had the decency to blush.

"And long as we're telling secrets, there's something that I should have said years ago. Rosemary, he wanted you to shoot him," Mrs. Vitelli said quietly.

"What?" Grandma Rosemary looked at Mrs. Vitelli incredulously. "Why would anyone want to be shot? By me or anyone else?"

"Because he'd been diagnosed with cancer. The doctors gave him a year, but he'd have started going downhill long before that. They told him to get his affairs in order." Mrs. Vitelli clasped her hands in front of her, standing as tall as a little old Italian woman could.

"And was the affair what he was supposed to get in order?" Grandma Rosemary stood, too. She wasn't that much taller, and the two women looked surprisingly alike. Same reddish hair, same dancer's build. Basil had a definite type.

"We couldn't have any children. Back in those days they didn't have the ways to figure out who had the problem, and there weren't many things to be done about it, either."

"And that pertains to me how?" Grandma asked.

"He didn't let you find out he was married to someone else until he knew you were pregnant, did he?" Rose said, her head cocked to one side.

Grandma shook her head. "We'd pretty much just figured it out."

"And he made sure you knew where his gun was before that, didn't he?"

Grandma nodded. "We were in New York. He wanted to make sure I could protect myself if I needed to do so."

"Don't you get it? And you always thought you were so damn smart." Rose chuckled.

Grandma started across the room. "Who are you calling stupid?"

"The woman who hasn't figured out how the wool was pulled over her eyes forty-five years ago. I know you've thought about it. I'm guessing you haven't thought about too much else, based on how you've led your life." Mrs. Vitelli didn't back down an inch. She just stood there, staring at Grandma as if she was daring her to punch her in the nose. "You still love him, don't you? That's why you never married. You loved Basil and nobody else could be Basil for you. I understand. I feel the exact same way."

I have never seen anyone take the wind out of Grandma's sails like that. I have seen her back mean drunks into the corner with just a stare. I have seen her make my mother freeze in place without raising her voice. I have seen her quash fights between Cinnamon and me without any more threat than a raised eyebrow. I had never seen anyone shut her up until that moment.

"I did," she said softly, sinking down in the chair next to Mrs. Vitelli. "I loved him and I killed him. I didn't deserve to have someone else."

Mrs. Vitelli sat, too. She took Grandma's hand. "What you did was a mercy, and it took more bravery than he or I had. It's why he chose you: your beauty and your fire. He knew you could do it."

"He wanted me to kill him?" Grandma's voice sounded higher and clearer than it had sounded in my life. It was as if all the whiskey had washed right out of it.

"He didn't want to face what was coming, and he set you up, I'm afraid. I even abetted him. I could have come to the Artichoke Festival with him, but I knew it would be better if I didn't."

"What about that, Jamie?" I said. "That was a heck of a secret. Little Mrs. Vitelli has been carrying that one around for forty-five years, and she's not pulling a gun on anyone."

Jamie picked at her veil. "It's pretty good, but it's old. Who cares about anything that happened that long ago?"

Grandma Rosemary stood up, clearly incensed. "*I* care. But if you want something a little fresher . . ." She pointed one of her long elegant fingers at Justin Esposito. "That boy there owes me fifty thousand dollars, and he's messing around with my granddaughter."

Ashley stood at her table. "Justin?" she said, her voice small.

Justin stood up and looked out at the crowd. "I'm Sage Zimmerman's father."

"You're what?" Ashley shrieked.

"I'm sorry, Ashley. It was eight years ago. I only just found out." Justin put his arm around Cinnamon. "But I want to make it right. I want to be Sage's father."

"You can't do this." Ashley stamped her foot. "You can't just leave me."

"Let him go, Ashley," Troy said, walking closer to her. "Let him leave. Come to me."

"Troy, you live in a trailer. I just can't do that."

"I won't be in a trailer much longer, Ashley. I've got a big chunk of money coming." Troy's jaw hardened. "I've got some pictures I'm going to sell."

Ashley's eyes narrowed. "What pictures?"

"My pictures." Courtney Day stepped out from behind one of the tall potted plants at the doorway to the ballroom. "So you'll finally sell them to me?"

"Courtney?" I said. That one surprised even me.

"Hey, Ginger," she said, flashing me that famous grin. "How's it going?"

"I've been better," I said.

"I feel you," she said, shaking her head. Then she turned back to Troy. "What's with the sudden change of heart?"

"It's your body, Courtney. It's your business." Troy's shoulders slumped. "Trying to do the right thing is getting me nothing. I might as well go along for the ride."

"What pictures?" Ashley shrieked.

Jamie swung the gun toward Ashley. "Buy a freaking vowel, Ashley. I'm guessing they're naked pictures of Courtney when the two of them were an item back in high school." She turned back to Courtney. "Am I right?"

"You got it. And Mr. Law Man here doesn't want to give them up." Courtney rolled her eyes.

"I'd be happy to give them up, Courtney," Troy growled. "I'm not so happy about giving them up to be published, and then having you pretend to be all shocked and dismayed about the whole thing."

"It's show-biz, baby. I keep telling you that. It's not for real."

"Wait a minute," I said. "You *wanted* the pictures published? I thought you wanted them to keep them from being published."

"What are you, crazy? I was eighteen. My ass will never be that high and tight again. If those pictures hit the tabloids and I can get all pissy about them, Brett and I will be on the cover of all the supermarket magazines for months, and teenage boys will be downloading me for all eternity." Courtney shook her head over my naïveté.

"And I end up looking like more of a creepy perv than Lamont," Troy said.

"Hey," Lamont said, clearly offended.

"Shut up, Lamont," Troy, Lamont Sr., and I all said in unison.

"Ohhh," Jamie said, nodding her head in comprehension.

"I love you, Ashley," Troy said. "Lose that deadbeat. He's done nothing but run up gambling debts since he came back to town. At the rate he's going, all that money that means so much to you will be gone in a year."

"Justin, is that true?" Cinnamon turned to look at him.

It looked for a second like Justin was going to deny it, then he said, "Pretty much. I don't know how it got so out of hand. I started out winning pretty often and it was an incredible rush. Everything else felt so . . . flat. Gambling was more exciting than anything else in my life."

"Thanks tons, Justin. You weren't exactly rocking my world either," Ashley broke in.

"Hush, Ash," Troy said, his voice low and gentle. He put his hand on the small of her back and she quieted.

"But . . . then I started losing and the pit just seemed to get deeper," Justin went on. "I couldn't stop. I want to. I hate it now. I don't know how else to get out of debt, though."

"Grandma?" Cinnamon turned to where Grandma Rosemary now sat with Rose Vitelli.

"Not on your life, dear," Grandma rasped. "That boy has been the best protection I've had in years."

"Protection?" Justin asked.

"It keeps your father and his cronies off Grandma's back," I said. "Believe me, anyone with a business in Santa Bonita needs as much protection from your dad and Lamont Gilman and Police Chief Schulte as they can get."

Justin turned to his father. "Dad?"

The Honorable Mayor Esposito put his head in his hands and said, "Don't say another word, Justin. For once in your life, keep your mouth shut. You and Lamont have been expensive enough recently."

Troy began inching slowly closer to Jamie. As I caught his eye, he made a "keep it rolling" motion with his hands.

"That's okay, Justin," I said. "I think Ashley has something to tell you, too."

Ashley pursed her lips. "I do not."

"Ashley's pregnant, you idiot," I told Justin.

Justin jumped back. "She's *what*?"

"She's pregnant. Ashley's pregnant."

"She can't be."

"Well, she is." I paused. "And the baby's not yours."

Everyone gasped. Troy paused for a moment and then continued his silent movement toward Jamie.

"Cinnamon figured it out," I said.

Ashley snapped, "What about you, Ginger? Don't you have any secrets?"

All eyes turned toward me.

"Not really. I seem to be the repository for everyone else's secrets."

From the corner of my eye, I could see Troy easing his way around the tables.

"What about this?" Cinnamon pulled a manila envelope with a smear of jelly on it out of her enormous purse and slapped it down on the table. My Envelope of Freedom from San José State University.

"Where did you get that?" I asked.

"From our garbage. Why did you throw it out?"

"Because that's generally what people do with garbage." I suddenly felt very, very cold.

"You threw out your acceptance package from San José State?" Brian asked. "Why?"

"I can't go, Brian. I'm so sorry, but I can't do it."

"Why?"

It wasn't my secret to tell, but every way I turned, someone else's secret was blocking my path. I looked across the room to where Craig sat with Kendra. Keeping someone else's secret had closed that door in my face. How many more doors was I willing to have slammed in front of me?

I took a deep breath. "Mom has multiple sclerosis."

"Ginger!" Mom gasped. "No!"

"She has what?" Cinnamon looked at me as if I had just announced that Mom was from the planet Alpha Centauri.

"Mom has remitting and relapsing multiple sclerosis. That's why Dad quit the Surf Daddies. She's sick. She needs our help."

Cinnamon turned to Mom. "Is that true? Are you sick? Why didn't you tell me?"

Mom reached for Cinnamon, but Cinn drew back. "I didn't want to worry you. Your dad's here. That's all I need."

"Except that tricky part about Dad still drinking," I said.

Dad's head dropped onto his chest. "Ginger," he said sadly.

Mom turned to Dad. "You're still drinking?"

"No," he said, emphatically. "I am not drinking. I did fall off the wagon but I swear I'm back on it, Cassia." Dad took Mom's hands between his and looked directly into her eyes. It was like the rest of the room dimmed a little bit.

My head fell back in frustration.

Brian took my hand. "There are other people to help take care of your mom, Ginger."

"No, there really aren't, Brian."

"What about Cinnamon?"

"Yeah, what about me?" Cinnamon asked, her hands on her hips.

"Will you answer your cell phone in a crisis if you're off with Justin? You didn't for your daughter. Why would I think you'd do it for Mom?"

Cinnamon's head tipped forward in a mirror of the gesture Dad had made in his moment of defeat before my steamroller of truth.

"You can't even take care of your own daughter without me here. How on earth would you take care of Mom, too?"

"Excuse me, little girl." Grandma's raspy voice cut through the murmurs around us. "Can I not be of assistance in taking care of my own daughter?"

"Oh, Grandma, I so wish you could. But when you're doing time for running an illegal card game in the back of your restaurant, you won't be able to do much. I don't think the fact that the mayor's son owes you a buttload of money is going to protect you forever."

Justin put his hands to his face. "Ginger."

I lost it. "Don't Ginger me, buddy—I don't owe you anything. In fact, I don't owe anything to *any* of you people, and I'm sick to death of all your damn secrets! Because of them, I'm going to be stuck here forever. It's just a matter of time before I have an illegitimate child, and all the good spice names are taken, so I'll have to name her Oregano! You want to know my real secret though?" I asked.

My family nodded back at me.

"Go on," Jamie said.

"I *hate* hair." It felt so good to finally say it out loud. "I hate the smell of it. I hate the feel of it. I hate feeling like little bits of it are stuck in my throat all the time. And I'm afraid I'm going to start hating all of you, because I don't see any way to get away from it."

Mira Wexler stood and shakily said, "Last winter, I drove

away from a gas station with the nozzle still in my gas tank. I didn't realize it until I'd pulled the whole gas pump over. I was so freaked out and scared, I just kept driving, and I never stopped."

Tessie Hamilton stood up. "I steal Cinnamon and Ginger's magazines from their mailbox at the salon. I put them back after I'm done reading them."

No wonder we got our *People* and *Us Weekly* so late!

"*Stop it!*" Jamie screamed, her hands covering her ears. "You're like a bunch of little mice running around in my head with your sharp little teeth and claws, ripping ripping ripping at my brain! Stop it! Stop it! *Stop* it!"

That was the moment that Troy lunged for Jamie. She swung around, the gun waving wildly. Troy grabbed her arm and the two struggled for a moment. Troy was so much bigger and stronger, there seemed no doubt about the outcome. Then Jamie bit him, and there was a loud crack as the gun went off. Troy clutched his shoulder and fell to the floor as the wedding cake behind him burst in a cloud of buttercream and marzipan flowers.

Brian leapt up, cloth napkin in hand, and rushed to Troy's side, ripping open his shirt and pressing the napkin to the wound to stop the bleeding. Everyone else stood or sat in stunned silence, hands pressed to their mouths to stifle screams and gasps.

Everyone, that is, except Ashley.

As the whole room stared in horror at Troy lying on the floor in a growing puddle of his own blood, Ashley took off running from her table. In a move worthy of an NFL linebacker, she put her shoulder down and barreled into Jamie, knocking her flat. Chest heaving, she grabbed the gun from Jamie and pointed it high over her own head.

"Just because it's your Special Day," Ashley growled, "doesn't mean you get to shoot my boyfriend."

"I have never seen that many people arrested at one wedding," Mom said in a wondering tone, as she played with the broken centerpiece on our table.

Dad shook his head. "Remember that wedding the Daddies played back in eighty-seven? On that beach near Santa Cruz? I think there may have been more arrests at that one."

"Well, what did they expect? If you want to have a nude wedding on the beach, you have to go to a nude beach. You can't just drop trou any old place you feel like it and get married." Dad stroked her cheek and she smiled at him.

"I can't believe you're so cavalier about it, when one of the people arrested was your own mother," I said.

Mom shot me a look. "She beat a murder rap. Do you really think she can't beat this illegal card game thing? Have a little faith in your grandmother."

"She'll make an ideal witness against Mayor Esposito, Police Chief Schulte, and Lamont Gilman in their corruption trials," Brian said. "She may be the keystone that brings them all down. It doesn't hurt that that paparazzi dude was following Courtney and got the whole thing on tape."

"I'm worried about Jamie, though. It's pretty hard to turn things around when you've shot a police officer."

"She only winged him," Brian said. "It didn't hit anything vital."

"Plus, I think he may actually have pulled the trigger," Dad pointed out. "You know, when she bit him."

I looked over to where the bullet had hit. Sage was happily eating pieces of the exploded cake, and I got up to stop her. It just seemed like a bad idea to eat a cake that had been shot.

As I approached her, Craig Esposito stopped me. "Your niece has the birthmark, doesn't she?" he asked. "That's why you kicked me out of your bed, isn't it? She has the Esposito wineglass on her back. You saw it on me and thought I was her father."

I stared up at him. I didn't know what to say, so I just nodded.

"And you couldn't tell me because you were keeping your sister's secret for her," he continued.

I nodded again.

He ran his hands through his hair. "And I acted like such a jerk. Demanding explanations, and not listening when you said you couldn't explain. I'm sorry, Ginger. I'm so sorry."

"No, I'm sorry. I leapt to all kinds of conclusions when I saw that birthmark. I should have known that you weren't that kind of guy. It's just that everybody had been warning me, saying all kinds of things about your family . . ." I broke off, realizing what I was saying.

Craig was in the same boat as I was. Everybody assumed he was a certain kind of person because of who his family was, just like they did about me. "If anyone should have known better, it's me, Craig. I'm the one who's sorry."

He brushed my hair off my cheek and tucked it behind my ear, his hand lingering along my jaw. "Maybe we should take each other out for dinner to apologize."

"I don't know, Craig. That may not be the best idea."

"I can't think of a better one right now," he said, his voice a soft caress.

I felt that electrical buzz starting up and I took a step back from him. "Well, I'm not sure anyone's thinking too clearly, after almost being shot by an identity-stealing bride having a psychotic breakdown."

He laughed. "You have a point."

I said good-bye and turned back to where Sage was licking buttercream icing off her lips. Justin had knelt down next to her and taken both her hands in his, and was speaking earnestly in a low voice. I saw her jaw start to jut out, but then she smiled and nodded at him. They walked back to the table together.

I went back to the table, too, and said to Brian, "Have you ever gotten exactly what you wanted, and discovered it was even better than you thought it was going to be?"

"Yeah," he said. "That would be you."

CHAPTER NINETEEN

"That's it?" Natalie asked. "That's all you're taking?"

I put my two suitcases in the trunk of her Camry and my box in the backseat. "That's it," I said. "I'm traveling light." I felt twenty pounds lighter with the weight of everyone's secrets off my shoulders. I got in on the passenger side.

"Are you ready?" she asked.

"I've been ready my whole life," I said.

She was just pulling away from the curb when I saw someone running up the sidewalk toward us. "Hold on a second."

Craig ran up to my window and I pushed the button to lower it.

"Hey," he said, and thrust a CD toward me. "I made you a mix CD. Traveling songs to speed you on your way."

"Thanks," I said, smiling.

"You know, Stanford's not far from San José State. Forty-five minutes tops." He leaned in the window, and I felt the heated rush I seemed to always get when he was near, the electrical vibration that revved up into a *zing!* whenever he kissed me.

"You've mentioned that," I said.

"Plus there's Thanksgiving and stuff," he said. "Now that we're practically family."

"Ewwww," Natalie said.

"Not in an icky way," I assured her. I turned back to Craig. "I'm thinking your family isn't ready to invite mine for Thanksgiving dinner. Your aunt seems pretty bent out of shape about your uncle getting indicted based on my grandmother's testimony."

He smiled. "Maybe yours is ready to invite mine, though."

"We'll see," I said.

"Yeah," he said, and leaned in and kissed me.

We pulled away from the curb. We weren't even to the highway when my cell phone rang. "Hey, Brian," I said.

"Hey, yourself," Brian said. "Are you on the road yet?"

"Yep."

"Excellent," he said. "I'll see you tonight."

We hung up.

"You're sleeping with both of them?" Natalie said, cracking up.

"Don't be gross. I'm not sleeping with either of them." *Anymore.* "I'm keeping my options open. I have quite a few of them, you know."

Now that I didn't have all those secrets to keep and tend, the road in front of me was wide open. I didn't know exactly what my future looked like, but I could see some basic shapes taking form. Like looking at a bride's face through all the layers of tulle; I just knew it was going to be beautiful when it was finally unveiled.

"And do your options all know about each other?" Natalie asked.

"Absolutely. I'm done with secrets. You know why?"

"Why?" She slid the mix CD Craig had given me into the player.

"Because the truth will set you free." I was ready to ride.

Up Close and Personal with the Author

WHERE IS SANTA BONITA?

Wouldn't you just love to know? I know I would! Sadly, Santa Bonita doesn't exist outside of my fevered brain. It may, however, bear a bit of resemblance to certain California coastal towns, particularly Half Moon Bay. This is my first made-up locale. In my previous books, I've used real locations. I decided to come up with my own town this time for several reasons. First, I didn't want anyone (like maybe the mayor) suing me because I'd said they had some kind of nefarious secret. Second, I wanted to add some quirks to the town and didn't want to be tied to what already existed. I didn't, however, make up the Moss Beach Distillery where Justin and Ashley have their wedding reception. That place and its attendant ghost, the Blue Lady, are real. I couldn't make up anything better than a haunted restaurant that used to be a speakeasy. Sometimes fact is just way better than fiction.

Making up Santa Bonita was a blast. Naming it was less so. It sparked an argument in my household about appropriate names for California towns that became as heated as any argument that has ever raged there, and only ended when I said that my imaginary friends were going to live wherever I told them to, regardless of logic and language. I think we all felt so stupid after I said that that we dropped the whole topic and never discussed it again.

WHAT'S UP WITH ALL THE MOVIE QUOTES?

I wanted the sisters to have a shorthand way of communicating, and movie quotes seemed like a way to do that that would be accessible to readers. My sisters and I often have entire conversations that are strings of in-jokes from TV shows, books, and movies we've shared, but more often from shared experiences. With one sentence, we can communicate a whole set of ideas. People around us don't know why we're promising to keep in constant contact in thick Russian accents, but we get the joke and the sentiment immediately. I thought that using movie quotes would be a way to do that without having to key a reader into a bunch of flashback stories about great aunt Guite, or what happened that time at the Greek restaurant.

WHAT'S UP WITH ALL THE MONKEY COMMENTS?

That is quite possibly me getting terribly carried away. A friend had given me a copy of *Mother Nature* by Sarah Hrdry and another friend had given me a copy of *Woman: An Intimate Geography* by Natalie Angier. The parallels they drew between monkey behavior and human behavior fascinated me. I told one of my sisters that I felt we are like bonobos. I was referring to the way that we help with one another's children and have a very cooperative lifestyle and deal with our conflicts without getting angry.

She took offense, as she felt I was calling her slutty. The whole thing cracked me up and started the running joke with Craig comparing Ginger to a bonobo, but in a nice way.

WAS IT HARD TO COME UP WITH ALL THOSE BRIDES?

No! It was hard to keep the number of brides and their stories and secrets down to a dull roar. A wedding is one of those events that seems to bring everyone's craziness to the surface. I don't know anyone whose wedding didn't have some kind of drama. Any event that brings large numbers of people (especially people who are related to one another) into one space has the possibility of becoming dramatic. Unlike funerals, however, where people are generally reined in a little by propriety, weddings seem to encourage everyone to indulge themselves in interesting ways.

WHAT'S YOUR SECRET?

It wouldn't be a secret anymore if I told you, now, would it? But you're right in assuming that I think everyone does have a secret. I was amazed when I started talking to people about secrets, how pervasive they are. Some of my favorites are the secrets that aren't secrets, the ones that everyone knows but pretends not to in order to spare someone's feelings or self-respect.

It all made me think about the millions of secrets we keep, the big ones and the small ones, the important ones and the trivial ones. It also made me think about why we keep them and who is good at keeping them and who isn't. The best secret keeper in our family is the one who won't even let on that he has a secret that he's keeping. I also thought a lot about how keeping secrets changes our relationships with some people. Letting someone into your confidence is a huge sign of trust. Excluding someone from your confidence can be tremendously hurtful.

WHAT IS THE COURTNEY?

I have no idea! I pored over wedding magazines and bridal websites looking for something that could be The Courtney. I never found anything that really worked. I think it's a special haircut that only Cinnamon's hair magic could create.

Life is always a little sweeter with a book from Downtown Press!